Praise for the RACHEL PORTER
Mysteries by
JESSICA SPEART

"Fresh and close to the bone. [Speart's] characters
breathe with the endlessly fascinating
idiosyncrasies of living people."
Nevada Barr

"Each of Speart's books is a great read and a
lesson in endangered species conservation
and wildlife law enforcement."
Pittsburgh Post-Gazette

"Chills and laughs galore."
James W. Hall

"The author portrays stark
atmosphere . . . vividly . . . There are
plenty of appealing characters, not the
least of which is Rachel herself."
Publishers Weekly

"[Speart's] mysteries take readers to all sorts of
interesting places . . . She has a real flair for bringing
colorful characters to life on the page."
Connecticut Post

"Speart's stories ring true. And, as a bonus, each
story delivers a powerful conservation
message . . . Speart not only tells a great story,
she teaches me about a seldom seen world."
Charleston Gazette Mail

Other Rachel Porter Mysteries by
Jessica Speart

JESSICA SPEART

COASTAL DISTURBANCE

A RACHEL PORTER MYSTERY

AVON BOOKS
An Imprint of HarperCollinsPublishers

This is a work of fiction. Names, characters, places, and incidents are products of the author's imagination or are used fictitiously and are not to be construed as real. Any resemblance to actual events, locales, organizations, or persons, living or dead, is entirely coincidental.

AVON BOOKS
An Imprint of HarperCollins*Publishers*
10 East 53rd Street
New York, New York 10022-5299

Copyright © 2003 by Jessica Speart
ISBN: 0-380-82062-5
www.avonmystery.com

First Avon Books paperback printing: March 2003

Avon Trademark Reg. U.S. Pat. Off. and in Other Countries, Marca Registrada, Hecho en U.S.A.
HarperCollins® is a registered trademark of HarperCollins Publishers Inc.

Printed in the U.S.A.

10 9 8 7 6 5 4 3 2 1

Acknowledgments

Thanks go to USFWS Special Agent Pat McIntosh for allowing me to ride shotgun and showing me how to walk through the marsh; Dr. Greg Masson for teaching me the fine points of contaminants and how to collect evidence when knee deep in water; Barb Zoodsma, with the Georgia Department of Natural Resources, for imparting her knowledge of manatees; Anna Ashwood Collins and Sue Morrison for inviting me into their home and sharing their friendship and wine; my editor Sarah Durand for jumping in and treading lightly; and to Carol Fuca who is always there to provide encouragement, listen to me kvetch, and play second mom to Max and Tallulah.

COASTAL
DISTURBANCE

One

Someone was crying outside my bedroom window last night. I got up and ran out, only to find nobody there. Some say the devil you know is better than the devil you don't. In which case, I should have been feeling completely at home right about now.

"Well, hot damn! This here says you're some kinda special federal law enforcement agent with the U.S. Fish and Wildlife Service. Is that so?"

The local sheriff hypnotically wove my ID card between his fingers with the ease of a professional card shark. "And just what is it that brings you to our peaceful little town today?"

"I thought I'd do some fishing," I answered; flashing what I hoped was a seductively beguiling smile.

"Well, aren't you the lucky one getting Labor Day off?" He grinned, giving the distinct impression of a cat on the prowl who'd just caught himself a mouse. "So, what are ya'll fishing for anyway?"

Naturally, he'd have to ask. It was a pastime that I knew almost nothing about.

Mayday! Mayday! The distress call shot straight to my brain as the sheriff continued to study me.

1

"Catfish," I responded, in my best imitation of a Southern drawl.

His meandering gaze vainly searched my vehicle for any sign of a fishing pole. "Too bad you don't seem to be having much luck," he shrewdly observed.

So much for charming the man into submission.

I'd been following up a hot tip concerning some illicit commercial shrimping in the marsh. So far, everything had gone just as I'd hoped. The suspect had docked his boat, unloaded the illegal haul, thrown it in the trunk of his car, and taken off. His next stop would probably be a shady commercial fishmarket just over the state line in Florida.

I'd been hot on my perp's tail, determined to catch him in the act of selling the goods. That is, until a siren began to howl behind me like a surly cat in heat. I'd had no choice but to slam on my brakes and pull off the road. Fisherman Joe slowed down just long enough to flash me a digital good-bye in his rear view mirror. After that, he'd left me behind eating his dust.

There was no question but that I'd brought this upon myself. I'd been driving with my eye pressed against a video camera that was precariously balanced on my shoulder. As a result, my Ford Explorer had swerved back and forth like a drunk on a roll. This was crack law enforcement at its best.

The sheriff's gaze now came to rest on the camera nestled beside me.

"There's some great scenery around here," I lamely offered, hoping to tap dance my way out of this mess.

This was the one thing my topnotch informant had warned me about. Trust no one in the backwater community of St. Mary's Bluff, where everyone knows everything about everybody. It was a given that the locals were all involved in a melange of illegal activities. The surprise ingredient was Sheriff Tom "Quick Draw" Magraw, best described as Georgia's version of the local Godfather. Word had it he received a kickback from everyone, including the local paper boy, who also happened to be his own son.

He eyeballed me now. "Don't take this wrong, but I'm gonna have to run your license, just to check and make sure everything's on the up and up. You know what I mean."

Absolutely. He was a master when it came to ensuring that his compadre made a clean getaway.

I watched Magraw walk back to his vehicle with both feet turned out like a haughty ballerina. The sight was ironic, considering he had the body of a wrestler gone to seed. What wasn't so amusing was when he picked up the microphone in his patrol car and flipped on the outside speaker.

"I got a little lady here and darned if she isn't trying to fish without the use of a pole. I'm still trying to figure that one out. Anyway, she claims to be a special agent with the U.S. Fish and Wildlife Service. Says her name is Rachel Porter."

Magraw had just cleverly alerted all of St. Mary's Bluff to my presence.

"So she *is* with Fish and Wildlife? Okay then, no problem. I'll let her get on with her work."

Fat chance of that. Sheriff Magraw sauntered back, as if nothing the least bit unusual had taken place. I suppose nothing had, except that any undercover operation I'd hoped to mount was now blown.

"Sorry for the inconvenience. You enjoy the rest of your day. And don't hesitate to let me know if I can be of any assistance," he politely offered, placing my license and ID in the palm of my hand.

"Thanks, but I think you've done more than enough already."

That was a mistake. I knew it as soon as the words left my mouth. Magraw's eyes flashed like detonated gunpowder, even though a smile remained plastered on his face.

"Are you referring to what happened back there? Sorry about flipping on that outside speaker. These clumsy fingers of mine get in the way and do that every now and then. But don't worry."

Magraw handed me one of his cards. "The fact is, it would make life a whole lot easier if you filled me in on exactly what you're up to. You may not know it yet, but you need someone like me in the area to keep an eye out for things."

The man sounded so sincere, I nearly believed him.

"Think it over. It could work to both our benefit." His eyes locked on mine and I suddenly knew exactly what he meant.

"Thanks, but that won't be necessary. I've already got everything I need," I bluffed. Hell, why stop there? I patted the camera, purposely yanking his chain.

Sometimes I'm not as clever as I like to believe. The sheriff's eyes zeroed in on their target.

"That sure is some fancy piece of equipment you got there. Nothing a country sheriff like myself can afford."

Who was he kidding? The video camera was a scuffed-up, secondhand bargain basement special. Magraw could have probably bought his own yacht with all the kickbacks he received.

"Mind if I take a look at it?"

He left little doubt that this was a demand, rather than a request.

"It's not mine, so please be careful," I responded, and reluctantly handed over the camera.

Magraw's agile fingers immediately went to work, deftly hitting the release button, so that the film cassette popped out and fell to the ground.

Crrrrrunch! echoed the sickening sound.

I looked down at where his heel expertly ground the cassette into the blacktop.

"Goddamn, I'm sorry!" he apologized, and bent down to pick it up. "Wouldn't you know these big ol' fingers of mine would mess up something again? Tell you what. I'll scrape five bucks out of petty cash and buy a new cassette for that fancy camera of yours."

Magraw couldn't have made his warning any more clear. *This is my banana republic. Now get the hell out of it!*

I took a deep breath, aware that the situation called for something I normally detest—the utmost diplomacy. "That's all right. No harm done. I've got plenty more cassettes back at the office."

"Well, that's mighty nice of you. Why don't you give me a call next time you're down this way, and I'll buy you lunch?" Magraw magnanimously offered, having successfully defended his territory.

Then he strode back to his patrol car, where he waited until I took off.

Two

The late afternoon sun filtered down through the pine trees, as if raining tears of gold. It was time to call it a day and head home. I turned the Ford around and began to drive north. No question about it. I'd have to come up with a different tactic when investigating cases in St. Mary's Bluff. With that in mind, I punched a number into my car phone. My call was answered on the eighth ring.

"This Spud's for *youuuu*," drawled a voice that sounded as if it had just woken up.

It was none other than Spud Bowden, my crack informant. A down-home sleaze, Bowden made his living dealing drugs, illegally fishing, and being paid by various state and federal agencies to turn on his friends. Spud had once shown me a collection of business cards, revealing exactly whom he worked for as a paid informant. I wish *I'd* had this guy's connections.

"I'm calling to thank you, Spud. What did you do? Tip off Magraw that I'd be around today?"

"That you, Porter?" he asked with a raspy chuckle.

I listened to what sounded like chicken feet digging through a pile of gravel. It was probably Spud's fingers scratching at the scrawny excuse for a beard that crawled down his neck.

"Hell, it ain't my fault if you have trouble making an easy collar."

"Let me give you a piece of advice, Bowden. Playing both sides will only get you burned. I'll not only put word out that you're a paid informant, but will also make certain that no other agency ever uses you again," I threatened.

"Hey, hey! Chill, will ya?"

I listened as another body part proceeded to be scratched.

"Tell you what. I'll give you a hot tip free of charge. Will that straighten things out between us?"

What a *mensch*. "It all depends on what you're offering."

"Okay, how's this? Some joker out here is whacking clapper rails from his motorboat at this very moment."

"How do you know?"

"How the hell do you think? My place is on the marsh and this numbnut just flew past my damn bedroom window. Can't you hear?"

Spud was right. The sound of gunshots exploded in the background.

A local bird, clapper rails are also called "marsh hens" because of the way they fly low and slow when not hiding behind tall blades of grass while sportsmen are on the prowl. It's considered a definite no-no for hunters to crank up their engines to flush the birds out. Rather, game law requires that they turn off their motors and pole through the marsh at high tide. But there are always those few who decide, *No way in hell. That's too much work!* Instead, they rev their engines and deliberately speed through the water at full throttle, scattering a slew of the birds.

"Don't say I never gave you something for nothing," Bowden muttered and hung up.

Spud's location was only a ten-minute drive from here. I threw the Ford into gear and spun out.

I was once again working at a new station, though this time, the decision to transfer had been my own. Even so, I couldn't help but wonder if I'd made the right choice.

The problem was that part of my heart had been left behind in Montana, having become involved in a relationship that didn't pan out. As a result, I was afraid it would affect my work. How could it not? I'd fallen in love with the tribal game officer for the Blackfeet Reservation. I still cared for the man and knew that he loved me, as well. There'd just been one major hitch—I was also deeply involved with somebody else.

Hearts can be fragile as finely spun sugar; emotions as highly charged as shooting stars. A choice had to be made and I'd followed my head, remaining with the man who'd always stood by me. No doubt about it—love triangles really suck.

I'd been hoping to get posted somewhere in proper New England, where my morals could be overhauled and firmly set back in place. I should have known that wasn't to be the case. The head honchos in Washington apparently consider it their patriotic duty to toss me about from state to state.

It's common knowledge that I'm viewed as a pain-in-the-ass to be gotten rid of, and that the right transfer just might do the trick. That's the only reason I could figure as to why I was once again back in the deep South. This time I'd landed below the gnat line, where the crackers aren't crisp, bread never gets stale, your clothes refuse to dry, and bugs are everywhere. My new posting was southern Georgia, home to good ol' boys, swamps, gators, and ticks.

I veered off old Highway 17 and onto a winding dirt road that headed straight for the marsh. Ramshackle shanties, topped with corrugated metal roofs, dotted the land like so many discarded tin cans. A broken-down backhoe, resembling an ancient dinosaur, sat slumped in one family's front yard, while others boasted rusty swing sets.

A woman as slight as a passing breeze hung laundry on a worn-out rope lazily drooping between two trees. However, most of her time was spent futilely slapping at a troop of voracious gnats. She'd cleverly freed her hands by sticking clothespins in her mouth, where they dangled like primitive wooden teeth.

Nearby, a little boy leaned against a wishing well that wearily sagged on a patch of brown lawn. His face was so smudged that it blended perfectly with the dirt. Every now and then, he'd attempt to slide down inside the deathtrap, as if determined to shatter the boredom.

"Buddy, stop that this instant!" the woman wearily warned, shooting the wooden projectiles from her mouth.

My guess was that if she could have made a wish, it would have been to get the hell out of this place. It was an area where history perpetuated itself: women got pregnant young, married young, divorced young, and died young. The men didn't fare all that much better. They lived off the land, like their daddies and granddaddies before them. Only these days, the purchase of a double-wide mobile home was the major goal in life to be aspired to.

The houses soon gave way to marsh, and the road came to a stop. That was where a shiny silver Lexus SUV sat parked. Attached to its rear was an empty boat trailer. It appeared that Spud's sacrificial lamb was still around.

Grabbing my binoculars, I stepped outside, where a pungent smell filled the air, and a slight breeze rippled through a lush ribbon of golden fringe. A flock of pelicans, plump as rich millionaires, blithely wheeled overhead, their brown bodies reflecting in water bright as polished glass.

I stood and searched the skyline as the light slowly began to dip. The marsh was soon glowing as if on fire, the maze of channels glistening blood red in the setting sun. I closed my eyes for a moment and listened to the sounds around me. Hundreds of tiny fiddler crabs scurried about, their feet crackling in the mudflats, while the spartina grass gently rustled like a field of prairie wheat. A pulse rhythmically pounded beneath my feet, much like a heartbeat, as the marsh took a deep breath and came to life.

Maybe meditation isn't such a bad thing after all, I mused, never having been one for yoga.

But any delusions I had about breaking into a soulful *ohm* were interrupted as a hyenalike cackle raucously filled the air. The clamor was picked up and repeated over and over in mocking fashion until I felt like the butt of some great cosmic joke, only to realize the laughter was coming from an unseen flock of clapper rails.

BOOM!

The roar raced across the marsh, with the intensity of a cannonball, as a covey of rails exploded out of the grass like feathered firecrackers heading toward the sky. That was followed by a motorboat, which sped into sight bearing two figures. One man stood tall and imperious, maintaining perfect balance, as he chambered and shot another round. He shouldered the rifle's recoil, absorbing the blast as if it were nothing more than a nudge. However, a number of clapper rails weren't so lucky. The birds spiraled out of the sky in a dead man's dive.

Some people grab your attention because they exude power. Others are noticed due to their looks. Then there are those who ooze charisma. Mr. Sportsman appeared to have it all. Topping it off, he was the perfect fashion plate in his precisely pressed khakis, crisply starched stonewashed shirt, and stylish safari vest.

I turned my binoculars next to the elderly black man steering the boat. He paid little attention to his companion, but instead focused on the marsh. Only something must have tipped him off that he was being watched, for he now turned and stared in my direction. I responded by waving him in, only to be mistaken for an admiring onlooker. The driver casually returned my wave. It was time to set things straight.

Pulling out my badge, I tilted the shield so that it caught the rays of the setting sun. Then I waved once again. But rather than head back, the driver simply slowed the craft, as his companion began to question him. A brief exchange took place, and he followed the driver's finger to where it pointed in my direction. Mr. Sportsman deliberately turned and squeezed off a few more rounds, so that another two clapper rails fell into the marsh like oversized raindrops. Only then did the boat make its way back toward land.

All the while, the hunter never sat, but maintained a regal pose as though he were Washington crossing the Delaware. Perhaps he simply didn't want to soil his clothes. Even from this distance it was easy to tell they were first-class threads.

This was the challenge—dealing with arrogant hunters determined to do whatever they damn well pleased. I could usually predict their reaction just by the way they approached—along with their shock that a woman had been given the power to step on their neck.

The elderly driver jumped out and sloshed about in the

water, as he pulled the boat's nose onto land. Only then did Mr. Sportsman deign to leave the craft, his handmade Le Chameau leather-lined chasseur boots stepping firmly onto dry ground. I'd seen them worn only by the wealthiest hunters around. They must have set him back a good four hundred bucks, placing him in a most exclusive category. I took a closer look at the man I'd soon be dealing with. Appearing to be in his late fifties, he was tall and fit, sported a full head of dark hair, and had intensely blue eyes. He wasted no time, but strode purposefully toward me like a Humvee on a mission.

"My driver indicated you were urgently waving us in," he spoke as he walked. "He also thought you were holding up some sort of badge. I certainly hope you didn't end an excellent run of hunting on this fine Labor Day without good reason. Just tell me that you're not one of those errant females who's lost and in need of directions," he affably joked.

Had any other man said that, I would have taken offense. But there was something about this guy that was different— and it wasn't just his disarming smile. It immediately became clear that he knew how to play to an audience. I also had the distinct impression he usually got whatever he wanted. That alone made me all the more determined to stick to my guns.

I flashed my badge, trying hard to ignore that his clothes were spotless, while mine hung plastered with sweat against my skin. Even worse was that my shield didn't get the reaction I'd hoped for. The hint of a smile flickered across his mouth.

"I'm afraid I have to ticket you for shooting clapper rails from a running motorboat," I informed him. "You must be aware that's a violation of federal game laws."

The words didn't merely roll off the man; they brought a full-fledged smile to his lips.

"Surely that's not necessary. In fact, it seems a bit overzealous," he lightly reprimanded. "Isn't there some way we can work this out?"

He spoke with such supreme confidence that I felt almost like a contrary schoolgirl. Equally annoying was that there was something oddly familiar about the man, though I couldn't quite put my finger on it. Clearly, we didn't travel in the same social circles. Everything about him shouted *noblesse oblige*, while I was more a Wal-Mart type of gal. Hell, even his rifle reeked of money with its diamond inlays, etchings of oak leaf clusters, and back-slanting tips of rosewood. It was obvious that my sporty friend was some sort of fat cat. Every detail about him shouted privilege, breeding, and wealth. Even the way he stood, so perfectly calm, revealed he believed it was his God-given right to walk away without paying a fine. I couldn't help but wonder what it must be like to feel so entitled. My guess was that I was about to find out.

"I'm afraid that's not possible," I coolly responded. "I'll need to see your license."

He remained silent until his identification had been firmly placed in my hand.

"Not even as a professional courtesy?"

It was then that my eyes caught sight of the name on the license. I now realized just who it was that I'd caught. No wonder the man was grinning from ear to ear, certain that he'd be let off. Clark Williams was a former Undersecretary of Interior for Fish, Wildlife, and Parks.

My stomach clenched at the dilemma that I suddenly found myself facing. Either ticket the man as I would any ordinary Joe. Or let him walk, reinforcing the belief that if a violator is rich and powerful enough, he was beyond the law.

I knew that Williams was watching me closely, silently betting I would play the game. An old joke among agents floated through my brain.

Bust the wrong hunter and you'll find yourself transferred to the Okefenokee swamp.

That was convenient. It just so happened the Okefenokee was only about forty miles away from here. Besides which, there wasn't much further I could slide down the Service's totem pole. I tried not to think about that—or what could be gained if I agreed to play along. Instead, I wrote out the ticket and gave him a fine.

I didn't look at Williams until after I'd handed him the flimsy piece of paper. His complexion was mottled with rage. Then I chose to further provoke the man by flippantly spouting instructions that he clearly already knew.

"You can mail in a check, unless you decide to appeal. In which case, you'll be notified of a court date and time."

Williams continued to stare at me without a word.

"By the way, I'll take those birds," I cockily added, pointing to the lifeless clapper rails that lay in his boat.

"Eight Ball, bring them over here!" he commanded, his eyes never leaving mine.

The old man hopped to it, having thoughtfully strung the birds together during this time. He handed the clapper rails to Williams and I reached out to take them, only to be met with steely resistance. It wasn't that Williams pulled away; he just wasn't ready to release them yet.

"What's your name, young woman?" he ominously questioned, his voice balefully soft and low.

Damn! No matter how it was said, the word "young" always warmed the cockles of my heart.

"Rachel Porter," I staunchly replied.

"Well Agent Porter, it appears you've still got a good deal to learn. These damn birds are going to wind up costing you a hell of a lot more than they're going to cost me."

A chill went through me, but I was damned if I was about to back down now.

"Is that a threat?" I challenged.

His eyes never flinched, making it perfectly clear that our showdown was far from over.

"It's much more than a threat. It's a guarantee. You'll soon discover this isn't the way to get ahead in your agency. Enjoy Georgia while you can, because you won't be here for long."

It was my turn to smile. He should only have known my history.

Williams spun around on his Le Chameau boots and strode back to the Lexus, leaving his lackey to do the dirty work. The elderly man finished maneuvering the boat onto its trailer, and then hesitantly made his way toward me.

A slight figure, his skin was slate black like a chalkboard and his posture stooped, as though he'd been carrying a heavy burden for far too long. Wrinkled fingers nervously plucked at the legs of his pants like the slim beaks of baby birds, and his lips rhythmically moved back and forth across his gums.

"'Scuse me, Miss. But you gonna give me one of them tickets, too?" he asked in a voice that crackled like creased tin foil.

Whatever the man was being paid as a weekly wage, it certainly wasn't enough.

"Do you work for Mr. Williams?" I inquired.

"Nah. I got me a job over at DRG."

I knew DRG to be a chlor-alkali plant in Brunswick, not far from the local U.S. Fish and Wildlife office of ecological services. The plant processed salt water, turning it into caustic soda and chlorine that was then used by paper mills as a bleaching agent.

"But Mr. Williams, he hires me to take him out hunting in the marsh every now and then," he continued.

There was no way I could give the old man a ticket. I wouldn't have been able to live with myself.

"Tell you what. If you give me your word not to speed in the marsh anymore, I'll let you off without a fine."

"I'll try my best," he replied, his eyes veering toward the Lexus.

No more needed to be said. I instinctively knew what he meant.

I watched as he slowly walked back to the SUV and climbed into the passenger seat. He'd barely had a chance to close the door when the Lexus took off. Then I got into my own vehicle and set off for home, increasingly aware that I was about to be engulfed by an impending firestorm.

Williams's history with Interior had been notorious, to say the least. Stories still floated around concerning his flagrant disregard for the law when it came to fulfilling the desires of the rich and politically connected. Word had it that he'd been wined and dined by high-priced lobbyists every night of the week. I didn't know how much truth there actually was to the rumors. But his philosophy when it came to the preservation of wildlife was well known.

If you can't hook it, shoot it, or screw it, then it's not worth conserving.

Three

The sun was already gone by the time I headed north along the coast to my new home on Tybee. Eighteen miles outside of Savannah, it's the very last in a chain of islands strung together by causeways stretching across the marsh. The temperature had grown cooler, allowing me to lower the Ford's window. I took a deep breath, and the nighttime scents magically infused my soul. Then I crossed the bridge over Lazaretto Creek and made a wish, knowing that I was now home.

I drove past bungalows on wooden stilts that looked like long-legged flamingos. Warm orange light poured from each one, as if they were Halloween pumpkins all lit up in a row. I'd grown to love the island, partly because it had the feel of a place that time had forgot; partly because it reminded me of the much-neglected Jersey shore. Tybee certainly had its share of cheap roadside motels and stores selling cheesy souvenirs. On the other hand, there were no golf courses, gated villages, color-coordinated houses, or luxury resorts. Instead, the island preferred to cultivate what was alluded to as "ticky Tybee tacky."

This was a beach bum community in the truest sense—a place of delicious eccentricity filled with colorful characters ranging from rich to poor, redneck to gay, all the way to celebrities, artists, and fishermen. Those in the know affectionately referred to the island by its nickname—the Redneck Riviera. Even the pirate Blackbeard had once hung out here. Legend had it he'd not only headquartered his crew on the island, but that his treasure was still buried beneath its sands. We must have been former soulmates, since I'd immediately felt at home on my very first visit.

I turned down a narrow alley where it looked like some of Blackbeard's crew probably still lived. Lush foliage crept onto the gravel road, covering what little civilization there was in unruly undergrowth. Live oaks, dripping with Spanish moss, resembled impoverished royalty draped in remnants of tattered refinery. All the while palmettos conspiratorially hovered behind their drooping fronds, as if quietly plotting a coup.

I pulled into the carport of the house I was renting, a tiny bungalow with a turquoise metal roof. Vines crawled up along the abode's wooden walls, competing for space with the mildew, while an old ship's chain lay stretched across the length of yard. Each day its metal links seemed to sink into the spongy ground a little deeper. I felt certain that one day I would wake to discover I'd been swallowed up by the marsh.

Hopping out of my Ford, I found myself serenaded by music coming from next door, where a player piano pumped out "You Light Up My Life." Debbie Boone, eat your heart out. The lyrics were warbled by a thin voice that held all the delicacy of a reed instrument, and belonged to my present landlady, Marie Trumble. A true aficionado of music, she'd once been a well-known torch singer.

I glanced over to where Marie sat near her living room

window, dressed in her usual evening attire—a faded blue beaded gown. There appeared to be fewer beads on her dress with each passing month, and a fake diamond tiara was perched atop her head as she trilled songs that sounded oddly like Muzak.

Marie's house was as flamboyant as she was, with a pagoda roof, stained glass windows, and seashells lining the walkway. Her black cat, Houdini, lent an air of mystery to the place. His amber eyes tended to freak visitors out by following them every-frigging-where they went. Right now, the feline was taking a much-needed snooze on the hood of Marie's beloved old Cadillac Eldorado, with its humongous fins and white pebbled roof. Houdini lay sprawled out like a fat inkblot on the yellow bomber.

I skipped up the steps and entered my own abode, only to wonder if I was in the right place. Dancing lobster lights had been strung around the kitchen, their claws silently clicking as if in rhythm to a Spanish tune. Candles were lit and the table was set with two chipped, mismatched plates. Funny, how I used to dream of drinking wine from Waterford crystal and eating haute cuisine off Lenox china. These days I preferred to eat my frozen meals straight out of their Hungry Man plastic containers. That way, there were fewer dishes to wash.

Forget the plates, forget the lights. Far better was the man standing in my kitchen. This was the real reason I'd left Montana—to try and make a go of it with the longtime love of my life, Jake Santou.

I watched as he concentrated on stirring a pot, his hands covered in lobster mitts. They made him look like some kind of half-man, half-shellfish that had come from out of a deep lagoon. He quietly hummed along to Marie's medley of tunes, his mop of dark, curly hair shining in the reflected glow of the lobster lights. The strand of plastic crustaceans seemed equally determined to light up my life as well, whether I wanted them to or not. Right now the numero uno thing on my mind was a martini. I figured I deserved it. Heck, I'd not only duked it out with "Quick Draw" Magraw, but also ticketed Clark Williams, very possibly blowing my career sky high all on one holiday afternoon.

The bottle of vodka beguilingly beckoned. I was so focused on making my way over to it that I momentarily forgot about anything else in the room. What stopped me were a pair of sinewy arms that wrapped themselves about my waist and held me in place.

"Whoa! Hold on there, chère. What's this? Here I'm cooking you dinner and I don't even rate a hello?"

Santou twirled me around to face him, and bent me backward in a mock embrace.

"Where have you been, woman?" he joked. "It's getting late."

I planned to respond with a witty rejoinder, only to have my breath taken away. Santou knew exactly what to do; he slowly began to kiss my neck. I was a goner as Jake seductively worked his way down toward my breasts, sweeping me over the edge.

"Dinner can wait," he growled.

Scooping me up, he carried me into the bedroom. I forgot about clapper rails, powerful officials, and crooked sheriffs as Santou pulled my T-shirt over my head. My jeans quickly followed, falling past my feet and onto the floor. The frustrations of the day melted away as I willingly gave myself over to the moment. The sheets grew damp beneath our flesh and the skirmish continued in a struggle worth fighting for. I finally found relief as I softly fell into a deeper part of myself, and my demons temporarily crept away. I could tell that Santou felt the same way. It was then, when we were both fully satiated, that we became one with the quiet throb of the marsh outside the window.

It wasn't until afterward, when the day's events came rushing back, that I again had the urge for a drink. Jake must have felt me move against his chest, and his fingers entangled themselves in my hair. Last year had been a turning point in our relationship—we'd very nearly tanked. It was then that we'd realized how much we truly meant to each other and decided to take the plunge. That was when the C word had come into play—Commitment.

Marriage was still more than I was ready for. After all, we were two independent people who needed time to adjust to the etiquette of sharing the same place. We'd already discovered that it required diligence, patience, and stamina. But what neither of us had counted on was that other C word. It proved to be far more difficult than I could have ever anticipated—the horror of Compromise. Sometimes I wished the word had been altogether banned from the English language. Just divvying up the damn closet space required the skills of a United Nations ambassador.

"Are you ready for dinner?" Santou lazily murmured.

I nodded. Whatever he'd been cooking smelled terrific.

We took a quick shower, threw on our robes, and headed into the kitchen, where Santou put the burner back on and gave the pot a quick stir. I made good use of the time to pour myself a hefty glass of vodka. Add a splash of vermouth, an olive, and *voilà*! I had my own rock 'em, sock 'em version of a martini.

"You planning on drinking for two?" Santou questioned, with a disapproving look in his eye.

"I've had a rough day, is all," I gruffly responded, feeling slightly guilty without knowing why.

"Then I guess your day didn't quite go as planned."

I looked at the man as I sipped my martini and began to relax a little more. What was his problem, anyway? How could something that made me feel this good possibly be bad?

"Actually, I'd say it was one for the books."

Santou dished his homemade gumbo into two bowls filled with rice, and my stomach began to growl.

"I was rousted by the local sheriff of St. Mary's Bluff and run out of town. After that I ticketed a former Interior official on a game violation."

Santou chuckled, and I took another sip of my drink. Maybe it was the vodka kicking in, or perhaps I was just beginning to mellow, but living together was starting to feel like the norm. I leaned over to give Jake a kiss on the cheek, as I wondered why we'd waited so long.

Santou turned in time to catch my lips, and then smiled. "You're right. That's not bad for a day when you weren't supposed to be working at all. In fact, I'm beginning to think you had an ulterior motive for us living together. At least this way, you know one of us will always be employed. I guess I'll just have to wait until you no longer have a job before you finally learn to cook and clean."

"Very funny," I caustically retorted, all the while knowing he was probably right. Jake put my own halfhearted attempts at cooking to shame.

I listened to Santou breathe as he slept beside me that night, unable to sleep myself, beleaguered by the thoughts of the day. Jake seemed to sense my unease and slipped an arm around my shoulders, pulling me close. Before long I began to nod off, knowing that for the first time in years, I finally felt at home.

Four

I rolled over in the morning to find that Jake was gone. Then I remembered he'd mentioned an early meeting today. It had taken a good deal of finagling on his part to get transferred to the FBI office in Savannah. What had helped was that the head man also happened to be Cajun.

"And you know us Cajuns. We like to stick together," Santou had joked.

But it had cost Jake plenty. He'd turned down a prestigious job that the FBI had wanted him to take in D.C.

I pulled myself out of bed, showered, and got dressed. Wouldn't you know? It was another warm, sunny day. Cold weather and snow were two of the things I didn't miss about Montana—though I had to admit, there was one thing in particular that I did.

I headed into the kitchen and opened the pantry door, knowing it was important to get a nutritious start to the day. Mmm, mmm, mmm. A lone Pop-Tart sat waiting in its box alongside the last dregs of Cap'n Crunch cereal. I figured that ought to tide me over for at least an hour.

It was as though my landlady, Marie, had read my thoughts. Her timing couldn't have been better as she tottered in the door with a plate of danishes in her hands.

"Good morning, my dear. Thomas tried to hide these from me, hoping I'd eat a proper breakfast. So, I played along and made a show of having a bite of cereal. That proved enough to throw him off the track." Her eyes twinkled from within their bed of wrinkles. "You think he'd know me better after all these years. As soon as the pastries reappeared, I ditched the Shredded Wheat, grabbed the plate of goodies, and hot-footed it over here. Now I can enjoy my morning cholesterol in peace with you, while having as much caffeine as I like."

Marie was a piece of work, which was exactly what I enjoyed best about her. She knew it as well, and her face puckered up in a mischievous smile. Her appearance was made all the more merry by feathery wisps of red curls arranged as carefully as newborn chicks in a nest on her head.

Her age was the only thing she was rather touchy about, a subject we never brought up. However, I'd once snuck a peek at her driver's license. It revealed Marie to be eighty-seven years old, though she only admitted to seventy-one.

She looked particularly chipper this morning, attired in a jaunty red top and blue-and-white Capri pants. The combination gave the illusion of a ripe strawberry on a Delft china plate. Though she spoke incessantly of Thomas, I'd never yet had the opportunity to meet him. But then again, there was a perfectly good reason. It wasn't that he was reclusive or unfriendly. Rather, Thomas was her former husband who'd been dead for the past ten years.

Marie strongly believed there was little distinction between the living and the dead, maintaining it was no more than the finest line which could be easily crossed. Perhaps that thought gave her comfort as she continued to lose loved ones over the years. God knows, it certainly came in handy whenever she misplaced things—an occurrence that happened on a regular basis. Keys disappeared, a week's worth of bras and panties vanished, her wallet absconded without a trace. Pity the well-meaning soul who dared suggest that Marie might possibly have mislaid them. Her response was always the same icy stare, followed by the curt explanation that it was an impish prank being perpetrated by Thomas.

Interestingly enough, Thomas hadn't interfered when Marie officially ended her mourning period by taking up with Alfred—a younger man of seventy-five, whom she referred to as her "boy toy." But then Thomas had always been very progressive about such matters, Marie had carefully explained. Besides, since she was only "seventy-one" years old, what did he expect? That she wouldn't have a sex life?

"Here, take another," Marie urged, pushing the plate of pastries toward me.

"But don't you want to save some for Alfred?" I asked, scarfing down a cheese danish.

"Heavens, no! He doesn't need to gain any more weight. Not when I keep him around for his good looks," she teased.

However, I knew their relationship was much more than simply skin deep. I could see it in her sprightly walk, the way she smiled, and the attention Marie gave to her makeup and clothes. Alfred was the man who applauded her singing each night, marveled at her youthful, dewy complexion, and brought milk and cookies to her in bed. He made Marie feel vibrant and happy, and she clearly did the same for him.

Marie once revealed the secret as to how Alfred had finally won her heart. He'd kissed her liver spots one by one and lovingly referred to them as "freckles."

That was the kind of relationship I also wanted with a man. It was the way I hoped to grow old with Santou.

I left Marie to savor the last of the pastry, as I jumped in my Ford and took off for work. An enormous fireball had already risen high in the sky, as if it had vaulted straight out of the earth's molten core. The deep-dish sun leisurely beat down upon the marsh, which luxuriated in a briny saltwater bath—an event that took place twice daily during high tide.

Shrimp boats busily worked the channels between the islands, floating silent as water spiders while spreading their gossamer nets. The only noise came from a flock of carpet-bagging pelicans that peeled out of formation and dive-bombed the boats, in hopes of a tasty snack.

I crossed tidal rivers and creeks radiating in a maze of serpentine fissures, like an immense circulatory system driven by a huge pumping heart. *McQueens, Wilmington, Whitemarsh, and Oatland.* I held my breath as I drove over flyways connecting each of these small islands, taking note of the marsh to my left and the ocean on my right. My Ford exuberantly barreled down a one-lane road on which there was little traffic, evoking the feeling that this land was all mine.

Nearly four hundred thousand acres of salt marsh stretch along the Georgia coast to create a watery cradle of life. Fish, reptiles, birds, and mammals all reside in this unbroken forest of tawny green that works like a Band-Aid for my soul.

Soon I left the coastline behind to travel a very different sort of road—one occupied by an invading army of paper mills and chemical plants in a fast-food strip of industry. Together they produced an odor similar to overcooked cabbage on St. Patrick's Day. I'd once asked a local if he knew what the scent was, only to be told it was the smell of money.

I passed in and out of Savannah in no time, skirting the

center of the city as I made my way east. Before long, I arrived at Fish and Wildlife's Refuge Office, where I unlocked the door and entered my own private room. Flipping on the lights, I turned on my computer and took a stab at brewing a decent pot of coffee. No sooner had the java begun to drip than my phone started to ring.

"Special Agent Porter speaking," I answered in my best professional tone.

"Cut the crap, Porter," barked an irate voice.

I should have expected the call. It was my boss, Jim Lowell.

"I'm going to be fair and listen to your side of the story before I pull an Ozzy Osbourne and chew your head off."

Lowell tried so hard to be cool that it made him terminally square. I hated that he considered himself to be an aging rocker all because he'd played guitar in high school eons ago. In truth, Lowell was a die-hard company man through and through—a bureaucrat who'd kissed enough high-powered political rear ends to be deemed a first-rate groupie.

Rather than speak, I chose to remain silent until clued in to exactly which incident Lowell was hell-bent on bawling me out about. I didn't need to give the man any further ammunition.

"I know perfectly well what happened with Clark Williams, so quit your stalling, Porter. For chrissakes, what in hell did you think you were doing out there yesterday?" he snapped, taking aim at my jugular.

"My job," I retorted, giving it right back to him.

"Let me tell you a little something about your job, Porter. You're lucky to still have one, considering the number of enemies you've made in the Service so far."

Wow, this guy really knew how to make a girl feel special.

Even Ozzy could have taught him a thing or two when it came to people skills.

"You know what your trouble is?"

While I probably could have guessed, I felt certain I was about to find out.

"You have real difficulty accepting supervision," Lowell eagerly filled me in. "That's why you've been bounced around the country so much."

I had to grit my teeth to keep from telling him what the real crux of the matter was: I hated being controlled by someone who'd never been out in the field. Jim Lowell was of that special breed willing to say or do anything in order to get ahead. As a result, he'd been promoted through politics.

"But I now realize your resentment goes far beyond those of us within Fish and Wildlife. You can't get along with anyone in a position of power," Lowell theorized.

"Oh, come on. It's only human nature for someone to complain when they receive a ticket," I retorted. Hell, it was the standard reaction. Do nothing and people were happy. Enforce the law and they got pissed off.

"Then maybe you should be more careful with what you perceive to be a violation. It wouldn't hurt if you stopped and thought twice before handing out a fine to just anyone."

For a moment, I couldn't quite believe what I'd heard. Then it began to sink in.

"Are you telling me only to ticket those people who don't have the clout to cause problems?" I challenged. I'd be damned if I'd bend the rules just so my boss didn't have to deal with any high-level bitching.

Lowell immediately launched into attack. "Let me tell you what your grandstanding has done. That little stunt you pulled out in the marsh? Well it opened up a whole can of worms for this agency. Clark Williams is now planning to push for a congressional oversight hearing on Division of Law Enforcement excesses based on what happened yesterday."

I started to laugh, sure this had to be a practical joke. What did Lowell think? That he was going to scare me into submission?

"I'm not kidding," he informed me, cutting my laughter short.

"But how can Williams claim my actions were excessive when he clearly was in the wrong?" I asked, in amazement.

"You mean you really don't know?" Lowell fired back. "Then it's high time you became better acquainted with who's who in this world. For your information, Clark Williams is on the board of directors for the National Hook and Bullet Association."

Oh shit. Talk about having a nail driven into my coffin. I knew NHBA to be a high-powered hunting group that boasted eight hundred wealthy and politically savvy members, none of whom liked to be told what they could or could not shoot. NHBA's agenda was simple—to relegate all federal wildlife law enforcement agents to nothing more than desk duty. In other words, they were putting the screws to Fish and Wildlife with the intent of shutting us down.

"I already received an angry call from their lawyer this morning. He insists your behavior proves that NHBA members are being targeted by a bunch of overzealous agents out to hang a fat cat trophy on their wall."

"That's patently untrue!" I argued in my own defense.

Surely not even Lowell could fall for such blatant intimidation.

"But wait, you haven't heard the rest of the news," Lowell

imparted in a lethally sarcastic tone. "Your charges against Clark Williams are being dropped."

"That's impossible!" The words flew out of my mouth before I could stop them. "I caught him on an ironclad violation, the same as I would have anyone else."

"That's real interesting, Porter," Lowell drawled.

Call it paranoia on my part, but I could have sworn the man was enjoying this.

"No, it's much more than that," I insisted, refusing to let the matter drop. "It's totally hypocritical to apply one set of rules to some poor slob, only to let a big shot like Williams wriggle off. If you don't back me up on this, I swear I'll take it all the way to the top."

My threat hung in the air like a hangman's noose.

"Back off, Porter. I'm not the villain here," Lowell warned in a near hiss. "This wasn't my decision. Charges are being dropped on the basis of a strategy known as the DeLorean defense."

The tactic could have been called the O.J. defense for all I cared. In fact, it would have made more sense, since it felt as though I were getting shafted.

"What's that?"

"Think back. It was a tactic successfully used to free John DeLorean, an exotic car maker. Cocaine conspiracy charges against him were dropped when it was discovered that the FBI had done something not in accordance with their own policy."

"Which was?" I asked, having no idea where all this was headed.

"FBI agents set him up to buy drugs. It was a clear case of entrapment."

"I'm sure that's fascinating. But I still don't understand what it has to do with me. It's not as if I threw Williams in a motorboat, raced the engine, and suggested he gun down a bunch of clapper rails."

"Maybe not. But what you did was just as illegal," Lowell maintained, expertly dangling the bait.

Naturally, I took it. "Oh yeah? And would you like to tell me exactly what that was?"

"It's simple. You weren't authorized to work on Labor Day. By doing so, you operated outside the scope of your job. That's grounds enough for the case to be thrown out."

A dull thud resounded in my brain. It was the sound of my jaw hitting the floor.

"You've got to be kidding me."

"Do you hear any laughter?" Lowell shot back.

"So, that's it then? Case closed?" I asked, feeling oddly numb.

"Not quite. There's still the matter of your insubordination. I believe I'd made it perfectly clear that your request to work the holiday had been turned down. What the hell's the matter with you anyway, Porter? Is your personal life so lousy that you have to be out in the field all the time?"

I bit down hard on my lip to try to keep from sniping back. *Oh, screw it!*

"No, It's just that with so much dead wood around, I'm left to pick up a lot of the slack."

My response was met by a moment of stony silence.

"Then let me say this in language that even *you* can understand. You're skating on thin ice, Porter. One more screwup and I'll personally see to it that the Service has to deal with one less loose cannon. You'd be wise to watch your step from now on."

His words were followed by a sharp click, after which the

sound of a dial tone buzzed in my ear. Damn! Lowell had actually hung up on me.

I stared at my computer as the screensaver kicked into gear. Dozens of colorful yo-yos sprouted wings and now flew across my monitor like birds in an evening sky. The screensaver had been a present from my former boss, Charlie Hickok, along with a note.

Never forget how this agency works. When the going gets tough, "you're on your own."

I now realized my mistake. I should have run straight to the nearest U.S. Attorney's office with the paperwork after ticketing Williams, and gotten the Justice Department involved. That was the surest way for special agents to survive in the political backstabbing world within Fish and Wildlife. Only then could I have safely said to Lowell, Williams, and the entire NHBA, *"Thou shalt not mess with me."*

The phone rang in a series of sharp staccato screams, jerking me out of my reverie.

"Special Agent Porter," I growled.

"Call off the hounds of hell! Whatever I did, I'm sorry."

I laughed in spite of myself. It was Gary Fletcher, the Fish and Wildlife contaminant specialist calling from his office in Brunswick, Georgia.

"Sorry about being mad. Believe me, it's got nothing to do with you."

"Great. Now you sound like my last girlfriend just before she dumped me. Okay, Pepper. Spill the beans. So, what's wrong?"

I hated when he called me Pepper. It was the name of Angie Dickinson's character in her old TV series, *Police Woman*. No way did I look anything like Angie, with my long frizzy red hair, scuffed-up boots, and kick-around clothes. In addition to which, I was loath to admit I'd been old enough to watch the show.

"I had a run-in with a former Interior Department bigwig, Clark Williams, and just learned that he won the battle. I got the news from Lowell, who handed me my head for having had the nerve to give him a ticket."

"Clark Williams, huh? Yeah, he was always a bureaucratic weenie, the same as your boss. Tell you what. Why don't you come here to the office, and I'll fill you in on what Williams is up to these days."

"No way. I was just down in your area yesterday. That's how I got into all this trouble."

"Aw come on, Porter. It's only an hour's drive," he wheedled. "Besides, screw that crap. I've got something much better for you to lose your job over."

The man cleverly knew how to lure me.

"Oh, yeah? What's that?"

"You've got to see it yourself to believe it," he continued enticingly. "It won't be a waste of your time, I promise. In fact, you really need to get your rear end down here pronto. Oh yeah, and you're gonna want to bring a camera along."

That did it. I went for his come-on hook, line, and sinker.

"Okay, okay. Give me an hour and a half."

"What, are you getting old and slow, Porter?" he teased.

"Damn you. I'll be there in sixty minutes."

It was only as I sped along the coast, with my windows rolled down and a hot wind slapping my face, that my mind started to wander. That's when my thoughts once again turned to the conversation with Jim Lowell and my curiosity became newly aroused. Just how *had* Clark Williams managed to learn so quickly that I hadn't been authorized to work yesterday? And if not Lowell, then exactly who within Fish and Wildlife had taken a stand against me, deciding that charges should be dropped?

Five

I drove along the coastal road that wound in and about the marsh, though there was no question this was the longer route. Still, where else could you find places with names such as Two Way Fish Camp and Mudcat Charlie's? I flew past old Texaco stations, feed stores, and antique shops with signs announcing DEAD PEOPLE'S THINGS FOR SALE. A neighborhood BBQ joint, that better resembled a shack, declared itself to have THE BEST RIBS IN THE SOUTH. A poster next to it revealed the place also doubled as a beauty parlor and tanning salon.

Rising Son Missionary Church stood on Rising Son Road next to a group of condos sprouting up. The structures were as abundant as daffodils in the spring, gobbling every square inch of space along the marsh. Locals blamed the building frenzy on "damn" Yankee money that was said to be pouring in. They groused that Northerners were snapping up cheap land in their unending quest for pretty spots to build along the coast.

I pulled into a 7-11, locally referred to as *Stop and Robs*, and walked inside to grab some quick lunch. Hurrying past bags of potato chips and pretzels, I snubbed day-old sandwiches filled with mystery meat, determined to press on. I

36

had the best of intentions as I headed toward the rear section with its fresh fruit, yogurt, and cottage cheese. That is, until I ran smack into a display rack of Moon Pies.

Oh, my! It now appeared they came in three tempting flavors—vanilla, banana, and chocolate. The only way to solve this dilemma was to taste test each one.

The Moon Pies took care of my starch requirement. Now I needed some protein in my diet. That proved easy enough. Striding over to a metal pot, I removed the lid and lowered a slotted spoon into the vat of hot water, ladling a batch of salty boiled peanuts into a Styrofoam cup. Add to that a large plastic bottle of Coca Cola and, *voilà*! I had lunch. After paying, I got back in my Ford and drove with one hand, while cracking shells open and popping peanuts into my mouth with the other.

It was a short distance from the 7-11 to I-95. A billboard for a strip club that exclaimed WE BARE IT ALL marked the exit for Brunswick. Formerly a commercial fishing fleet center, the town had sold its soul to industry long ago, and now made the industrial strip around Savannah look pristine. Smokestacks towered above live oaks, belching prodigious amounts of fumes to conjure up visions of Dante's *Inferno*. The acrid odor wafted past my nose, carried on a gentle marsh breeze.

The Fish and Wildlife contaminants office lay just beyond a Sunbeam Bread Outlet and a Michelin tire store. I parked in front of the squat building and continued my taste test by polishing off a banana Moon Pie. Then I walked inside to find that the door to Gary's office stood closed. A cautionary sign pasted on its surface bore the admonishment, WARNING! HAZARDOUS WASTE SITE. CLEAN UP IN PROGRESS. ABSOLUTELY NO ENTRY!

I didn't bother to knock, but gave the warning all the respect it was due by kicking open the door. It immediately became apparent that the sign was no joke. Files, charts, and books covered every bit of three long tables, as well as most of the floor. The place was a virtual storehouse of information with folders strewn everywhere, in sky-high tottering piles. My eyes followed the trail to its natural paperclad end. That's where I found Gary Fletcher intently hunched in front of his computer.

One arm rested on top of a mound of paperwork marked *Crisis de Jour*, while his other hand roamed through a scant head of hair. Two large mugs sat next to his mousepad, one of which contained day-old coffee, while an array of Weight Watchers desserts in open boxes lay scattered about his desk. I just hoped Gary didn't have any delusions about becoming their next spokesperson. He was far from a walking advertisement for their diet, weighing in at close to two hundred pounds.

Crumpled Big Mac wrappers roosted where they'd missed the edge of the garbage can, while petrified French fries had become part of the room's decor. It was clear that Gary had broken the building's *no smoking* rule. The place smelled like the den of a donut-eating, coffee-drinking, something-might-be-dead-in-this-place Marlboro Man.

I cleared my throat and raised a skeptical eyebrow as Gary popped a Weight Watchers brownie into his mouth.

"Hey! Glad you could make it." He smiled, revealing lightly chocolate-tinged teeth.

Holy cow, the man was also a junk food junkie!

"How many of those have you had today?" I asked, knowing full well I wasn't one to reprimand with a vanilla Moon Pie hidden in my glove compartment.

"I'm trying to cut back on calories and still maintain my energy. This is as lowfat as I can get. Want one?"

Then again, who was I to refuse such a generous offer?

"Besides, it's my lunch," he explained, handing me part of his stash.

"Very unhealthy," I tsk tsked, and proceeded to devour it.

We headed outside, taking an extra few cookies with us. Since Gary's vehicle was misbehaving, we settled on traveling in my Ford. He climbed into the passenger seat, accompanied by the sound of peanut shells crunching beneath his shoes.

"I gotta hand it to you, Porter. You run a real class act," he dryly noted.

"Okay, so where are we headed, Scotty?" I asked, riffing on the fact that he was a closet Trekkie.

Besides being a big believer in UFOs, Gary maintained there were aliens walking among us. I still shivered at the remembrance of something he'd once said. *You know you've been abducted when you look at your footprints and your feet aren't in them anymore.*

"Point your starship toward St. Simons Island, Pepper."

I followed his instructions, beginning to think that perhaps being compared to Angie Dickinson wasn't such a bad thing, after all.

St. Simons is just one of the barrier islands hugging the Georgia coast like an expensive strand of pearls—green buffers protecting the Lowcountry from the ever-changing whim of the Atlantic Ocean. They'd become part of my dreams with such evocative names as Sea Island, Blackbeard, Cumberland, and Jekyll. The chain had originally been dubbed the Golden Isles by Spanish conquistadors—a name that remained perfectly valid today. Having once been

vacation hot spots for the likes of the Rockefellers, Carne-
gies, Goulds, and Morgans, they continued to be places
where the wealthy came to play.

That's what made it all the more surreal as I drove down a
generic strip in Brunswick, passing a McDonalds, a Wal-
Mart, and a shop called Guns 'R Us. Brunswick's poverty
lay in direct contrast to the wealth of St. Simons and Sea Island, which were separated from the mainland by a mere
four miles of marsh. Yet they couldn't have seemed farther
away.

I turned onto the F. J. Torras Causeway and headed for St.
Simons now, crossing over five tidal rivers. My arrival was
marked by a marina off to my left, while the Gisco shrimp
docks lay to my right. Two cormorants sat perched on a
group of wooden piles, where they stretched their shiny
black wings and basked in the sun like a couple of lazy
tourists.

Once an island of cotton plantations and slavery, St. Simons was still a land of privilege. Only now it had evolved
into an upscale suburb by the sea, complete with shopping
centers, golf courses, and houses vying for space with ar-
madillo, deer, turtles, and marshes.

"Turn here," Gary instructed, and I swung a left onto
Frederica Road.

We passed small, exclusive stores with wares as tempting
as Godiva chocolates, and probably just as expensive. The
landscape slowly changed as the shops grew fewer and the
houses stood farther apart. Soon we entered a section of
maritime forest where laurel oak, red maple, and sweet gum
trees perfumed the air, each mingling its distinctive scent.

Vines sinuously wrapped themselves around tree trunks

like the limbs of sensuous women, while ancient live oaks wept tears of Spanish moss. My mother had long ago told me that the gray wavy strands were remnants of an old man's beard that had caught on trees as he'd chased young girls through the forest. Only later did I learn it was a bromeliad used by Henry Ford to pad the seats of his first Model Ts. The fibers had also come in handy for stuffing bed mattresses—an interesting tidbit, since chiggers love to nest in the stuff as soon as it hits the ground. I giggled upon hearing that it was the origin of the saying *don't let the bedbugs bite!*

It wasn't long before we reached the island's northernmost end, an area with little development. Having run out of Weight Watchers goodies, Gary now passed the time smoking a cigarette.

"Are you going to clue me in to exactly where it is that we're going?" I asked.

"I just recently learned about this place, myself. It seems they've been requesting a permit to expand their facility. What's interesting is that their application was put on the fast track by the Corps of Engineers and the state of Georgia."

That in itself was enough to raise suspicion. I pretended to patiently wait as Gary blew a smoke ring. It was the restless tapping of my fingers on the steering wheel that gave me away.

His eyes slid toward me, and a sly smile crossed his face. "The only problem is that nobody bothered to bring it to Fish and Wildlife's attention. But then again, it's pretty easy to understand why after my initial visit here this morning."

I was about to press him for more details, when I spotted some sort of entranceway up ahead. *Huh, that was strange.* I hadn't known there were any commercial ventures on this end of the island. Yet, it didn't look like it could be anything else.

Two large statues now came into view, framing either side of an archway. It wasn't until we drew closer that I realized they were giant replicas of manatees. Constructed of plastic, they stood on their tails and wore sequined bras and gauzy harem pants. Proof positive that no matter how much money someone has, it's still no guarantee of good taste.

Slap happy smiles were drawn on each creature's pudgy face, and their flippers pointed toward the archway. The concrete portal itself was garishly festooned with cartoon versions of sea life. But it was the sign hanging from it that caught my attention.

MANATEE MANIA WET 'N WILD WATER PARK
THE WAY MOTHER NATURE INTENDED IT TO BE!

We parked in the lot and walked toward what I imagined to be an extremely tacky tourist trap. Tacky maybe—but one with a hefty price tag. The entrance fee was fifty bucks. I flashed my badge and we proceeded inside for free.

Visitors were first herded through the gift shop. Very clever. It would also be the last place people would stop before they'd leave. Our entrance into the store was hailed by a trio of mechanical manatees singing Beach Boys tunes, which they strummed on fake guitars. But manatee mania didn't stop there. Every single gift item had a picture of the creature on it, from coffee mugs to tee shirts to scarves. I was growing ever more curious as to what this place was about, as we exited the store and entered the park.

A giant Ferris wheel on our right jerked into motion, eliciting a barrage of screams. So did an attraction called *Wet 'n Wild Insanity*, which encouraged hyperactive kids to barrel down a steep water slide. We continued past yet another ride with people in bumper boats, before reaching a large man-made lagoon surrounded by a fence. A sign announced that a separate fee was required for entry. Instead, we dodged the busy gatekeeper and snuck inside.

Techno music boomed from two enormous speakers as a crowd deliriously jumped in and out of the water. What seemed unusual was that everyone wore flippers and scuba masks.

I drew closer, wondering what all the fuss was about, only to spot what appeared to be enormous boulders lying below the surface. That is, until these ghostly gray shapes suddenly came to life and started to glide through the water.

I pushed my way forward as the objects now began to take form. For a moment I could have sworn they were giant Pillsbury Dough Boys floating face down in the pool. No, wait! They were more a cross between mutant Idaho potatoes and Goodyear blimps. Only these tater tots had the thick hides of elephants, must have been ten feet in length, and weighed close to two thousand pounds.

Swiftly dropping to my knees, I leaned over until my face nearly touched the surface. My heart pounded and my breath caught in my throat, my mind insisting that I must be imagining things; it simply couldn't be. Then two founts of water sprayed high in the air from out of a bewhiskered snout, and a pair of tiny black eyes emerged like twin periscopes to look back at me.

My brain screamed, *no way!* as someone shouted, *watch*

out! But I couldn't move, much less speak. I stayed firmly rooted in place, staring in amazement at the creature's face, which was part walrus, part hippo, and squared off in shape.

I stretched out my hand, wanting to feel its snout, needing to make certain that my vision was real. But the mammal promptly slid back beneath the water. Jumping up, I raised my camera and began clicking away, knowing I had to document what I'd just seen.

My actions were met by a tooting sound blasting in my ears like a high-pitched scream, determined to get my attention. No problem there. I spun around, ready to pounce on some ill-mannered kid. Instead, I came face-to-face with a bikini-clad bitch of a Baywatch babe wearing little more than a whistle around her neck.

"Hey! You didn't give me your ticket to get in here," she brayed, her hands firmly grasping two bony hips. "This section isn't included in your entrance fee. The sign on the fence says it's an extra seventy-five bucks to swim with the manatees. Or, can't you read?"

I was tempted to give her something, all right—a punch that would rocket her off to Timbuktu.

"Are you out of your mind?" I began to sputter, only to have Gary intervene.

He steered me out of the lagoon and back toward the bumper boat ride, where a couple of morons sat behind two of the crafts, each cursing a blue streak while acting out road rage.

"Incredible, huh?" Gary remarked, as the two boats collided, shooting a spray of water my way.

Great. Now I looked like a contestant in a wet tee-shirt contest.

"Didn't I tell you it would be worth the trip? Just wait till you meet Wendell, the guy who runs the park."

"What are you talking about?" I exploded, wondering if I were the only sane person in this place. "You *do* realize those were manatees in that pool? Remember, endangered species? For chrissakes, what's going on here is totally illegal!"

"No shit," Gary agreed. "Why do you think I called you? But try telling that to Wendell. I walked out of his office this morning feeling as though I'd been on an acid trip."

"Let's go see this idiot," I darkly decreed.

Wendell would be lucky if *he* wasn't extinct by the time I finished with him. I stormed past the water slide and Ferris wheel, following Gary.

What a lousy way for a dying breed to spend their last remaining days. This was a creature whose relatives dated back fifty million years. Even their name was ancient, spawned from the pre-Columbian Carib Indian word for *woman's breast*. These were the original mermaids, for chrissake! It wasn't their fault if a bunch of sex-starved sailors had mistaken them for women with fishtails, all because they nurse their young in an upright position.

Large and slow moving, manatees are the least-ferocious mammal on the planet, having no natural enemies. Except for man, of course. Once hunted to near extinction, laws were finally passed so that people could no longer slaughter them. Civilization has come a long way. Now it's motorboats that knock manatees off at a record rate.

Each year hundreds die, crushed by speeding pleasure boats and lethally slashed by sharp propellers. If they survive that obstacle course, there's always the chance they'll become entangled in fishermen's nets and drown. That is, if eating polluted sea grass and swimming in toxins doesn't kill them first. Extinction from natural forces at work is one thing. But the toll taken on manatees by humans and their actions is nothing less than marine mammal genocide.

Three thousand, two hundred, and seventy-six manatees are left, with more dying each year than are born. If I had *my* say, Wendell Holmes and his Wet 'n Wild Water Park would soon be the ones going the way of the dodo.

We bounded up a set of rickety wooden steps to a double-wide mobile home built on concrete pilings. I could already tell that Wendell was a classy kind of guy. His mobile home was one of those fancy models covered in wood siding.

A cardboard manatee cutout met us at the top of the stairs with a sign in its fins that read, ALL MERMAIDS PLEASE ENTER. Gary must have thought that applied to him, as well. He didn't bother to knock, but simply opened the door and walked in.

I already had a preconceived notion of how I imagined Wendell would look. Of course, he was nothing like I'd expected. The image I'd conjured was that of a human shark, sleek and lean with a keen sense of cunning to match. Instead, my eyes fell upon a bloated version of an old Robert Mitchum—with one minor addition. His face appeared to have had a run-in with a Mack truck.

Wendell was easily in his mid-sixties, with a ruddy face, eyes that were bleary, and a nose that could have passed for a piece of bruised fruit. The baby-blue polo shirt covering his chest was adorned with coffee stains that dribbled down the front. The fabric itself was worn and frayed where it stretched across his expansive belly. Perched jauntily on his head was a sailor's cap embroidered with a Manatee Mania logo. Upon second glance, I realized that Wendell dressed a lot like the Skipper on *Gilligan's Island*.

"You back again so soon?" he groused, catching sight of Gary.

"Yeah. Why? Did you miss me?"

I walked through the door as Holmes pulled his massive hulk from his chair, with a demeanor like that of a grizzly. However, his scowl promptly vanished as he saw me standing there in my wet tee-shirt, dripping water onto his floor. Funny, how a little thing like that will work wonders on a man. Wendell's eyes began to twinkle, and his growl softened into a smile.

"My, my! So there really *are* mermaids in this world. And just who might this be?" he inquired, bringing a hand to the brim of his cap.

Okay, so I still got a rush knowing I could have that kind of effect on a man—even if they were older and fatter these days.

"Sorry about the water, but I was a victim of a splash-and-run by some bumper boats. I'm Rachel Porter," I responded and shook his proffered hand. My first clue should have been when he didn't let go.

"Don't apologize, sugar. You're dressed perfectly for the occasion. After all, how else would a mermaid appear? Except *au natural*, of course," he joked. "Besides what else is a water park for, if not to have fun?"

"I guess that all depends on what your definition of fun is," I replied, trying to remove my hand from his grasp, only to have Wendell clasp it in both his own.

"It seems we not only have us a mermaid here, but a Yankee one at that. It's a real pleasure to meet you, Rachel. My name is Wendell Holmes."

You can tell a lot about someone from their handshake. I revised my first impression as his grip warned me that he wasn't a man to be screwed with.

"I bet you didn't know there are three kinds of Yankees in this world."

However, he could have been part shark with the way his eyes devoured me. I jerked my hand from his clasp with enough force to produce a suction sound.

"You got your regular Yankees up north. Then there are damn Yankees that come down here to visit. And finally we got us God damn Yankees, who come down here and then won't leave. However, I'm hoping you're among the latter," he flirted with a wink.

"Then it seems your wish has been granted," I responded in kind, as sugary as presweetened iced tea. "In fact, I expect you'll be seeing quite a bit of me."

"Oh, really." Wendell leaned forward as lecherously as the Big Bad Wolf. "And why's that? Have you found something here that you like?"

"Actually, I'm the law enforcement agent for the U.S. Fish and Wildlife Service in the region."

Wendell drew back as if he'd just been doused with a bucket of ice cold water.

"Which brings me to why I'm here today. I'm sure you realize that manatees are an endangered species and protected under federal law. That being the case, maybe you can explain not only how you obtained them, but exactly what they're doing here.

Wendell shot me a look as if to say, *For chrissakes, isn't it obvious?*

"I guess I have them 'cause I like the name Manatee Mania. Otherwise, I'd have to call this place something else like—oh, I don't know—Dolphin Delirium, or Panda Passion, or Wacky Walrus World," he clowned.

Only neither Gary nor I were laughing. Wendell quickly reassessed the situation and took a different approach.

"*Of course*, I know they're endangered. That's the whole reason this park exists," he genially explained. "Those manatees are like my very own children. Every single one of them was either injured or orphaned when they were found. It's just pure luck that I managed to rescue them before they died. You know, it seems to me that someone like yourself should be mighty happy that I was able to save them. In fact, you might wanna give me some sorta medal, and tell more people about this park. Or is helping animals a crime in the eyes of Fish and Wildlife?"

Wendell sure had one hell of a knack for being at the right place at the right time when it came to rescuing injured manatees.

"It's not a crime, though you *are* supposed to have a permit. However, it *is* a violation when you don't inform the proper authorities. It's also illegal to keep manatees as a tourist attraction for customers to swim with at your park."

Wendell placed his hand on his heart. "I gotta tell you that I consider myself to be a true-blue environmentalist. Not just in word, but in deed. Are you saying that I should have twiddled my thumbs and watched helpless manatees die just because I didn't have the government's authorization on a lousy piece of paper? You tell me what's more important: going through the proper channels, or taking action to save these critters' lives?"

Either I was having a bad day, or Holmes was actually

starting to make sense. Especially since I have a tendency not to go through the proper channels, myself. Maybe he really *did* care about the species.

A blast of techno music quickly brought me to my senses. Clearly, Holmes was a master at dodging questions and screwing with people's minds.

He now raised his hands high in the air like a sinner who'd found religion. "It's God's work that I'm doing here, devoting my life to rehabbing these critters."

Oy vey. Who was he kidding? Manatee Mania was nothing more than a rank commercial venture hiding behind the guise of a mercy mission.

"Oh, you mean *that's* what's going on out there in that lagoon," I sarcastically replied. "And here I thought the manatees were just being used as a moneymaking attraction."

Wendell shook his head, as if I had sorely disappointed him. "See there, darlin'? That just goes to show how wrong you can be. What we got ourselves here is an educational facility. The only difference between you and me is how we approach the problem. And as far as I can see, the Feds haven't done too well when it comes to saving manatees. In fact, I do believe their numbers have been going down."

I took a deep breath, sorely tempted to whack him across the side of his head. "Okay, Mr. Holmes. Let me see if I can explain this to you one more time."

But Wendell cut me off at the pass. "First you gotta call me Wendell. Otherwise, I'll think you don't like me. And second, you need to know I've developed an exciting new concept to build awareness of the manatee's plight. It's a little something I call the 'Adopt a Manatee' program.' "

"Trust me. You're going to want to hear about this," Gary

softly murmured, as Wendell grabbed a brochure and waved it in my face.

"Go ahead and take a look. Then let's hear what you have to say. I think you're gonna be mighty impressed. Who knows? Fish and Wildlife might even want to hire me as a consultant," Wendell boasted.

The pamphlet was nothing more than an advertisement for the water park, providing hours of operation, scheduled activities, and a price list.

"Very informative," I caustically noted.

"You're looking in the wrong place!" Wendell brusquely insisted, grabbing it from my hands. He turned to the back, where his finger impatiently stabbed at a short paragraph.

Adopt a manatee and become a proud parent! Receive an authentic adoption certificate, an 8X10 autographed photo of your very own manatee, and its personal biography. You'll also receive valuable coupons toward your first visit, where you can swim with your new special friend. All this for the very affordable annual fee of just fifty dollars! Discounts given to groups of twenty children or more.

The pitch ended with the snappy slogan, *Once you come nose to snout, you'll be hooked without a doubt!!*

Not only was Holmes a con artist, but he wasn't even very original, at that. The adoption concept was already in use by a legitimate manatee organization actively working to conserve the species. Enough was enough. It was time to call Wendell's bluff.

"I've got to tell you, Wendell, it's great that you single-handedly managed to rescue all those manatees. Though I've never heard of anyone being able to do that before."

Wendell proudly flexed his bicep. "It's cause I'm a strong guy. You wanna feel my muscle? Go ahead. But I gotta warn you. One squeeze and you're gonna want more."

Wendell deserved to do time just for bad come-on lines.

"You obviously care about manatees. Which is why I'm certain you've now taken the time to get all the necessary permits. After all, you wouldn't want to keep them here unless they could be properly rehabilitated. What good would that do? Except to rake in money for Manatee Mania as long as they stayed alive."

Wendell remained silent as I proceeded to look around the room. "That's odd. I don't see any of those certificates displayed. I'm afraid I'm going to have to ask you to show them to me."

Only a few proven facilities, such as Sea World, have ever been allowed to obtain manatees. Call me crazy, but I didn't believe Manatee Mania fell into that same category. Wendell stared off into space, as if expecting the certificates to materialize out of thin air, before finally answering.

"I'm afraid I can't do that right now. They're in a locked case inside a safe deposit box at the bank, along with all my other important papers."

"Then that's a problem, Wendell. They're supposed to be up on your wall. Otherwise, how do I know that you really have them?"

Wendell slowly scratched his stomach. "You gotta good point. I guess I hadn't thought about that. Tell you what. I'll have them up the next time you stop by for a visit. Course, first I gotta find the key to the case. I'll be damned, but I can't seem to remember exactly where I put it."

How convenient.

"Don't screw with me, Wendell. I plan to go straight back to my office and check to see if you're telling the truth. Wasting my time will only add a hefty fine onto the violation that you're already going to get hammered with," I fibbed.

Holmes tugged on his cap in frustration. "For chrissakes, were you always such a hard-ass?"

"Should I take it that means you *don't* have the proper paperwork?"

Wendell's head sagged onto his chest. "I really do love these critters, and am only trying to teach people about them."

His voice quivered, causing each word to end with an emotional flutter. The guy was a pro. I think even *he* was starting to believe his own pack of lies.

"But you know how the public is. You gotta amuse them. So what I offer is good, wholesome family entertainment. After all, that's the American way, right?"

Wendell must have been a carny in a prior life, with the way he so easily slipped in and out of each fast-talking sales pitch.

"I got an idea. What say I show you around the park? That way you can see for yourself what we do here."

Now I knew what Gary meant when he'd said that dealing with Wendell was like being on an acid trip. I tottered between feeling flabbergasted and absolutely furious. At the same time, I decided why not give the man more rope with which to hang himself?

Six

We followed Wendell down the steps and across the grounds to a structure painted like a circus tent. A manatee cutout stood near the door with a menu board lodged in its flippers.

"This is Manatee Mania's healthy fast-food café," Holmes proudly announced.

I took a gander at the menu. Every item was deep fried—right down to the manatee burger.

Wendell caught my eye. "Don't knock it till you've tried it. Those critters are mighty good eating."

I must have registered my surprise, causing Wendell to break into a hearty round of laughter. "I'm just joshing with you. We don't actually cook the rascals. It's just what we call our special burgers."

Mmm, mmm, mmm. My stomach quietly growled as I noted they were topped with bacon, mayonnaise, and American cheese. It certainly sounded healthy enough to me. I made a mental note to stop by sometime for lunch before closing this dump down.

Next was the "petting zoo" that featured goats, sheep, and cows, all looking pathetic as kids ran wildly among them playing a game of tag. The one thing there was no shortage of in this park was half-clad girls, all of whom must have been getting degrees in physical fitness. Each wore Daisy Mae short shorts and little midriff tops with Manatee Mania emblems stitched across the chests. Working as glorified baby-sitters, their main mode of kid control was to blow hard on their whistles. Between the babes, brats, and bedlam, I quickly reached my limit with this place.

"Let's stop wasting time and get down to business," I demanded. "I want to see where the manatees are kept."

Wendell shot me a look of annoyance, as he proceeded toward a building that housed a large aquarium.

"This is where the manatees spend their 'down time' when they're not swimming with our guests. Not bad digs, huh?"

The manatees were apparently all in demand, since the tank stood empty.

"Exactly how many manatees do you have at the park?"

"Five little beauties," Wendell beamed. "Dasher, Prancer, Donder, Vixen, and Rudolph. I named them myself."

"Then I guess you must be Santa," I dryly remarked.

"You'll just have to wait until Christmas to find out," Wendell bantered. "Of course, you're also gonna have to be a good girl, if you know what I mean."

Holmes turned his attention back to the tank. "Actually, I like to refer to this place as their salad bar. Manatees may be vegetarians, but those cows can chow down as if there were no tomorrow. You'd think this stuff was Chinese food, what with the way they're always hungry again an hour later."

Manatees pack away a good hundred pounds of greens in the wild every day. The water inside the aquarium was littered with remnants of romaine lettuce leaves. However, most of it appeared to be old and spoiled.

"Of course, that's not all they eat. You'll see that the girls give them plenty of other treats."

"Speaking of which, why don't we see what the manatees are up to?" I curtly suggested.

We left the aquarium and walked to an enclosed area with a small pool. It was here that people had their pictures taken with the manatees for twenty-five bucks a pop. A family of four was in the water now, their arms draped around one poor animal's neck, as a *Baywatch* babe pretended to be a photographer.

"As you can see, the critters are expertly cared for by our staff," Wendell gestured in the babe's direction, managing to maintain a straight face. "Not only are they trained professionals, but the girls also provide plenty of eye candy for us boys who are more grown-up," he added, giving Gary a playful nudge.

I saw him point as "Dad" now picked up his own camera and began to snap some shots of the babe. She posed while feeding the manatee an apple slice that was held in her mouth. That bit of good clean fun only cost the family an additional ten bucks.

Even Gary watched slightly slack-jawed before turning back to Holmes. "Don't stop there, Wendell. You haven't yet told Rachel why you want to expand the park."

Holmes irritably tugged on his cap. "Hell, you can see all the people that come here to visit. Well, they gotta stay somewhere. It's cause we need a hotel on the grounds, of course."

"And?" Gary purposely egged him on.

Wendell took a deep breath, as if girding for an oncoming battle. "There are also plans in the works for a breeding facility."

Now I knew that I was dealing with a certified lunatic. "Have you totally lost your mind? What do you think you're going to do? Raise manatees that you can then sell to other amusement parks?"

Bingo! I knew I'd hit my mark as his face turned beet red.

"Well how else are you going to get these sea cows off the damned endangered species list?" Wendell countered. "Or are you afraid if that happens you'll lose your cushy government jobs?"

That did it. I'd somehow get *his* rear end out in the marsh for a few weeks so that he could see just how cushy it was.

"On top of which I keep telling you that Manatee Mania isn't an amusement park," Wendell stubbornly insisted. "It's an educational facility."

"Oh, yeah? I guess that's why you need the miniature train ride and roller coaster that you have blueprints drawn up for," Gary sniped.

"Okay, you wanna play hardball? Then explain this to me. How come it's all right for people to swim with manatees in Florida, but not here in Georgia? Huh? As far as I'm concerned, it's got something to do with the fact that *you* people like to go down there."

I silently wondered what kind of people it was that he meant—Northerners, Jews, or both.

"That's easy, Wendell. Those manatees aren't kept in captivity but live in the wild, where they're free to come and go as they please. In addition to which, the areas are officially sanctioned by Fish and Wildlife."

What I didn't tell him was that even then, manatees were still harassed. Some swimmers chased the mammals while others clung to their necks, forcing the manatees to take them for a ride. It was ecotourism at its best and worst, providing tour guides and diving centers with a way to make big bucks in the name of conservation.

"That's one helluva piss-poor argument," Wendell spat. "Our critters live better here than they do in the wild. Fact is, they'd probably refuse to leave if we tried to kick 'em out. Besides, you got people swimming with dolphins all over the place. They're even at Disney World, for chrissakes! And you don't hear anyone screaming their damn fool heads off about that."

"For the last time, Wendell, it's because manatees are an endangered species," I said, in near exasperation.

"Which is exactly why I'm trying to save them! Why else do you think I have a staff of crack marine biologists on board here?" he indignantly sniffed.

So far, I hadn't seen anyone working at this park who appeared to be over twenty-five. "And just where would this team of crack biologists be?" I skeptically inquired.

"Why, we got ourselves one right over there." Holmes smugly pointed to the *Baywatch* babe/photographer.

"You've got to be kidding. *That's* your marine biologist?"

"I believe your prejudice is showing, Missy. Didn't your mama ever tell you it's not nice to judge people based solely on their looks?"

That was funny coming from Wendell, since every one of his employees seemed to have the exact same measurements—thirty-six, twenty-four, thirty-six.

"Hey, Candi! Would you mind scooting over here a minute, sugar?" he called to his ace marine biologist.

She wiggled toward us, having apparently achieved a master's degree on how to swing her hips.

"She's also a real Georgia peach, if you know what I mean," he snickered, in an aside to Gary.

I glanced over to find my pal could barely keep his tongue in his mouth.

"You oughta see her playin' with the manatees. One of them even rolls over when she gives it a treat. But then take a look at her. Hell, I'd do the same myself."

I was tempted to arrest her, if for nothing else than that she made me feel like roadkill. There wasn't an ounce of fat on her five-foot, six-inch frame, while she had plenty of curves in all the right places. As for her tan, it was a perfect caramel as opposed to my own skin, which was a lovely shade of red.

"Candi Collins, this here's U.S. Fish and Wildlife agent Rachel Porter and her associate, Dr. Gary Fletcher."

Candi Collins. Even her name was tailor-made for a lay-out in *Playboy*.

Candi adroitly sized up her audience, knowing just how to play it. She charmed Gary with a smile, and flashed me the evil eye.

"Wendell tells me that you're one of the marine biologists here at Manatee Mania," I began my interrogation.

"Actually, I'm the *head* biologist. Isn't that right, Wendell?" She slipped her arm through his, while batting her big blue peepers.

"Absolutely," he enthusiastically agreed.

"So, where did you get your degree?" I inquired, figuring it should be easy to trip her up.

"University of Florida in Gainesville."

"And your master's?"

"Mote Marine Laboratory in Sarasota," she smoothly responded, without having to think twice.

Damn! I'd thought for sure I'd catch her on that one. But Candi confidently flicked her luxurious mane of long blond hair, nearly whacking me in the face.

"Well, it was nice to meet you both. Just let me know if I can be of any further assistance."

Even I couldn't help but stare as she sauntered back to the pool, her hair swaying in rhythm with her hips.

Don't hate me just because I'm beautiful, they seemed to say, mimicking an old TV commercial.

Actually, it seemed a good enough reason to me.

For chrissake, Rachel, get a grip! So what if you're no longer twenty-five and parts of your body wiggle when you don't want them to?

Oh, shut up! I snarled to my rational inner self.

"Meanwhile, all this expansion is taking place on wetlands," Gary added, bringing me back to earth.

"For pete's sake, are you beating that dead horse again? Nobody ever gave a damn when this place was called a swamp. So why should they care now that you're calling it a *wetlands?*" Wendell huffed. "I don't know why you have such a beef with this place, anyway. After all, the state's on board with my plans."

"Gee, I wonder why? Maybe because they're greedy for the revenue that they hope will roll in from tourist bucks," Gary jabbed.

"Damn straight. And what's wrong with that? There's gonna be a helluva lotta jobs created," Wendell righteously added.

I drew closer to the pool where the manatee now lolled, only to see that she had a calf by her side. The mother gently nuzzled the youngster, who responded in kind with a series of squeals, chirps, and squeaks. Once again, I found myself seduced as the baby looked up at me with a pair of dewy basset hound eyes. It was all too easy to see why people felt compelled to make a physical connection. Still the question remained, should a place like this be allowed to make a profit, turning endangered species into moneymaking pets?

I received my answer as the manatee mom tenderly enveloped the baby in her flippers and they slipped beneath the surface to steal a moment of privacy.

It was then that another realization hit—neither animal bore any sign of a fresh scar.

I turned and looked at Holmes. "One more thing, Wendell. How did these manatees come to be injured in the first place?"

Holmes puffed out his chest, looking remarkably like a large pigeon. "Why, from boat propellers, of course."

If that were true, then why hadn't I seen any marks?

I decided not to tip my hand yet, as another family now climbed into the pool. Only mama manatee wasn't in the mood for photos. She tried to pull away as her baby started to cry. But the family solved that problem by tightly wrapping their arms around her neck. The despondent creature's spirit finally broke, and she gave up her struggle. Maybe I was imagining things, but I could have sworn the manatee looked at me with sad, pitiful eyes.

What the hell was I doing, anyway? Screw Wendell, screw the water park, and screw trying to be nice. It was time to bring this freak show to an end.

"Okay, that's enough! The photo shoot is over," I angrily intervened, flashing my badge as they began to protest.

"It's alright, folks. Just come on back later, and the session will be free," Wendell offered, doing his best to smooth things over.

I irately confronted him. "I'll be reporting what I've found to Fish and Wildlife's regional office. If I were you, I'd prepare for this park to be shut down."

However, Wendell's reaction surprised me as a sly smile crept across his face.

"Oh, I sincerely doubt that. You see, I've got everyone from the Chamber of Commerce to the county and state behind me. Not to mention some mighty powerful friends in very high places. But ya'll come back any time, you hear? Why, I'll even arrange for you to get some free passes."

Wendell looked way too pleased with himself as he walked back to his office. So much so that he reminded me of the Cheshire Cat. Only this tom behaved as though he'd just caught, plucked, and deep-fried a couple of unsuspecting chickens. It made me all the more determined to get this park closed down pronto.

We headed out, passing the Ferris wheel, the fast-food café, and the gift shop. Each was filled with a steady stream of customers eager to part with their money. The manatees apparently had more glam power than I would have thought. That was further confirmed as we passed the entrance booth, where a line of people impatiently waited to shell out fifty bucks. There could be little doubt that business at Manatee Mania was booming.

We climbed into my Ford and drove back down the road, past a new sign for the park. All the while, I continued to be amazed by what I'd just seen.

"Where do you suppose Wendell ever got the money to open a place like Manatee Mania? I mean, he doesn't strike me as someone who's rich. Just look at his office and the clothes that he wears."

"Yeah, and you haven't even seen the trailer he lives in. From what I hear, the girls at the park call it his Viagra Palace."

I raised an eyebrow, wondering how Gary had managed to get *that* piece of information.

He caught my expression and laughed. "I can be quite charming when I put my mind to it. Speaking of which, don't let Wendell fool you. The guy is clever as a fox."

"I don't doubt that for a second. I also noticed there's no love lost between you two. In fact, you certainly learned to push his buttons pretty fast."

"What can I say? It's an innate talent. I like to think of it as one of the simple pleasures in my life. As for where he got the money, it's interesting you should ask. Remember I promised to fill you in on what Clark Williams has been up to? Well, your buddy's been a busy boy since leaving the Interior Department."

My curiosity kicked into high gear at the mere hint that there could be some sort of tie-in.

"Tell me about it."

"Well, after the Interior Department, Williams worked as a lobbyist for a high-powered PR firm in D.C.—which, by the way, is owned by his father-in-law."

That was nothing unusual as far as politics and nepotism were concerned. Still, I found the association to be an interesting one. "His father-in-law's a heavy hitter?"

Gary nodded. "Yeah, it seems daddy-in-law dearest has quite the moneyed clientele. We're talking heavy-duty industry groups like oil, timber, mining, natural gas, and development concerns. Now imagine that his hotshot son-in-law suddenly becomes part of the firm, bringing with him all his

Interior Department connections. Clark quickly became the new golden boy, helping to skyrocket Daddy Warbucks into the position of chief fund-raiser for your favorite political party."

"Okay, you've nabbed my interest. But I still don't see how Manatee Mania fits into all this."

Gary gleefully rubbed his hands together like an overgrown kid with a secret.

"Here's the best part. Daddy and Williams had a falling out a few years ago. Evidently, Clark was caught with his you-know-what in the company cookie jar."

"You mean they found that he was filching the firm's money?"

"No, worse. Clark was screwing his father-in-law's favorite secretary. Anyway, Williams left D.C. with his tail between his legs, and decided to strike out on his own. That's when he came down here to the Golden Isles in search of gold, and damn if he just didn't find it."

Gary paused, letting the tension mount until I thought I would burst.

"Tell me what it is, already!"

"Consider what was relatively chcap down here just a few years ago, and yet virtually guaranteed to rise in value."

"I hate riddles," I growled, figuring that should be warning enough that I was in no mood for games.

'L-A-N-D. Land." The word reverently tripped off his tongue, as though it were a priceless gem.

"You mean, Williams has his own development company?" Maybe it was because I had always scraped by that I couldn't help but feel a certain grudging amount of respect.

"Uh huh. The Golden Dreams Development Corporation, and it's fully lived up to its name. Everything the business touches turns to gold. Golden Dreams has been gobbling up enormous parcels of land all along the coast. Williams is now concentrating on buying whatever's left on St. Simons."

"Is there much?"

"Believe it or not, there's still a good chunk of undeveloped real estate along the northern end. That's why he joined forces with Holmes. It was Golden Dreams that provided the seed money for Manatee Mania. Williams is betting the water park will continue to be a great draw as far as attracting families. Think of it as his hook for getting them interested in St. Simons. Pretty smart, huh?"

Absolutely brilliant. "So then, Williams is the real owner of the water park," I concluded.

"I'd say he's more the landlord," Gary explained. "That's the real reason Wendell is pushing so hard to expand Manatee Mania. He wants to make it a top-notch tourist destination, and Golden Dreams is willing to invest the money right now. It's all part of their master plan to convince newly affluent people to buy in the area."

"And why not? It's a beautiful spot, with the added advantage of built-in entertainment for the kids. What a great marketing strategy for selling luxury houses."

"We're not talking just houses. They've also got drawings for a couple of golf courses, churches, and a senior assisted-living facility. Hell, from what I hear, there's even going to be a fancy-schmancy condo complex. But that's only part of Clark Williams's grand scheme for taking over the universe. You care to take a stab at what else he's got going on?"

"Don't make me guess, or I swear I'll corner the market on Weight Watchers desserts and not let you have any."

"Okay, okay," Gary laughed. "It's common knowledge

that Williams is planning to make a run for Congress."

That bit of news took me by surprise. If it were true, no wonder my boss had been nervous.

"Do you seriously believe he'd jump into that arena after his experience in Washington?"

"Are you kidding? He's already got a campaign office set up in downtown Brunswick."

Well, well. Whadda ya know? It seemed I'd hit a double header. No wonder Wendell had bragged of having friends in high places. Not only was Williams the driving force behind Manatee Mania, but he was also a political contender. Thank goodness my visit to the water park had been made before learning of Williams's involvement. Otherwise, I might have been accused of intentionally trying to harass the man yet again. Just wait until he learned that I planned to close down his crown jewel.

I dropped Gary back off at his office.

"All I want after a day like this is to go home, groom my horse, and wash down a bunch of Weight Watchers chocolate eclairs with an endless bottle of scotch." Gary paused. "So, how about it? Wanna join me?"

For the first time, I realized how lonely he probably was. Gary's wife had died of a heart attack a few years ago, and the shock of her death had taken its toll. Why is it that we spend our time mourning those who've passed on, when it's the ones left behind that need us the most? I'd learned for myself that with each passing death, another piece of our soul is lost. Since then, Gary's life had come to revolve around two things—caring for his horse, and drowning himself in work. It was a reaction that I thoroughly understood.

As tempting as his offer was, more pressing was my need to head back to the office. I wouldn't be able to rest until I'd written the report, faxed it to my boss, and knew that Manatee Mania would be promptly closed down. No way did I want those mammals to remain in that hellhole one moment longer than necessary. I was fully determined to get them back in the wild where they belonged.

Gary picked up on my hesitation. "Don't worry about it. I know you're busy. Besides, you've got that man of yours at home to attend to."

Great. Talk about your whopping sense of guilt. I'd been so busy that I'd barely seen Santou this entire week.

"You're right. Then you don't mind if we do it another time?"

"Absolutely not." Gary grinned. "Just try to leave your office before midnight. Otherwise, I'm afraid you'll turn into a pumpkin one of these days."

The man knew me far too well. I'd learned early on that twenty-four hours, seven days a week, wasn't nearly enough time to get all my work done. Not when I was the only game in town, as the sole field agent in Georgia. In truth, it was all too easy for me to identify with endangered species—basically, because I felt like one, myself.

Seven

I battled my way through rush hour traffic, finally reaching my office, where I unlocked the door. Once inside, I groped around in the dark. This was the government's way of letting me know that I wasn't permitted to work overtime. Six o'clock was the magic cutoff hour when the overhead lights were automatically shut off.

I solved the problem by plugging my own lamp into a wall socket. Then sitting at my desk, I quickly wrote my report, after which I e-mailed, faxed, and shot a hard copy off to my boss in Atlanta. I didn't give a hoot about Clark Williams, or who his contacts in Interior might be. I was determined to make this case, no matter what. Best of all, it was only a little past eight o'clock. That still left plenty of time to have dinner with Santou.

I dialed all of his numbers, one by one—cell, office, car phone, and house. But he was nowhere to be found. Jake was clearly unavailable. That being the case, I decided to head into Savannah and eat at my favorite down-and-dirty barbecue spot.

I drove into town and ditched my car, knowing Savannah is a city that demands to be savored. What better way to explore its cobblestone streets than on foot? The historic district was my favorite spot. I trod its sidewalks now, hoping to spy something new and exciting with each twist and turn. Tonight a group of jugglers performed in front of the old cotton warehouses lining the waterfront.

From there I worked my way north, past an architectural hodgepodge of houses ranging from Greek and Roman Revival, to Federalist, Victorian, and Regency. What I loved best were the intricate cast iron railings festooning an array of deliciously ornate balconies.

This was a city that had managed to resist progress throughout its history for a very simple reason. One day its founder, James Oglethorpe took off for England after issuing the proclamation: *Don't do anything until I return.*

Of course, he never came back and the city never changed. It's still a place where tea is taken at noon, voodoo is practiced at midnight, and socialites sip martinis while sitting in front of poet Conrad Aiken's grave. Where else can you find a cemetery whose pathways are lined with "voodoo bricks" designed in a maze, their purpose to keep the spirits from escaping?

But then, Savannah is one of the most haunted cities in the U.S., the souls of those who've died here unable to rest, ever since Union soldiers desecrated their tombstones while marching with Sherman to the sea. As a result, the dead still haunt the streets vainly searching for their graves. Only when they find their proper burial place will they finally be able to sleep.

A veil of Spanish moss grazed my face, and I quickly hurried along. Each house that I passed now sprang to life, having turned ghostly in the dark. The sound of heavy footsteps abruptly came from behind, falling into rhythm with my own. I've learned the need to face down my demons when they approach and swiftly turned around, only to find I was alone.

A sigh escaped my lips, and the thumping of my heart slowed down. Once again, I'd managed to slip past Savannah's specters that were haunting the streets on their nightly rounds.

I scurried up the few remaining blocks and turned into an unmarked alley. From there, I followed my nose. Night was in full swing, and the moon now lit my course.

The smell of barbecue grew stronger, prompting my feet to rap-tap-tap along the cobblestones toward a beam of yellow light that dappled the street up ahead. A lightbulb's rays streamed through a screen door to create a pattern of tiny tic-tac-toe boards. I pulled the screen open and stepped inside the one and only Mo's BBQ Joint.

Sheets of fake red brick sagged where they leaned against the walls, tired as tuckered-out hound dogs, and an ancient fan creaked like the bones of an old man, its blades rasping as they circled overhead. Five steps and I reached the counter, placing my order with a woman so old that the ceiling fan seemed spry. She walked with a limp, wore a fancy gold bow in her hair, and had a face as wrinkled as a dried-up apple.

I chose ribs, red rice, collard greens, okra, and tomatoes—all for the price of seven dollars. Then I slid into a booth at one of three rickety tables and watched her go to work.

The old woman puttered about, murderously hacking away at the ribs with such vengeance that I was taken by surprise. Even more startling was the lethal look in her eyes. Her mouth moved, uttering the same word over and over, as I focused in on what she said.

Clarence, Clarence, Clarence.

The chant tripped from her lips with each fall of the cleaver, appearing to give her great satisfaction. I imagined Clarence to be her husband, and wondered if he were already dead.

She then spooned soggy greens from a battered old pan. The veggies hung limp as wet noodles, having experienced a slow, painful demise after cooking on the stove for several hours.

A tiny black-and-white TV angrily blared where it sat on a decrepit Formica table. Even here, there was no escaping the Auburn–Georgia football game. My dinner was served as Auburn scored a few extra points before halftime. My hostess clucked her tongue in disgust, and irritably turned the channel. Oh goody. I got to watch Robert Stack narrate *Unsolved Mysteries*, instead.

I polished off the last of my meal, dipping a slice of foam rubber disguised as white bread into the remaining barbecue sauce. Yum. Then I attempted to track Santou once more. Damn. The man wasn't anywhere to be found.

Oh, Rachel!

The lights mischievously called from where they danced upon the cobblestones. Only now they'd moved farther down the street and playfully urged me to come along.

While I didn't mind being alone, I wasn't yet ready to head home. Instead, I tripped the lights fantastic and headed to Pinkie Masters's bar.

A local watering hole, Pinkie's is easy to find. The neon Pabst Blue Ribbon sign shines like a beacon in the dark. I entered the smoke-filled bar where the jukebox competed with the halftime show of the game on TV.

Bellying up to the bar, I ordered the house special—a can

of Pabst Blue Ribbon straight out of the cooler on the floor. Then I slid onto a stool and joined the locals, none of whom would have been caught dead ordering a mixed drink in this place. Pulling off the tab, I hoisted the can—no glass, thank you very much—and surveyed my nocturnal companions.

Savannah's pioneers had mainly been exiles released from debtors' prisons. Though that was centuries ago, not a whole lot had changed. These days, Savannah's aristocracy still tends to be one of shabby gentility, many of whom are eccentric enough to belong in a Tennessee Williams play. This gathering of unconventional souls is what gives the city its unique flavor. What other place can lay claim as home to both Juliette Gordon Low, the founder of the Girl Scouts, along with Lady Chablis—better known as *Midnight in the Garden's* ever-loving, party-crashing drag queen?

I knocked back my second beer as the football game resumed, ratcheting the noise level up another few notches. The racket succeeded in driving me out of the place. It was just as well. The guy next to me had become too friendly, and the hour was getting late.

Dragging my rear end off the stool, I walked to my Ford and drove out of Savannah on motorized wings, past the historic district and run-down projects. I waved sayonara to the paper plants, leaving the trappings of city civilization behind. Then, taking a deep breath, I exhaled all of the day's frustrations. And, just like that, I found myself running on Tybee time.

I flew between strands of land, pulled by the gravitational force of the ocean.

Oatland. Whitemarsh. Wilmington. McQueens.

The name of each tiny island ran through my brain like a

mantra, and I chanted them out loud, feeling as though I were a child again. The only thing that slowed my flight was the drawbridge that suddenly rose up into the sky, piercing the heavens like an angry hackle.

Shrimp boats bobbed off to my right, masquerading as fallen stars in the night, their lights forming a strand of diamonds that floated on the black water. I spent the time counting each vessel, while impatiently waiting for a large barge to crawl by. The drawbridge barely came to a close before my foot hit the gas pedal and the Ford continued to soar. I crossed over Lazaretto Creek into Tybee, feeling like one of Blackbeard's invading pirates.

Yo ho ho and a bottle of rum!

The moon cast ghostly shadows that came to life, swaying and dancing in its light, like a gang of drunken buccaneers in search of buried treasure.

The figures trailed me through the night, as I parked under the carport, ran up the steps, and bolted myself inside, only to discover that the house felt strangely empty. Then I realized why. Loneliness had craftily followed me home, stalking my every move. It edged closer as I saw a note lying on the kitchen table.

Had to take off for destination unknown. Should be back in a day or two, chère.

The loneliness that had been peering over my shoulder now brazenly slipped inside my bones.

There was only one thing to do when the darkness and solitude began to loom. I reached for the vodka bottle and poured myself a hefty drink—no ice, thank you very much.

Hell, I didn't even bother with a splash of vermouth. Forget the olives. No need to add juice. Instead, I drank it straight down until nothing was left. Then I poured myself another.

I was in a state of sleep so deep, it's as close to death as one can get, when the strangest sound awoke me. I opened my eyes to discover darkness surrounding me everywhere. I must have nodded off, having forgotten to turn on my night light. I hate when that happens. It gives my demons the freedom to run amuck through my home, my dreams, my psyche.

Tiny shivers ran up my back as I heard the sound yet again. I know my demons inside and out. In return, they've learned to plumb all my weak spots and like to torment me. However, these moans didn't belong to them.

Heartbreaking sobs wound themselves around me tight as a steel band. Their sorrow and pain infused my heart, their wails racked with despair. The cries had come before in the night, always when I was alone. Whoever they were, whatever this was, they clearly wanted me on my own. I had little choice but to leave my bed and go outside to further investigate.

I walked into the night where my feet were pillowed by darkness, though the cathedral ceiling was littered with glittering stars. It was almost as if children had gleefully tossed handfuls of sand high over their head, and the grains had magically adhered to the black velvet sky.

I blindly pursued the sobs where they led, following a trail down along the marsh. The moon had risen, fat and round as a well-fed tick that had been busy feasting on the night. It cast its light over the land like a sheet of black-and-white film, creating a photograph in which I now took part. The air was so still, I could have sworn I was in a trance as I kept walking, having lost all sense of time.

I finally stopped in front of a liquid field of spartina grass, each blade blanketed in a golden net of moonbeams. It was here that the sobs died, replaced by a primal throb that rose from deep within the marsh. The vibration filled my body until my frame hummed along in perfect pitch. Then its beat overflowed to mournfully fill the night. At that moment, the marsh came alive in a symphony of pops, rustles, and plinks. The mud awoke with one great gulp. Even pistol shrimp contributed to the concert, clicking their claws loudly together and snapping at the air. That's when the hairs on my neck stood on end. I could feel that I wasn't alone.

Rachel! A voice called to me from somewhere in the marsh.

It was as if an invisible cord bound us together. Against my better judgment, I began to walk toward the sound. The water lapped at my toes like tiny, wet kisses, but still I didn't stop. Not until the low belch of a tugboat punctuated the air, joining the music of the night. Only then did the spell burst like a fragile bubble, causing my feet to come to an immediate halt. I looked down at where a patch of shiny black mud lay before me.

Then I carefully scanned the area. But the tugboat was the only thing in sight, along with the commercial barge that it steadily pushed upriver. I followed them with my eyes, as they continued toward Savannah. Only when the boats reached their destination could they rest for a while, secure in the knowledge that they'd finally found safe harbor.

Eight

The sun played hide-and-seek, knowing that I wanted to sleep, yet refusing to let me lie in bed any longer. My throat was parched, while my tongue felt like an alien object in my mouth—something akin to a wooly caterpillar. The pounding in my head reminded me to never again mix Pabst Blue Ribbon beer and vodka. But it was the scent emanating from between the sheets that vividly jolted my memory of last night's foray.

Ohmigod! I smelled exactly like the marsh!

I rolled out of bed and jumped in the shower, where the water beat down upon my head. It washed away the pungent smell that stubbornly clung to my arms, my legs, and my hair. The only thing it couldn't rinse away were the cries I'd heard in the dead of night, while tracking sorrowful ghosts through the marsh.

I toweled off, dressed, took two aspirin, and stripped the bedsheets. Then I headed into the kitchen, planning to dine on yesterday's untouched breakfast—a small bowl of Cap'n Crunch.

Opening the fridge, I rooted around—not that there was all that much to dig through. I could have been a stand-in for

Old Mother Hubbard, herself. You know—the one whose cupboard was always bare. But that's what happened whenever Santou went out of town.

I pulled the milk container from behind a couple of beer bottles, opened the carton, and poured some over my cereal. Then I dug into the bowl and popped a spoonful in my mouth—only to spit it back out. The milk had already turned sour. What the hell. There was still a stale Pop-Tart to gnaw on.

I chewed on the dried dough and gummy jelly, only to have it remind me of the mud I'd nearly tramped through in the marsh last night. One thing led to another, as I again replayed what had happened in my mind. There was one person who might provide an answer as to exactly what it was that I'd experienced. Even so, I didn't know if involving her was the wisest thing to do. It could very well stir up more trouble than would prove worthwhile.

I was still tossing the pros and cons back and forth, as my feet carried me toward my landlady's house. Houdini met me halfway, where he loudly purred and rubbed against my legs. Then the cat leapt back up onto his favorite spot—the hood of Marie's mint-condition Eldorado.

The only problem with the car wasn't mechanical; rather, it had to do with its driver. I'm sure Marie could have navigated just fine, if she would have swallowed her pride and stuck a pillow under her rear. Without that additional height, she couldn't see above the damn steering wheel. The result was that whenever she drove, the car appeared to be traveling under its own power.

Though she'd never yet had an accident, it had more to do with the neighbors' precautions than anything else. They'd thoughtfully placed big orange cones along both sides of the road. Their hope was that Marie would take the hint and follow them, like a plane going down the runway.

Even so, something was bound to happen sooner or later. It was just a matter of time. That was the reason parents warned their children to run whenever her yellow bomber came cruising down the blacktop. However rather than flee, it had turned into a game that local kids loved to play. Skipping into the street, they'd join hands and loudly chant,

You better get back
You better get back
Before you end up a big, wet splat.
You better hide
You better run
Or you'll get hit by Marie and be squished like a bug.

The last child to race off the road was declared the winner. That is, unless someone's mother caught them first. Then the kids would scatter at her angry warning:

Watch out! Marie's behind the wheel and she's gonna cream ya but good!

I always loved visiting Marie's house. She was constantly collecting things, so that I never knew what I might find. I traipsed up the walk toward a carousel horse that stood on her porch, as if waiting to take me on a daredevil fantasy ride. Whirligigs dangled from the rain gutters and metal cutouts of dragonflies flew everywhere. Marie said they represented happiness, strength, and courage—three of the essentials for getting by in this world.

I knocked on her front door but received no answer. No

matter. I knew exactly where she would be if not inside. My feet crunched down the seashell-lined walkway, as I now headed for her backyard.

Brightly painted birdhouses sat atop tall wooden poles, helping to guide the way. Though the lot wasn't large, Marie had still managed to make room for two items that were near and dear to her heart.

The first was a small pond edged in purple brick, and gaily trimmed with glass stones and glitter. Nothing unusual there. Except that it held a nude mermaid statue adorned in Mardi Gras beads—a figure for which Marie claimed she had once posed.

The other object was a freestanding deck that rose high above the metal rooftops of all the surrounding houses. It provided Marie with an unparalleled view of the ocean on one side, and a panorama of marsh on the other. The deck's permanent residents were a couple of pink plastic flamingos, along with a knockoff of the famous Waving Girl statue from Savannah. The sculpture stood looking out to sea. Legend had it that her fate was to forever greet approaching ships, while waiting in vain for the return of her lover.

I heard the *squeak, squeak, squeak* of a creaky porch swing and looked up to see Marie and Alfred rocking away, holding hands like a couple of lovebirds. I still remembered our initial meeting. But then, how could I not?

I'd answered an ad in the local Tybee paper concerning a house for rent, and drove by one night to check it out. What I'd found was an old Eldorado parked in the driveway, rockin' and rollin' as though it were possessed. I figured there were probably a couple of kids inside, trying to steal the radio. My plan was to sneak up and scare them. However, *I* was the one who nearly had a heart attack, as I peeked through the fogged-up windows and saw more than I could ever have dreamt. The juvenile delinquents turned out to be my future landlady and her boyfriend, both totally naked, and in the throes of making passionate love.

Talk about your trauma—not on *their* part, but mine! Marie later revealed it was one of the things that kept her young, and suggested that I try it sometime. What the heck. She even said I could borrow her Cadillac.

I sprinted up the steps of the deck, as Marie and Alfred fondly smiled down at me. Just the sight of them together always made me chuckle inside. Probably because they reminded me of a couple of puppets on *Sesame Street*. They were just so damn cheerful all the time. Marie constantly beamed as though she'd swallowed a lightbulb, while Alfred's happiness rose to the top of his head. The tips of his white hair stood up in the air, as if held there by static electricity.

Marie scooted closer to Alfred and patted the seat beside her.

"Come and join us, Rachel," she suggested and then took a closer look at me. "Is something wrong, dear? You look perfectly awful this morning."

She must have been right. Even Alfred's hair stood up a bit higher as he caught sight of me.

"I bet you haven't had your morning coffee yet, have you?" he thoughtfully inquired.

Not unless sniffing the last of yesterday's dried coffee grounds counted. I pathetically shook my head.

"Well then, why don't you girls talk among yourselves while I go and fix us all a cup?" he helpfully suggested.

I wasn't about to turn that down. Not when I knew there'd also be pastry involved.

Alfred gave my hand a sympathetic pat, after which he kissed Marie's cheek. Then he scampered down the steps with all the energy of a sixteen-year-old.

Marie winked at me. "I'm slipping him some Viagra. Now why don't you tell me what the problem is. Have you and Santou had a fight?"

That was just it. There wouldn't have been any cries outside my window last night if Jake had been home. It was then I realized that I was beginning to depend on the man.

I looked over at Marie's expectant face and knew I'd have to fill her in as to what had happened. I just hoped she didn't suck me into her web of wacky superstitions.

"I've been hearing strange sounds outside my bedroom window every once in a while," I tentatively began. "Have you ever heard anything like that over here?"

Part of me wanted her to say yes, so that I'd know I wasn't crazy. Meanwhile, my rational side wanted to believe it was nothing more than an overactive imagination at work.

Marie's eyes grew big as an owl's, and her mouth formed a silent O. "Sounds? What kind of sounds are you talking about?"

A quicksilver jolt of excitement clung to her voice that sent a shiver racing through me.

"It's the sound of people crying. I've heard women, as well as men. Sometimes I swear there are even children. But it's always the same thing. The wails start softly and gradually build to a crescendo." I now found myself admitting more than I had intended. "I followed them down to the marsh last night, where I heard them calling my name."

Marie slowly nodded, as if she knew exactly what I was talking about, while turning toward the marsh. "So that's where they went."

The chill inside me blossomed into goosebumps that broke out along my neck. "Then you've heard them, too?"

"Oh yes, my dear. They used to be outside *my* window until I sent them away. I haven't left this body yet and still need a good night's sleep, you know."

Marie was definitely beginning to freak me out. She seemed to realize it, and gave a reassuring smile. "Shall I tell you what it is you're hearing?"

I nodded, choosing not to speak over the growing lump in my throat.

"There used to be a slave hospital right over there that was originally built in 1767." She aimed her finger like a pointer toward the marsh and Lazaretto Creek, the area where I'd walked last night.

"I never knew there was a slave hospital here on Tybee," I responded, wondering if it were really true.

"Oh, yes. Amazing, isn't it?" Marie intently stared into the distance, as if she could actually see the old building. "That's what 'lazaretto' means. It comes from the Italian word for *pest house*. Lazaretto Creek Bridge was named after the quarantine settlement founded here during that period. This is where people who got yellow fever were left."

Yellow Fever. The words conjured up images of jaundiced patients, their bodies racked with fever, pain, and nausea, as they bled from their eyes, nose, and mouth.

"Ships would stop at Tybee and drop infected slaves at the hospital before continuing on to Savannah. In fact, not all boats even bothered to stop. Some captains simply pushed sick slaves into the river, forcing them to swim here on their own. If they made it to the hospital, they were taken care of. If not, they simply drowned. Those who recovered were later sent on to the slave market to be sold. And those who died were buried in unmarked graves around the marsh." Marie's voice fell to a whisper, her fingers lightly touching her forehead, shoulders, and chest to form the sign of the cross.

Though the day was already heating up, my teeth began to chatter.

"It's their cries that you're hearing, my dear. But don't worry. I'll take care of it for you."

Call me crazy, but I truly wanted to believe her. "How can you do that?"

Marie smoothed my hair back and gently kissed my forehead. "Why just the same as I did for myself, of course. All we need to do is sprinkle some special water on the ground."

"You're not talking about holy water, are you?" I asked in alarm, my stomach starting to churn.

I could just see it now. I'd have to break Marie out of jail for stealing holy water from a church.

Marie pretended to brush some lint off my shirt, as she leaned close and whispered in my ear. "That's what I let the spirits believe. But what I really use is Evian water. They don't seem to be able to tell the difference."

Then she pulled back and continued on in a normal tone of voice. "One other thing, dear. Don't ever do that again."

"Do what?" I questioned, wondering what I'd done wrong.

"Follow a voice outside in the dark. Especially one that's calling your name," she sternly warned.

I was about to ask why, only to be interrupted as my cell phone rang.

"That you, Miss Porter?" inquired a voice as dry as parchment paper.

"Yes, this is Agent Porter," I replied. "Who's this?"

"It's Eight-Ball. You remember me? I was running Mr. Williams's boat through the marsh the other day."

An image flashed through my mind of a slave bending over in a field of cotton, his back lashed and bleeding under the hot summer sun. Just as quickly, the vision was gone.

"Yes, Eight-Ball. I remember. What can I do for you?"

"For me? Nothing. You already done plenty by not giving me a ticket. I want to thank you again for that."

"No problem. Just don't go speeding through the marsh anymore."

Eight-Ball chuckled, and the laugh sat high in his throat, where it sounded like the clicking of bones.

"I'll try not to. But there's another reason I called. I wanna tell you what I seen out in the marsh."

My eyes wandered back to the spot where Marie had pointed and, for a brief second, I felt certain that I also saw the remnants of the old hospital.

"What's that?"

"A buncha dead birds, along with a coupla critters and stuff. I spotted 'em when I was fishing yesterday."

"Do you mean that some animals were shot, and their carcasses dumped there?"

"No, there weren't no bullet holes in them or nothin' like that," Eight-Ball's voice crackled like static electricity. "They just kinda looked like they keeled over, is all."

Some people have a built-in barometer when is comes to choosing what lotto numbers to pick, which horses to play, and what games to call. Mine works differently than that. It lets me know when I'm about to venture into a case that might swallow me whole. There it was now—the slightest twinge in the pit of my stomach. I pretended to ignore it—though that had never stopped me before.

"Where did you see all of this, Eight-Ball?"

"It's a place I like to go crabbing in Brunswick, called Purvis Creek. To tell you the truth, I seen other dead critters there before. I just wasn't sure who to call. 'Sides, I don't like to get involved in things, if ya know what I mean."

I had a pretty good idea. The best way to stay out of trouble was to keep your mouth shut. It was a lesson that I, myself, had been told to learn more than once.

"Thanks for the tip, Eight-Ball. I'll check it out. Also, would you mind giving me your telephone number? That way I can call, in case I have any questions."

"I wouldn't mind. Only problem is, I don't have a phone."

Though he didn't say where he was calling from, I figured Eight-Ball was probably already at work.

"Okay then, how about if I meet you somewhere later on? I'll take you for a beer."

"I usually go fishing at the end of the day. Course, you can come by the river and bring a six-pack with you," he suggested.

That sounded fine. Except that this was a big coastline. I'd need more specific directions than that.

"Are you talking about where you found the dead animals?"

"No, Miss. I ain't gonna fish there no more. Something's real wrong with that water. I'm stayin' with my cousin over on St. Simons. The best fishing around there is a place called

Village Creek Landing at the end of South Harrington Road. You know where that is?"

"Don't worry. I'll find it."

The twinge in my chest had now developed into a steady thump. No doubt about it, I was definitely on the track of something big. I put the cell phone away as Alfred reappeared, carrying a tray.

"For the two most beautiful women in Tybee," he said, serving us each a cup of coffee, along with cranberry muffins. "Sorry it took so long, but I couldn't locate the muffins anywhere. I finally found them stashed in the linen closet."

Marie resignedly shook her head as she took a bite. "Naturally. That's one of Thomas's favorite hiding places. If he doesn't start behaving, I might have to get rid of him, too."

"Don't say that, dear. He's really not a bad sort. After all, he lets me spend my time with you," Alfred gently reminded her.

I finished my coffee and said good-bye. It was only as I headed down the steps that I once again remembered Marie's warning. I quickly clambered back up, where I caught Marie's eye just as my head peeked above the floorboards. Her hand jerked, causing her coffee to spill.

"My goodness, Rachel. You startled me. You look like a decapitated chicken."

Alfred deftly blotted her off, and I plunged ahead with my question.

"Sorry, but there's something I wanted to ask. Why did you tell me never to follow an unseen voice at night that's calling my name?"

Marie's expression turned deadly serious. "Because it's dangerous. There's only one reason why a spirit would call to you. You're being beckoned to join them in the afterlife."

Terrific. I should have figured it would be something like that.

The chill that had passed through me now took up permanent residence.

Nine

I flew south on I-95, as much to flee unseen ghosts as to make good time, while punching Gary's work number into my car phone.

"All right, it's your turn to come out with me today," I said by way of hello as he answered the line.

"Oh, yeah? Whassup?" he asked, in pitch-perfect imitation of an annoying TV commercial. Okay, so it was actually funny the first few times.

"Remember the old man I told you about? The one who was ferrying Williams around the marsh? Well, he just called. It seems Eight-Ball's been finding lots of dead wildlife along Purvis Creek in Brunswick. And since you know the area, and have a boat, you're my main man today. He mentioned there were no discernible marks on any of the animals or birds to indicate how they had died. I thought you'd find that of interest."

"What? You mean nothing to show they'd been bludgeoned, stabbed, or shot by our local contingent of good old boys?" Gary joked.

"Nope. Eight-Ball seems to think it might have something to do with the water."

"Ah, so now he's also a part-time biologist."

"All I know is that Purvis Creek was his favorite fishing spot up until yesterday, and now he won't go there anymore."

Gary remained silent for a moment. "Then I guess he must be serious. In which case, it could be any number of things, ranging from a disease outburst to contamination of some sort. What say we take a few samples and see if there's any truth behind what your friend thinks? I'll have the boat hitched up and ready to go by the time you get here."

My Ford tore down the blacktop, bypassing rural towns on a concrete swath of highway that sliced sharp as a butcher's knife through Georgia. Billboards whizzed past, advertising everything from barbecued pork to pecan pie. My stomach would normally have been growling by now, but my mind was elsewhere. I was thinking of chiggers, black rats, and palmetto bugs and how they all liked to live in Spanish moss. In some ways, it was as deceptive as the beauty of the South. It always came as a surprise to realize that something unbeknownst was slumbering deep inside, cunningly biding its time before choosing to reveal itself.

My car phone abruptly rang and I jumped, having been caught off-guard.

"Hey, Porter. How's it hangin'?"

I instantly recognized the voice. The caller was Spud. How apropos—just when I was thinking of vermin.

"Everything's fine, Spud. What's up with you?"

"Nothing much. Just that I heard you found yourself some performing manatees yesterday. It sure as hell took you long enough. But congratulations, anyway."

It was as if someone had snuck up from behind, and jabbed me with a shot of adrenaline.

"Why would you think I found something like that?"

"Oh for chrissakes, cut the act, Porter. My old girlfriend

called and yelled at me. The bitch is convinced that I dropped a dime on the place."

I found it funny that his former sweetie should be just as big a blabbermouth as he was.

"And who might this old girlfriend of yours be?"

"A bimbo by the name of Candi Collins."

Well tie me up and knock me down. I quickly turned the wheel, as I came close to veering off the road. It just went to show there was no accounting for taste, on either of their parts.

"You mean to tell me that you once dated a marine biologist?"

Whatever Spud was munching on must have gone down the wrong way. I waited as he hacked it up, spat it out, and then took a slurp of something.

"Marine biologist, my ass! The only thing Candi knows about fish is how to serve it. And by that I mean, she waited tables at the Huddle House before this manatee water park gig came along."

Spud had a wonderful way of making me see things from a totally different perspective. I actually found myself beginning to sympathize with Candi.

"Is there a reason for your call, other than to pass some time and shoot the breeze?" I inquired, anxious to end the conversation.

"Yeah. I've got a helpful little tip for you. Why don't you ask Candi how they got all those ugly-ass sea cows in the first place?" he suggested.

"I've got an even better idea. Why don't you just spit it out and save me the time and trouble?"

"Who, me? I don't know nothing," Spud blithely responded. "I'm just trying to think of ways to help you along with your job. Sometimes the right word here and there is all it takes. Happy hunting, Porter!" he cheerfully signed off.

My guess was that Candi Collins must have recently dumped Spud's rear end, proving once again that pissed-off spouses and disgruntled ex-lovers always make the best informants. In any case, it was a connection worth checking out—if for no other reason than to hear Candi's side of the story.

But Spud's call had spurred more than just idle curiosity. My suspicions were newly aroused. Something odd was definitely afoot at Wendell's water park. All it took was one look at the manatees to see they bore no sign of recent injuries—and certainly none that required rehabilitation.

I arrived at Gary's office to find that he was already waiting outside, with his twelve-foot johnboat hitched up and pertly sitting on its trailer. I chuckled to myself as I caught sight of its tag. The S.S. *Lucille* had been named after his horse.

"Ah! Take a deep breath, Rach. Don't you just love the reek of chemical plants and paper mills first thing in the morning?" he asked, expansively thrusting his arms open wide. "Time's a-wasting. Let's get going."

I hopped out of my Ford and into his pickup, nearly squashing a box of Weight Watchers brownies in the process.

"Hey, watch it, Pepper. I don't work well without my requisite daily supply of snacks," he said, removing a brownie from its half-crushed box and taking a bite.

We headed out, taking a different route this time, down Newcastle Street, where we passed the defunct Kress Five and Dime, before motoring by old Victorian houses that had once been beautiful in their prime. Run-down bungalows now sprang up beside them, their shabby exteriors partially concealed by ancient live oaks. The trees themselves appeared to be on the move, anxious to leave for better environs, their roots breaking through slabs of concrete pavement to show their displeasure.

After that we drove by the projects, where poverty, crime, and hopelessness all crowded together in a morass of public and low-income housing. Downtown Brunswick was not unlike a chain of wobbly dominoes. One after another, local stores and businesses had taken a tumble, so that this once-thriving town was now struggling to survive.

We swung onto Highway 17 and set our sights directly ahead for the causeway leading to St. Simons. It lay unfurled like a glittering silver strand, and we quickly drove across, leaving Brunswick behind to enter the promised land.

Ba bump. Ba bump. Ba bump.

Each revolution of our tires brought us that much closer, as the reek and filth slipped away like so much fairy dust. Gary's pick-up veered onto an unmarked road, clearly knowing the way all on its own. We traveled down a concrete ramp that carried us straight into the marsh. Once there, Gary turned the vehicle around and parked. Then we unhitched the S.S. *Lucille*, and slid it ever-so-neatly into the water.

"It's all yours, Captain Kirk," I said, and sat back to enjoy the ride.

The engine kicked in, and a flock of black-and-white wood storks took flight, the graceful flap of their wings so heartstoppingly beautiful that I literally ached inside. I watched until my attention was drawn to a great blue heron that stood as if frozen in time. Thin and elegant, the bird looked as regal as one of the island's wealthy women, where it posed motionless in the water, silently stalking its prey.

Then bending its long graceful neck in an S curve, the heron lashed out without warning, neatly impaling a fish on its sharp, pointed beak.

The world changed yet again as Gary steered back toward Brunswick and Purvis Creek, where seething smokestacks angrily raged against the sky. A trailer park stood on the bank to our left, along with a few listless residents who whiled away the time with fishing poles in hand. Crab buckets merrily floated nearby, looking like little round coffins.

We continued on, puttering in the S.S. *Lucille*, until we rounded a bend where no one was in sight. Gary turned off the engine.

"Slip these on," he instructed, handing me a pair of latex gloves and boots, as he did the same.

"Why are we stopping here?" I asked, not seeing any dead critters on the bank.

"Take a look around."

I had already done so, but did again, hoping to appear smarter than I felt. Big surprise, it didn't help. I had no idea what I was supposed to be looking at.

Gary finally took pity and focused my attention in the proper direction. "See the grass over there?"

"Uh-huh," I responded, still not ready to admit that everything looked A-okay to me.

"Well, it's all the same height, except for one spot to the right where it's definitely a bit shorter. Not only that, but there's also a lot of brown and yellow grass mixed in with the green. It's enough to clue me in that the vegetation is stressed. Now take a gander over to your left and tell me what you see."

I stared hard, first squinting my eyes and then opening

them wide. Maybe I was just imagining things, but it was worth a stab.

"The grass appears to be much greener and the vegetation looks as if it's growing in a fan shape," I responded, feeling like a promo for Erma Bombeck's book, *The Grass Is Always Greener Over the Septic Tank*.

"Very good," Gary commented, sounding slightly surprised. "Those are some of the visual tip-offs for a contaminants expert. What it tells me is that something's not quite right in this place."

He stepped out of the boat. "Don't wander off, but stay close to me. Oh yeah. And try to walk in my footsteps."

I dutifully followed.

Squish, squish, squish.

My rubber boots gently sank into the soft marsh floor, as if I were walking on wet foam rubber. We hadn't gone very far when something caught my eye. A few dead fish were floating on their sides among a field of spartina grass. They looked as though they'd been steamed, and were ready and waiting to be served for dinner. It took a moment before I realized what was so strange about them. Their skin had been partially sloughed off.

"Hey, Gary. Over here," I called out.

He kicked his way back through the water like an overgrown kid wading in a mud puddle.

"Let's see what we've got here. Hmm, a couple of killifish that look like they've had a run-in with the Terminator."

My own skin began to crawl. If something around here was doing that to fish, what might it do to me? I instinctively patted myself, just to make certain I still had all my body parts.

Gary placed the fish in a plastic bag and we moved on.

Blades of spartina grass rhythmically slapped against my thighs as if in protest. They softly whispered that I was encroaching somewhere I didn't belong. Their sharp red tips bit into my skin to emphasize their point. We hadn't gone very far when Gary spotted a dead clapper rail that had been feeding in the marsh.

"Time for another body bag," he darkly joked.

A marsh rabbit lay on the bank, where it appeared to be catching ten winks. I plodded through the grass and carefully tapped it with my toe. Either it had downed one hell of a sedative, or the bunny was sleeping the sleep of the dead. Gary bagged and tagged the rabbit as well, and we continued with our search. However, anything else that might once have been here was now gone. Most likely, it had become breakfast, lunch, and dinner for a multitude of hungry critters.

Gary next pulled an acid clean jar from a satchel he was carrying and filled it to the brim with marsh water. Then he produced a stainless steel bowl and spoon.

"Here, hold this," he said, handing me a second clean jar.

Terrific. I was thigh deep in water and muck, only to have Gary turn into a saltmarsh version of Martha Stewart. I watched as he carefully scooped up some mud and methodically began to mix it in the bowl.

Add two eggs and bake at three hundred and fifty degrees, I silently mused, as he scraped his creation into the jar that I held.

"You want to make sure to stir your sample well. That way, whatever contaminants are lying at the bottom will be picked up," he explained.

"Well, aren't you prepared?" I lightly teased, though I was thoroughly impressed.

Gary grinned and placed those containers in his satchel before handing me a new jar. "It's the law of the six Ps. Surely, you know them. Proper Planning Prevents Piss-Poor Performance."

Bending down, he painstakingly removed some tiny snails from a few blades of spartina grass.

"Is there anything that you *don't* take samples of?" I asked, looking on in wonder.

Gary shook his head while adding that specimen to his collection, after which he pulled out yet another jar. "Nope. It's always best to remember that everything's got a story to tell. Some are going to be obvious and shout at you, while others are just going to whisper."

I silently vowed to remember that piece of advice.

He continued on, filling jar after jar with spartina grass, blue crabs, and fiddlers. I had a sudden image of what Gary must have been like as a child, and quietly laughed to myself. I'd once read about a boy who'd taken a jar full of spiders to bed, only to have the arachnids escape. They must have been busy during the night, since his mother found him covered in cobwebs the next morning. I had no doubt that Gary also slept surrounded by his samples.

"What say we head over there?" he suggested, pointing farther down the creek.

We trekked even deeper into the marsh.

My mind wandered as I journeyed through an endless field of spartina grass, pretending that I was a pioneer woman and this was my little house on the prairie. It's when I least expect it that I'm usually caught off-guard. That's what happened now, as a form mysteriously began to take shape. I squinted, and the marsh joined with my pulse to beat like a drum. I could have sworn that sticking up from the mud was a human hand. I warily edged closer, and it slowly transformed into the lifeless body of a juvenile egret.

Wuss! I chided myself.

I pointed the bird out to Gary, and he added the carcass to his collection. Lying nearby were long white feathers rimmed with black, clearly those of an endangered wood stork. Gary picked them up, as well.

"What are you going to do with feathers?" I asked, continuing to be amazed by all the different samples he was taking.

"It's another great way to test for contaminants. A bird's system will try to secrete toxins by storing them in their feathers."

Okay. Who was *I* to know the difference? Up to this point, I'd thought of myself as being incredibly thorough.

"I learned long ago that unless you look good and hard for something, you generally won't find it. That's why the bureaucratic weenies in Fish and Wildlife call me Dr. Doom and Gloom. They know once I get on a case, I don't let up until I've discovered the truth. Even when they prefer I didn't. I refuse to stop poking around until whatever's screaming to be found has been uncovered."

I knew there was a good reason why I liked this guy.

"So, what do you think is going on out here in the marsh, Doc?"

"We'll know soon enough," Gary said and gave his satchel an affectionate pat. "But whatever it is, I've got a gut feeling that it ain't good. There are a few too many dead critters."

He stretched and looked back toward the S.S. *Lucille* for the first time since starting our walk. "Oh shit!"

My stomach responded with a sickening lurch. "What is it?"

"The tide's rushing out. We have to head for the boat pronto. That is, unless you're particularly fond of this place and want to spend the rest of your day here."

The scent of mud and algae had already begun to heat up, coalescing into a foul-smelling brew tinged with a dash of rotten eggs. Though the odor might prove a good incentive when it came to dieting, this was a lousy place in which to be stranded.

"No thanks. Nothing personal, but I've got better things to do."

I began to take a step toward the boat, when Gary's hand wrapped itself tightly around my arm and sharply jerked me back.

"Uh, uh!" he warned.

"What the hell did I do wrong?" I asked, feeling mildly defensive.

"Take a look at where your foot was going to land."

Though I eyeballed the area, it all looked the same—a slimy, dark field of mud.

"Do you see how shiny that patch is right there?" Gary asked, pointing to the exact spot where I'd been about to step. "Now take a good look at the puddle of still water that's sitting on top of it."

"Yeah. So?"

"So, step into it and you'll probably sink right up to your eyeballs, if not clear over your head."

That image slyly preyed on my senses as I now envisioned soft mud plugging up my nose and mouth. Perhaps I imagined it a bit too well. I felt myself begin to gasp for air.

"You have no idea how many people don't pay attention to black mud when they're out here, and wind up dying that way. It's a hell of a lot easier than you'd think. Even if you only get stuck in it up to your waist. Sure, you might be okay, as long as you don't panic and try to fight your way out of the stuff—assuming you're not alone, or that some-body finds you in time. Otherwise, you're a real goner."

"How so?"

"Because sooner or later, high tide is going to roll in just like clockwork. Once that happens, you're bound to die a gruesome death."

"Well, that really sucks."

But I knew he was probably right. Tides in this area could fluctuate up to ten feet, and came racing in from three to nine miles per hour.

An army of little fiddler crabs popped in and out of the mud, where they danced in a frenzy around my feet. But it was the blue crabs that I feared. There were millions of them here in the marsh. I'd heard tales of how they would appear en masse and quickly devour a body. I imagined I could al-ready feel their pincers at work, sharply nipping away at my toes, legs, and arms.

"Thanks for the lovely vision," I wisecracked. "What are you trying to do? Sufficiently scare me so that I never again venture into the marsh without you?"

"What can I say? I like to feel needed," Gary quipped. "It's just a natural occurrence that happens as the tide washes back and forth. Water saturates the mud, breaking it down until it becomes ten feet thick and gooey. Those pud-dles of still water are letting you know that the gunk sitting there is in suspension."

I looked over and saw the S.S. *Lucille* tied to a bunch of spartina grass, where we'd left it. Only now, it was barely floating in a few inches of water. Even more frightening were the shiny black patches of glutinous mud that seemed to have popped up everywhere. They lay like deadly land mines between ourselves and the boat.

"Terrific. In that case, how do you suggest we get home?" I asked, pointing toward the ominous checkerboard.

"That's an excellent question," Gary responded, pretending to twirl an imaginary mustache. "It's exactly why I brought these along."

Tucked under his arm were a pair of paddles.

"What do you plan to do with those? Have us paddle our way through the mud?"

"Very funny, Rach." Gary chuckled, as though he were having the time of his life. "It just so happens these babies are going to act as a bridge to get us across the marsh."

My eyes nervously wandered back to the foreboding dark blobs. "Are you sure two paddles will be enough to do the job?"

"I don't see that we have much choice. If they're not, we'll have ourselves one hell of a mud bath, won't we?"

"In other words, I might die, but at least my skin will look great."

"You've got it."

"How consoling."

"Aw come on, Rach. I'm just joshing." He laughed. "You know I'd never let anything bad happen to you."

I looked over at Gary and knew that he meant it. An unspoken bond had sprung up between us these last few months. I completely trusted the man.

"Okay, Captain Kirk. Lead the way."

"What you need to learn is that walking through the marsh is somewhat akin to piecing together a jigsaw puzzle. You just have to find the right areas where it's safe."

I followed as Gary leapt from spot to spot like a billy goat, sometimes landing on both feet, sometimes balancing on just one. We continued to zigzag back and forth in round-about fashion, slowly drawing closer to the S.S. *Lucille*. That is, until we hit the last stretch where nothing but black mud lay spread out before us.

"This is where it's gonna be fun."

Gary slung his satchel around his neck, and then carefully placed one of the paddles face down in the mud.

"Just try to think of yourself as a tightrope walker. I find that image generally helps. Oh, yeah. And make sure not to step off the paddle without first checking for a patch of hard land on which to jump. Otherwise, it kind of defeats the whole purpose."

By now, my stomach had become one massive knot.

"No problem. I'll just follow in your footsteps." What the heck. Gary had been pulling this stunt for years and apparently hadn't died yet.

"Oh, yeah. That's the other thing. I'm afraid you'll have to go first."

"What!"

The rock-solid trust that I'd placed in the man instantly vanished.

"Have you gone totally loony tunes? Or did you take out a life insurance policy on me that I don't know about?"

"Listen Rach, I'd gladly go first but I can't. This sucker's gonna sink beneath me like a rock due to my weight."

"Well, thanks a lot for waiting until now to tell me this," I sniped.

"Hey, no sweat. I'll take the lead if that's what you want. Of course, the problem is that then *you'll* be left behind."

Gary blinked at me like an owl from behind his horn-rimmed glasses.

Shit! I should have suspected there'd be a catch. Naturally, I'd been the klutz that never made it across the balance beam during high school gymnastics.

"You can do it. Just be careful and keep your balance."

"Yeah, yeah, yeah," I muttered, throwing Gary a dirty look.

"Maybe you should try holding your arms out at your sides like I do," he helpfully suggested. "It kind of makes me feel like an airplane. Go ahead, you'll see."

"Great. Then I can feel like one that's about to take a dive," I snarled.

"Don't worry. I'll be right behind, as soon as you step off."

Fall off is more like it, I balefully thought.

I held my breath and tentatively placed one foot on the paddle. Not bad. That is, until my other foot joined it and the oar started to totter and sink. I instinctively jumped off.

Gary's fingers impatiently tapped out the Funeral March on his satchel. "I'm afraid you're gonna have to move faster than that, Rach. Otherwise, we'll never make it to the boat in time."

"One more word from you and I'll be using *your* body to get across this damn marsh."

Okay. Think of yourself as the star on the women's Olympic gymnastics team, I thought.

I did my best to imagine that I was being held up by ropes and couldn't possibly fall, as I stepped back onto the paddle.

To hell with women's gymnastics. Imagine you're Peter Pan and fly across this damn thing, my inner voice instructed.

That seemed to do the trick. I reached the end of the paddle before I'd even realized it.

"Remember, don't step off until you're sure that it's safe," Gary called from behind.

Black mud lay in all directions, except for one spot that appeared to be solid. The problem was, it would take a decent leap to get there. I had no choice other than to hope my guess was correct as I took a deep breath and said a silent prayer. Then I jumped, wondering how it would feel to be swallowed up by a chocolate mousse mud puddle.

My feet hit dirt, only to feel something shaking. No, it wasn't an earthquake, but the quivering of my legs. I'd managed to land on terra firma. I was tempted to fall down and kiss the ground but decided to play it cool, instead.

"Your turn," I said, pretending to stifle a yawn.

"Have I ever told you there are times when you're actually very cute?" Gary chortled.

I watched as he now held out his arms and proceeded to scamper across the paddle like an overweight version of Baryshnikov. Good thing he moved as quickly as he did. Gary had been right. The instant he jumped off, the paddle sank deep into the marsh.

"Okay, one down, one to go. Just make sure you reach the boat on this next round, or we'll both be sunk," he instructed, laying the last paddle across the mud.

"Thanks, no pressure there."

I mentally prepared myself the same as before. Only this time I froze, unable to take the first step, certain that I would fall. Gary instantly took note of the problem.

"You've got to keep going, Rach," my coach urged.

That's what I told my feet, but they still refused to move. It was then that I heard what sounded like the stomping and snorting of an angry buffalo behind me.

"Goddammit to hell, I should have known better than to

ever bring a woman out here in the first place," Gary roundly swore. "Fish and Wildlife was right to want to keep Special Agents an all-male force. They obviously knew they'd run into this kind of problem."

My skin began to burn, partly in anger, partly out of humiliation. I now had every intention of not only making it across the damn paddle, but then lifting it from the mud and whacking him with it.

Gritting my teeth, I placed one foot in front of the other, refusing to stop until I'd reached the end of the oar. Then leaning over, I grabbed hold of the boat and pulled myself inside. I stood up, determined to exact my revenge, only to find Gary oddly beaming at me with pride.

"It's amazing what a little reverse psychology can do, isn't it? Please, no applause. You can thank me later," he said, taking a bow. Then he proceeded to dart his way across the paddle.

Boy, was he in for a surprise upon his arrival. I was mad as hell. Turning around, I began to peel off my gloves when a loud commotion erupted. I looked up in time to see Gary lose his balance and fall off the oar. My heart lurched, and I held my breath, as he landed knee-deep in a pool of black mud.

"Oh my God! Are you all right?" I yelled, forgetting all about my anger. I was too afraid the mud would malevolently suck him down and gobble him up.

But rather than respond, Gary swiftly pulled the satchel from his neck.

"Here, just make sure this is safe," he instructed and threw the bag toward me.

I caught the satchel in both hands and carefully placed it in the boat, more for his sake than my own. All I cared about at this moment was saving the man.

"Okay. Now what can I do to help?"

"There should be a long pole somewhere on the bottom in there. See if you can find it."

The S.S. *Lucille* was about as clean as my Ford. We both deserved to be given tickets as litterbugs. I swiftly pushed piles of junk around until I finally spotted the pole peeking out from under a bunch of life jackets. I held the stick toward him, but it fell a few feet short.

"I think I can grab hold if I just stretch a bit more," Gary insisted.

"Don't do that. It's too dangerous. Let me bring the boat closer."

"No, stay where you are. Otherwise, you'll get stuck in the mud," he stubbornly maintained.

Gary was so obstinate that I'd have gladly knocked some sense into the man, if only I could have reached him. Instead, I was left with little choice.

"Okay, whatever you say."

I leaned forward while Gary lunged for the pole, only to lose his balance yet again. This time he fell onto his hands and knees like an impish child, causing mud to splatter on his face. I'd have been tempted to laugh, if I weren't worried sick.

Bracing myself against the side of the boat, I held the stick out once more. "Good move, Gary. I don't think I'd have tried that myself, but you should be able to reach the pole now. That is, if you still have the use of your hands."

"Don't say another word," he warned, carefully straining to pull himself up from the muck.

I'd have thought the stuff was Silly Putty, what with the way it clung to his limbs. He ever-so-slowly worked one arm free and grabbed onto the pole, as his other arm toiled its way out of the sludge like some primeval creature struggling to be born. I waited until he firmly had hold. Then, propping my feet against the boat, I began to pull. What progress we made was done in snail-like fashion. I felt certain my arms were about to give way when Gary finally hauled himself inside, where he sat huffing and puffing, minus his boots and covered in mud.

"Wow. Am I a lucky gal, or what? How many women can say they've actually been paid a visit by the Swamp Thing?"

"Very funny, Porter," he cracked, still trying to catch his breath. Once he did, Gary broke into relieved laughter. "That *was* a pretty aerobic workout. Hell, I should be able to eat a good half-dozen donuts without any guilt."

"Yeah, I think you deserve at least that much," I agreed with a grin.

Gary flipped on the boat's engine and began to steer out of Purvis Creek, only to stop at the crab pot that we'd previously passed. He took a quick look around and then snatched a few of the crabs, sticking them into a baggie.

"What's that for? Tonight's dinner?" I quipped.

"No, it's so I can test their tissue, wiseass," Gary smartly responded.

We continued into the Turtle River and back toward St. Simons.

Putt, putt. Putt, putt. Putt, putt.

The sound of the motor became a mechanical lullaby, mixing with the penetrating call of a kingfisher. The blue and white bird perched on a branch, sporting a bushy double crest that gave it the look of an avian punk rocker. It scanned the water's surface with large, piercing eyes before plunging headfirst into the water. A moment later, the bird emerged with a small fish in its daggerlike bill. Then the "King of the

Fishers" flew back to its perch and viciously beat its prey to death before devouring it.

"You wanna hear something really twisted? Now that I'm safe, I can admit that I actually had fun back there," Gary revealed.

"Yeah, me too," I reluctantly conceded.

"That's what's so insane about our jobs, you know," Gary now waxed philosophic. "These adrenaline surges that constantly push us to respond to the next crisis. Hell, I even begin to crave the high after a while, just like a junkie."

I knew only too well. Santou had once accused me of preferring to be at work rather than at home. Though I'd refused to admit it, he'd been right. There was something about the rush that came from dealing with danger that couldn't be matched by watching TV or doing housework.

"I mean, do you realize the number of man hours we put in each week?"

"I suppose I think of it as dedication," I responded, loath to confess that my obsession might actually be a problem.

"Bullshit. You can't fool me, Rachel. I may be a contaminants expert, but I'm just the same as the rest of you law enforcement junkies. Our jobs are our lives. It's what we eat, sleep, and breathe."

Gary was right. Work was the sole reason that I woke up in the morning. No sooner did I finish one case than I actively sought another. Santou had finally given up trying to change me.

"So, 'fess up. Don't you ever think you might possibly want something more out of life than just chasing after poachers and ghosts?"

A subterranean chill crept into my bones.

"Poachers and ghosts? What are you talking about?"

"Don't play coy. You know what I mean. There are poachers who are easy to catch, and then those ghosts that you're never able to snag—the ones that become your personal Moby Dick."

"You mean there's more to life than that?" I joked. "What happened to you back there in that mud, anyway? Did you have a divine revelation of some kind?"

"Come on, Rach. I'm being serious. I'm trying to tell you not to screw up your life for an agency that doesn't give a damn about you and never will."

I looked over at Gary and realized that must be what he felt had happened with his own life.

"I'm not doing it for the Service, Gary. I'm doing it for the critters."

At least, that's what I'd always told myself.

Our conversation ended as we arrived at the ramp and loaded the boat onto its trailer. We didn't speak again until we were headed back over the causeway toward Brunswick.

"I've seen too many agents neglect their personal lives," Gary continued, picking up where he'd left off. "They crash land when their career comes to an end, precisely because they've got nothing else going on that matters. I'm talking depression, alcoholism, even suicide."

"For chrissakes, Gary. Is *that* what you foresee in my future?" I asked, beginning to feel pissed.

"No, it's just that I don't want you to end up alone, is all. Let me tell you, it ain't pleasant."

"Do you know something about me and Santou that I don't?" I challenged.

"How could I?"

I remained silent and Gary glanced over.

"You're not mad that I'm talking about this, are you, Rach?"

"Of course not," I tried to nonchalantly respond.

But Gary was hitting a little too close to home. Santou had recently broached the subject of marriage again, and I had agreed to seriously think about it. Maybe Gary was right. Maybe I *was* so caught up with work that I didn't realize my life was slipping by.

Gary parked in front of his office and I began to hop out, when his hand locked onto my arm.

"You know that I only want the best for you. Don't you, Rach?"

I looked at the man and wasn't sure why, but my heart began to ache. It didn't matter that he was covered in mud. I leaned over and gave him a kiss.

"I know that, Gary. And I want the same for you."

His mouth split into a devilish grin. "Great. Then just make sure I'm next in line if things between you and Santou don't work out. But right now, I have to get busy testing these samples."

Giving me a wink, he grabbed his bag and headed inside.

I jumped into my Ford, slipped in a Bonnie Raitt tape, and took off, warbling along as she sang the blues of my life.

Ten

There was still plenty of time to kill before my late afternoon meeting with Eight-Ball. That being the case, I decided to grab some lunch at a local dive near FLETC—the Federal Law Enforcement Training Center in Brunswick, where rookies from every federal agency come to train.

A dark and noisy joint, *Sue's* was your basic cop bar. A police cruiser sat out front as free advertising, while inside a VCR continuously played old reruns of the reality show *COPS*. As if that weren't enough, the regulars hummed along to the tune "Bad Boys, Bad Boys," while stuffing donuts in their mouths.

I ordered an overdone burger, cavity-causing sweetened iced tea, and some greasy slip-from-your-fingers French fries. I was tempted to top it off with a jelly donut, until I took another look at the boys in blue around me. A few too many pot bellies did wonders when it came to curbing my appetite. Instead, I decided this was the opportune time to pay another visit to Manatee Mania and have a little one-on-one with their Huddle House–trained marine biologist, Candi.

I headed back over the St. Simon's causeway, my Ford flying past an array of palatial estates as I made my way toward the north end of the island. It was there that the two plastic manatees stood merrily balanced on their tails, as if awaiting my arrival. I parked in the lot, approached the gate, and flashed my badge, hoping to appear friendly while still exuding a professional *don't-mess-with-me* air.

"Mr. Holmes is busy at the moment. Should I let him know that you're here?" asked the elderly woman sitting in the entrance booth.

A grandmotherly figure, she had apple-red cheeks, tightly permed white hair, and a register bulging with cash. I had no doubt that Ma Barker probably also had a piece stashed by her side, in case of trouble.

"No, that's alright. I'll walk around and check back in with you to see if he's free in a while."

"That's fine," she responded, sending out a *don't-screw-around-with-me* vibration of her own. "Just please make sure that you do. Mr. Holmes doesn't like it when people spring unannounced visits."

She shot me a look as piercing as that of the predatory kingfisher. I gathered the last gatekeeper must have gotten into *mucho* trouble for having allowed just such a transgression. Hmm. That would have been when Gary and I stopped by for an impromptu visit yesterday.

I skirted the gift shop and headed directly for Manatee Lagoon.

"Is Candi Collins on duty today?" I questioned the glum-looking ticket taker. Her eyes lit up as she saw my badge.

"Wow, is she in some kind of trouble?" the young *Dukes of Hazzard* chick asked, a little too eagerly.

"Why? Would you like her to be?" I responded, willing to dig for information wherever I could get it.

The girl tugged at her Manatee Mania midriff top. "Of

course not. It's just that I can't move up in this place until one of the girls leaves, and I really want to work with the manatees."

"Oh, are you a marine biologist, also?"

She shook her head. "No, not yet. But Mr. Holmes promised to teach me everything I need to know. He's even going to give me private lessons. He said by the time we're through, I'll be qualified to work at any water park in the world."

Something told me that a number of the sessions would probably take place in Wendell's Viagra palace.

"Congratulations. In that case, I'm sure a few of the girls will be moving on soon." Especially since Manatee Mania was bound to be permanently closed down.

"Thanks. You must have some inside information," the girl cheerfully responded. "Candi's in there keeping an eye on the kids while they're swimming around. Just go right through the gate."

Acting as referee was more like it. One child was attempting to climb on top of a manatee's back and ride the creature like a motorized surfboard, while someone else's little darling was hell-bent on feeding them pizza—a food item not normally associated with the health and well-being of marine mammals.

Candi appeared to be beside herself as she frantically ran about blowing her whistle to no avail. I briskly took matters in hand, informing each parent that they'd be handcuffed and hauled off to jail for harassment of an endangered species unless they gained immediate control over their boisterous offspring. The situation cleared up in no time.

Candi Collins caught my eye and gratefully waved, before sauntering toward me in her official Manatee Mania bikini. I watched as she approached, trying to decide if her walk was a God-given talent, or a cultivated skill that even *I* could acquire. No way. She must have been the lucky recipient of an *I'm-too-sexy-for-this-world* gene.

"Thanks for your help. Sometimes the kids get a little wound up and need a firm hand, is all."

Personally, I would have opted for a lion tamer's whip and a chair.

"I believe Wendell's in his office, if you're looking for him. He mentioned something about being tied up in a meeting all afternoon."

"No problem. The truth is, I came to see you."

Candi's complexion instantly blanched, turning from a healthy tan to a pale shade of gray.

"What do you want with *me*?" she nervously asked. "Wendell's the boss. Any questions you have should be directed to him."

Funny about that. Only yesterday, she'd gladly offered her assistance.

"This is something I think we should talk about first. I received a phone call from Spud this morning."

Candi's eyes flickered, though her expression remained frozen. "Who? I don't believe I know anyone by that name."

"Sure you do. Spud Bowden? Your old boyfriend?"

"Oh, *that* Spud," she nearly spat. "What dirt did that scumbag come running to you with? Because let me warn you, you can't believe a word he says."

"He told me that you're not a marine biologist."

"Oh, yeah? Well there. That just goes to show what kind of lying rat bastard he is. Let him prove it," she righteously insisted, thrusting out a hip à la Bob Fosse.

God, I wished I could do that.

"He doesn't have to. I already called Mote Marine Laboratory and checked it out," I bluffed.

"Well, whoop-de-doo. Good for you. And who says I didn't have a different last name back then? It just so happens that I was married at the time."

Boy, was this girl good.

"Besides, that loser is out to bad-mouth me any which way he can, all because I dumped his sorry ass like a sack of rotten potatoes."

"Oh yeah? So why *did* the two of you break up?"

"Because I finally got tired of paying all his damn bills, that's why. I bet he didn't tell you about the last stunt he pulled, did he?"

I shook my head, curious to know just how bad to the bone Spud Bowden could be.

"I'm driving home one night, after a twelve-hour waitressing shift, only to see his clunker of a truck hightailing it like a low-life skunk away from my place. He didn't stop, didn't bother to wave, just pressed the pedal to the metal and kept right on going. But what really made me suspicious was when I saw my kitchen table lashed to the rear of his truck."

"He stole your kitchen table?"

"Hell, he stole a whole lot more than that! The table was sitting on top of all my other stuff, which he had hidden beneath a tarp. Not only did he ransack my place, but he even stripped the aluminum siding off my brand new trailer to pay off some debts! You can't get any lower than that."

No doubt about it. That definitely sounded like something that Spud would have done. He was probably lucky she hadn't plugged him full of buckshot.

"You certainly had good reason for dumping the guy. But

that still doesn't make you a marine biologist, Candi. Why did you ever lie about that in the first place?" I asked, more than willing to bet that Wendell had something to do with it.

"Okay, so maybe I didn't go to Mote. But there are lots of other places just as good," she angrily huffed.

"Name one."

Apparently, Candi hadn't done her homework quite as well as she'd thought. She paused, obviously stumped.

"You're not the person I'm after," I softly informed her.

"Then why in the hell are you pushing me on this?"

"Because I need to know the truth. So tell me, where *did* you go to school?"

Candi responded with a flow of expressions that ranged from a pout, to an uncertain smile, to an angry glare, before she settled upon simply bursting into tears.

"Wendell said it would sound more professional if I told people that I was a marine biologist, and there wouldn't be a problem."

Bingo!

"Besides, even if I *don't* have a bunch of big ol' degrees, I still love these manatees better than any of those damn scientists ever could!" Candi vehemently insisted. "For instance, I know that each of them has their own unique personality, like Rudolph over there."

I spotted a fuzzy muzzle bobbing around in the water. It slowly surfaced to expose a face as wrinkled as a shar-pei dog's, topped off with black button eyes. The animal's lips moved like those of a hand puppet as it laboriously chewed away on something.

"I raised him myself when his mother got sick. I even hand-fed him with a baby bottle. Now if *that's* not rehabbing, then I don't know what is."

"That's great. But what happened to Rudolph's mother?"
I inquired.

"Well, she got weaker and weaker until she finally died.
That's why I had to take over. He would have starved otherwise. It's just lucky that Wendell found them when he did."

Once again, Wendell had perfect timing. Either this girl
was just as much of a liar, or she'd been brainwashed into
believing his stories.

"There's something else I want to ask you. Exactly where
is Wendell finding all of these manatees?"

"What do you mean? I just told you. He's rescuing them
from around the area, of course," she skittishly responded,
switching her weight from hip to hip.

"Cut the crap, Candi. You know perfectly well what I'm
talking about. Wendell said they'd been hit by boat propellers. Only none of them have any sign of a recent injury,
which leads me to suspect one of two things. Either someone is illegally breeding these mammals and selling them to
Wendell. Or, they're being snatched from the wild."

Candi's lips drew tightly together, and she immediately
clammed up.

"Whichever is the case, that also makes you an accessory.
Is it really worth doing jail time over?" I asked, allowing the
question to dangle.

"Look, Ma!" came a loud shriek from behind us in the
pool.

I turned and saw a child pulling hard on Rudolph's neck.
One flash of my badge and his mother promptly dragged
him off.

"Listen, Candi. I love manatees also, which is why it's
important that we do what's best for them. And that's for
these creatures to be in the wild, not mauled to death by

crowds all day in an amusement park. Right now, they're nothing more than a moneymaking tool for Wendell. Is that really what you want for Rudolph and the others?"

"That's not true," she argued. "Wendell says this is a wonderful way for people to learn about them, and that the critters instinctively want to bond."

"Well, he's wrong. Manatees are naturally shy and hate noise. This sort of thing simply stresses them out. If Wendell *really* cared, he would have guidelines posted that instruct swimmers not to ride, poke, or harass them like that kid was just doing."

Candi cringed and I knew I was getting through to her. "By the way, did anyone ever perform an autopsy on Rudolph's mom to try and find out why she died?"

Candi shook her head as tears began to stream down her face. Her heart was clearly in the right place. I decided to try and appeal to her conscience.

"You know, there's a good chance it was the result of being kept in a pen and forced to swim with a bunch of tourists. You can help me with this, Candi. That is, if you really care about them as much as you claim. For chrissakes, this has to be stopped. Just look at what's going on in there."

I directed her attention to the pool, where one of the manatees now appeared to be swimming lopsided—probably because a child had hold of its tail and was forcing the mammal to pull him around in the water like some sort of manatee jet ski.

"Oh shit," she muttered and promptly jumped in the pool to stop him.

I felt a twinge of guilt, knowing that she was about to lose her job. On the other hand, nothing would give me greater pleasure than to put Manatee Mania out of business.

I imagined being the one to break the good news to Wendell, when I caught sight of something out of the corner of my eye—a person passing by the gate. Only this wasn't just anyone, but a man who was tall and lean, and moved like a well-oiled machine. Scratch that—make it an expensive Lexus. A closer look revealed it to be none other than Clark Williams. He had apparently been in Wendell's office and was now heading toward the exit.

Chalk it up to my contrariness, but I was consumed by an overwhelming urge to confront the man. After all, it was due to him that the entire Service was probably now gunning for me. Besides, I'd gotten as much as I probably could out of Candi right now.

"I'll be in touch," I hollered to her over my shoulder as I ran out, already focused on my next target.

Williams moved briskly, each of his steps as resolute as the next, like that of a man on a mission.

"Would you mind slowing down?" I called, rushing to catch up to him. "I'd like to speak with you for a minute."

Williams stopped dead in his tracks and turned around. Once again, he was impeccably dressed in a tailored pair of olive twill pants and a chambray ivory shirt, his feet attired in loafers made of the softest calfskin leather.

"Why, Agent Porter. What a pleasant surprise. What can I do for you today?" he congenially inquired, flashing a winning smile.

If someone hadn't known our brief history, they might have assumed we were friends. As it was, his strategy worked. I was momentarily caught off-guard, having expected him to be furious.

"I understand you managed to have that ticket I wrote up on you squashed. That's an interesting maneuver you pulled," I replied, internally scrambling to regain my composure. "What was it called again? Oh, yeah. The DeLorean defense."

"I wouldn't call it a maneuver, Agent Porter. Rather, I like to think of it as playing by the rules. You weren't authorized to work on Labor Day, therefore you had no business issuing a ticket in the first place," Williams responded, remaining perfectly cool.

"Right. Which brings me to another matter. Just how did you manage to learn about my work schedule so quickly, anyway?"

Williams arched an eyebrow. "I'm afraid you'd have to ask my lawyer that question. But what makes you think he didn't simply take an educated guess? After all, it was a federal holiday, and you know how the government hates to pay overtime."

Damn the man. I was hoping he wouldn't come up with that. Williams continued to smile, clearly enjoying the game, while he awaited my next move. It was almost as if he were already three steps ahead. What I wanted more than anything was to wipe that smug look off his face.

"I understand you might try to further exploit the situation by requesting a Congressional oversight hearing on Fish and Wildlife Division of Law Enforcement excesses."

"See? Now that's something you've got wrong."

I expelled an inner sigh of relief, unaware until then just how coiled up inside I'd been.

"I'm far beyond simply contemplating it. I've already decided to charge full steam ahead. You can fully expect to be called to testify before Congress. However, I'm also certain that you'll charm each and every member enough to stay out of trouble."

Was that a twinkle I saw in his eye? I could almost swear the man was flirting with me. Then I realized what was actually going on.

"You're doing all this as a prelude to your run for Congress, aren't you?" I charged, thinking out loud. "This is simply a warm-up to showcase your stand against any sort of government regulation."

"Is *that* what I'm doing?" Williams mused, in a lightly mocking tone. "I must say, I feel flattered. And here I thought you didn't know anything about me."

The next moment, his attitude changed yet again. He dropped all trace of sarcasm and thrust out his hand.

"You're a smart woman, Porter. And believe it or not, I'm beginning to like you. I actually think you could do quite well for yourself with the proper guidance. What do you say that we call a truce?"

I looked at the man, uncertain of how best to handle the situation—never mind that every fiber inside me warned that he wasn't to be trusted.

"At least for now," he disarmingly added.

I had little choice but to shake his hand.

"I hope you don't mind a minor observation on my part. You need to learn how to better navigate your way through the system. So far, you've done a pretty lousy job of it."

"Oh, really. And what makes you say that?"

Williams winked. Either that or the guy had a nervous tic.

"Word gets around. Besides, it's not as if you've managed to successfully work your way up through the ranks."

"It sounds as though you've done some research of your own. Is that supposed to make me feel flattered or threatened?" I parried.

"Most definitely flattered," Williams responded with a

roguish grin. "You know, I could be a good friend to you if you'd let me. God knows, I've had plenty of experience with the wheeling and dealings in government. It seems to me that Fish and Wildlife could use more people like yourself in supervisory positions at their headquarters in D.C. I'd be more than willing to help you, under the proper circumstances."

"And what would *you* get in return?" I asked, immediately suspicious.

"The satisfaction of knowing there are more than just bungling dolts attempting to run the government. Let's face it. Everyone in Washington is handpicked in one way or other. I like to think I'm one of those who has sense enough to want intelligent people filling those positions."

"Uh-huh. And I suppose it also wouldn't hurt if they just happened to owe you a favor or two."

Williams softly laughed and leaned in toward me, as though he were about to share an intimate secret. "But of course. Anyway, I can't imagine that remaining a field agent would be very rewarding for the duration of your career. And why should it be? Especially when given a closer look at those colleagues who have already surpassed you."

He was right. Call it vanity, but I couldn't help but be bothered at having been left behind in the dust.

I began to fantasize about being offered a position that included perks such as respect, power, and money. True, I'd no longer be out in the field, but I also wouldn't be booted around the country. Santou would definitely approve of such a move. We could finally have a permanent home. There'd be no reason not to get married or have a family. Maybe it was time that I *did* grow up and put down roots. After all, didn't everybody?

"Who knows? You might even come to think of me as your mentor, one of these days."

Those words rankled my nerves, like a sour note clashing against a tuning fork, causing my perfect daydream to shatter. They forced me to take yet another look at the man. Everything about him was seductive—from his voice, to his smile, to his laugh. But most enticing of all was what he seemed to be offering. I felt like a fly who'd nearly been caught in his web. I mentally shook myself free, having realized just what I'd been contemplating.

I watched him watching me, calculating what my reaction would be. Who was this guy, anyway? Darth Vader, tempting me over to the Dark Side?

"Thanks, but no thanks. You forget, I've recently had a taste of what you consider to be justice, and I can't say that I much like the way your version of government works. Speaking of which, how did your meeting go with Wendell today? Have the two of you cooked up a master plan for Manatee Mania's breeding facility yet? Or were you hashing out details for the latest luxury condo complex?"

Williams observed me for a moment in amused silence, as if I posed no more threat than a mere flea.

"Does that mean you don't approve of Wendell's new plans for his water park?"

"See? Now that's something *you've* got wrong," I sardonically responded, choosing to echo his own words. "My approval doesn't matter, since Manatee Mania is about to be closed down."

"You don't say. And why is that?" Williams asked, almost indifferently.

"For illegally harboring and exhibiting endangered species,

to say nothing of condoning their harassment. You may have won our first go-around out in the marsh. But I believe this second more important round belongs to me," I nearly crowed, ecstatic that I'd managed to one-up this guy. "I've informed Fish and Wildlife's regional office about this facility and they should be taking action any day now. Oh yeah. That's the other thing. Not only do I know about your development firm, but I'm also fully aware that Golden Dreams is financially backing the water park. Sorry, but I guess you'll be taking a hit on this one."

There. *That* ought to put a crimp in his development plans. Over half the wetlands in this country had already been destroyed, having fallen prey to the onslaught of industry and rapacious development in a brutal battle. I planned to do everything possible to keep any more in this area from vanishing under my watch.

"I guess Golden Dreams Development Corporation is just going to have to look for a stretch of marsh somewhere else to rip up," I giddily added, unable to keep my mouth shut.

"You really are pretty full of yourself, aren't you Porter?" Williams responded, skillfully bursting my bubble. "Do you truly believe that what you say actually carries any clout? If so, I'm afraid you're sadly mistaken. Manatee Mania will be expanding right on target, as will the condos, houses, golf courses, and everything else that's already in the hopper. It's what's known as progress, Rachel. And neither you, nor a few miserable manatees, are going to stand in its way."

The edges of my confidence promptly began to crumble like a disintegrating cookie. I wondered if he might not be right. I hadn't yet heard a word from my boss.

Williams voice continued to curl itself around me, his

tone smooth as a leather whip. "You should consider choosing your battles more carefully. I'm not your enemy unless you decide to treat me like one."

It was as if I hadn't truly seen Williams until this very moment. The man standing before me now snapped fully into focus.

"You worked at Interior once upon a time. What happened to make you so anti-environmental?" I asked, aware that the same could be said about any number of former high-level Interior Department employees.

Williams deigned to bestow a condescending smile upon me. "You've got it all wrong, Rachel. I'm not anti-environment. I'm just pro-business. Besides, you should be well versed in what Interior's current philosophy is by now. Compromise isn't the answer some of the time. It's the answer all of the time."

"In that case, no wonder endangered species don't stand a chance. Not when they're being compromised to death," I caustically retorted. "I now understand why so many rumors flew around about you, when you were Undersecretary. It was said that you could be bought. Apparently, that was true."

Williams's eyes flashed angry as blinking traffic lights, only to be deftly suppressed. "It's not a black-and-white world, Rachel. The fact that you insist on viewing it as such doesn't help your cause any. Which is why you'd be smart to consider my offer. It's a one-time deal. Either learn to run with the big boys, or get crushed."

With that remark, Williams swiveled on the heels of his calfskin loafers and left.

I stood transfixed, wondering what he possibly knew that

I didn't. Maybe a chat with Wendell would help shed some light.

I strode toward his office, past a group of kids that came barreling headfirst down the waterslide, screaming holy hell at the top of their lungs.

"I want to have at least two of those," Santou had recently informed me, as though he were placing an order for a couple of pies.

My response had been to wisely keep my mouth shut. What was so wrong with being consumed by my job, anyway? I'd have to have another discussion with Gary about that.

I continued on to where a yellow van sat parked near the stairs to Wendell's office. Hmm, interesting. It hadn't been there yesterday. Perhaps Wendell was planning a move of some sort. Walking over, I opened the van's rear door and quickly looked inside for anything of interest. The interior was fully lined with foam rubber. Other than that, it stood empty. Maybe it was still waiting to be packed.

I vaulted up the steps two at a time, hoping to catch Wendell in the act of stashing away incriminating evidence. The cardboard manatee met me again at the top of the stairs, but with a new sign stuck in its fins today.

DO NOT ENTER. INTERVIEW IN PROGRESS.

I'd be damned if I'd knock and give Holmes prior warning. Instead, I simply barged through the door.

Wendell was sitting behind his desk with a girl in his lap, looking for all the world like the King of the Double-Wide Motor Homes. The only difference in his appearance today was the color of the shirt he wore. Lime green, it was garnished with the same pattern of coffee stains running down the front. That is, what I could see of it beyond Daisy Mae's chest.

The babe nervously tittered upon my entry, and jumped off. Wendell's reaction was to gruffly clear his throat.

"Thank you for stopping by, Miss Robbins. I'll be in touch after I check out your references."

"But I thought you said it was a done deal," Miss Robbins primly reminded him, beginning to button her blouse.

"Of course. Everything's in order. Just consider it a formality," he hastily assured her.

"The job's already mine," she whispered, letting me know I didn't stand a chance as she slipped out the door.

"Hiring another marine biologist?" I dryly inquired.

"As a matter of fact, I was just admiring her credentials," he acknowledged with a grin.

It must have been tougher getting a job these days than I had imagined.

"So, to what do I owe the pleasure of this visit, Miss Rachel? Is it possible that you drove all the way out here just to see me?"

No sooner had he finished the question than his eyes darted back to the doorway. "Just tell me you didn't bring that cocky sonofabitch with you. What that boy needs is to find some good pussy and get himself laid. He oughta relax a little, if you know what I mean."

Rising from his chair, Wendell sauntered around and perched his rear end on the desk, way too close to where I was standing.

"At least, it always works for me," he said with a wink.

I promptly took a step backward.

"Now what can I do for you today, sugar?"

"I've learned some interesting things since my last visit,"

I informed him. "One of which is that Clark Williams and his Golden Dreams development firm are the real owners of Manatee Mania."

"Well, that's just a buncha horseshit. Who's filling your mind with that kinda rubbish?" Wendell questioned.

He didn't wait for an answer, but flung the accusation off with a dismissive wave of his hand. "He's just one of my financial backers, is all. The fact is, I'm kinda like that fellow up in New York. You know who I mean—that Donald Trump. I believe it's always smarter to run a business with other people's money than your own. Of course, I also give credit where credit is due. Clark is fully in charge of expanding the water park."

But my interest had been snagged by something he'd just said. "Then there are also other people besides Williams who have a financial interest in Manatee Mania?"

"Hell, when you put it that way, the entire *county* does. Do you know how many jobs we'll provide by the time we're through developing this place?"

Wendell pulled at the crotch of his pants, as if construction were also going on down there.

I averted my gaze, only to spy three black-and-white photos up on one wall. They must have represented a holy trinity of heroes for Wendell. The trio consisted of George Wallace, Strom Thurmond, and Lester Maddox. Hanging from a nearby pole was the former state flag of Georgia, embellished with its large Confederate X.

Wendell saw me eyeing the banner. "I never could figure out why we had to go and change the state emblem. Hell, as one of our senators said, *Pickup trucks, deer hunting, barefoot girls, and boiled peanuts—that's what the Georgia flag represents!*"

"Uh-huh. I think I read that in a history book somewhere," I drolly responded.

"Enough chitter-chatter. I believe I know the real reason why you're here," Wendell informed me.

"Oh yeah? And why is that?"

"You've come to make up and be friends," he coyly replied. "After all, it wasn't very nice of you to threaten to close down my water park yesterday."

"That wasn't a threat, Wendell. It's actually going to happen."

Wendell yanked on the brim of his cap. "What the hell have you got against this place, anyway?"

"Let's see. For one thing, you've got children swimming in that lagoon treating manatees like pieces of furniture. For chrissakes, they're even trying to feed them pizza!"

"You don't care very much for kids, do you?" he astutely observed.

"Not when they're unsupervised. In addition to which, there's not a properly trained person here who knows how to suitably care for manatees."

Wendell opened his mouth to protest.

"And don't give me any crap about Candi being a marine biologist," I tersely warned him.

"For crying out loud, do you mean to tell me that she's not?" he gasped, feigning surprise. "Well, how do you like that? And to think I never suspected she might be lying." He clucked his tongue and slowly shook his head.

I stared at the man in disbelief, remembering something my old boss, Charlie Hickok, had once said.

It takes forty-two muscles in your face to frown, but only four to smack an asshole upside the head.

Right about now, that suggestion was sorely tempting.

"The party's over, Wendell. You have no rescue and rehabilitation permits, no professional personnel, and no business making money off manatees as if they were a sideshow
attraction. I'm personally going to see to it that Manatee
Mania is shut down within the next forty-eight hours," I
fumed.

Wendell calmly strolled back to his seat, as if he didn't
have a care in the world. "My, my. I'm beginning to think
you could use a little relaxation yourself, Miss Rachel."

"*I'm* not the one that you should be worried about."

Holmes sank into the chair and clasped his hands behind
his head. "As for closing the water park, I don't believe
that's gonna happen. In fact, you might wanna check in
with your boss. Tell you what. You can even use my
phone."

Wendell propped his feet on the desk and pushed it toward me. "Go ahead. I don't mind eating the dime on a long-
distance call."

Something was definitely wrong. It was clear that Wendell had information I didn't by the way he was trying to set
me up.

"That's generous of you, Wendell. But the government
still pays for my phone calls."

"Maybe not for long," Holmes replied with an enigmatic
smile. "By the way, tell wonder boy Gary Fletcher that he
also better behave. Otherwise, your friend's gonna find himself in a heap a trouble."

A sickening feeling settled in the pit of my stomach. If I
didn't leave this instant, I might very well commit homicide.

"You'll be hearing from me soon," I vowed, and flew out
the door.

My feet hardly touched the steps as I raced down them.

The screams of children on the waterslide barely penetrated my ears. It was the dull thud of my shoes pounding against the ground that insistently drove the message home.

Something's wrong. Something's wrong. Something's wrong.

The thought consumed me as I rushed past the entrance booth.

"You didn't go and disturb Mr. Holmes, did you?" Ma Barker leaned out and yelled.

I didn't respond, but jumped in my Ford and tore down the road, jabbing at the car phone with trembling fingers.

"Agent Lowell speaking."

"Did you get the information I sent about Manatee Mania water park?" I demanded, forgoing all pretense of a cordial greeting.

My question was met with deafening silence. The only explanation was that I must have driven into a dead zone. I pulled off the road, my body shaking from anger and frustration. It was as if all the air inside my vehicle had been mysteriously sucked out as I tried to take a deep breath, hoping to slow the racing of my pulse.

Count to ten, I told myself.

Oh, to hell with that. I was about to hang up and redial when Lowell finally spoke.

"We're putting this one on the back burner for a while. I want you to lay off."

"On the back burner? That's such an interesting expression, I can't help but be curious. Exactly what does it mean in this case?" I caustically inquired, my fingers tightly gripping the steering wheel. If it hadn't been bolted on, I would have pulled the damn thing off.

"It means just what I said. No action is to be taken at this time."

"And why is that?" I persisted, refusing to back down.

"Because there are other things that take priority," Lowell replied between clenched teeth.

"Not in my book, there aren't. What's more important than extricating a bunch of endangered manatees from a rinky-dink water park, where they're being illegally held and commercially exploited?" I seethed. "Go ahead. Please fill me in. I'm dying to hear exactly what it is that takes priority. Or could it be political pressure that has you on the run?"

This time the silence nearly shouted, so palpable was the tension.

"I'm not the enemy, Porter. So stop pushing my buttons," Lowell curtly responded after a moment. "All right, I might as well tell you, since you're bound to find out anyway. Manatee Mania is receiving a belated permit giving them the right to exhibit manatees."

"What are you talking about?" I practically screamed. "How can that be? Didn't you read my report? Don't you know what's going on in that place?"

"I'm just repeating what I learned a few hours ago, myself. An emergency request was filed on their behalf after your visit yesterday. A decision has been made, and the D.C. office is granting them the permit," Lowell tautly informed me.

"That's total insanity!" I exploded, not wanting to believe that it was really true.

"Possibly, but there's also nothing you can do. So, I suggest you swallow the pill, bitter as it may be, and move on," Lowell instructed.

I almost thought I heard a note of regret in his voice.

"Listen, Porter. Let me give you a word of advice. It's a piece of commonsense philosophy that a former head of Interior regularly preached to us. *Compromise isn't the answer some of the time. It's the answer all of the time.* You may not like it, but I strongly advise that you learn to live by that rule."

It was my turn to respond in stunned silence. I'd heard those exact words from Clark Williams less than an hour ago. Either the coincidence was extraordinary or—I barely dared believe it—the two were conspiring against me.

"Oh, yeah. There's something else I need to tell you before I forget. You're going to want to pick up a copy of the local paper down there tomorrow morning."

"Why?" I asked, my mind still reeling from the discovery.

"Thanks to you, Fish and Wildlife will be making front-page news."

That bit of information jerked me right back to reality.

"What's going on?"

"Read the article and find out. Maybe it'll clue you in as to why Manatee Mania is getting their permit. One other thing. This is my last warning, Porter. Do yourself a favor, and stay out of trouble."

He didn't say good-bye, but simply hung up.

My shakiness returned, gripping me stronger than ever. Only now it was fueled by the burning desire to get to the bottom of all this. I had no intention of allowing the manatees to become pawns in a political power game, their fate to die a slow, undignified death.

I got back on the road and sped down the blacktop, as if racing away from a crime. Truth be told, one was already in progress. It was the destruction of a species for the price of admission to Manatee Mania Water Park.

If the resources could scream, maybe those in power would finally listen. As it was, I fully intended to do their hollering for them for now.

Eleven

I stopped at the first convenience store I passed, and picked up a couple of six-packs. Then I broke at least three different rules by popping open a can and drinking it down. What the hell. Having polished off the first one so quickly, I figured I might as well suck down a second. I sat on the store's front stoop and proceeded to do that, while mulling over the conversation I'd just had with my boss.

I now wondered if Lowell was out to get me. Was it possible that he'd surreptitiously sabotaged my case from the very start? Not just with Manatee Mania, but also by betraying me to Clark Williams. How else could he have found out so quickly that I wasn't supposed to be working on Labor Day?

Something was making me feel dizzy—either the heat, or the stress, or the beer. Still, I couldn't stop replaying the conversation in my mind. Nearly as bad was the realization that even *Wendell* had information from which I'd obviously been excluded.

You're simply being paranoid, my inner voice tried to rationalize.

But no matter how much I told myself that, I kept coming back to the same conclusion—someone up top was out to get me.

Heading back into the store, I grabbed a bottle of Mylanta and took a few swigs, then snatched a peek at my watch. It was time to hook up with Eight-Ball. I hopped in my Ford and drove off.

I followed Eight-Ball's instructions as best I could, though I was approaching from a different direction. Even so, the landmark he'd told me to watch for soon came into view—Bennie's Red Barn Restaurant.

I turned onto South Harrington Road and immediately found myself engulfed in a time warp, as stands of ancient live oak reached out with gnarled limbs to embrace me. No sooner was I pulled into their sphere than I traveled down a stretch of road, through wild, unruly country. This was a place where grapevines grew thick as men's thighs, and Spanish moss swayed in a hint of breeze like long, bristly horsetails.

Two giant hands formed the canopy above, whose interlocking fingers blocked out the late afternoon sun. A stand-in for Woody Woodpecker coyly hid in the foliage, where he hammered out a rhythmic tune. Meanwhile, resurrection fern curled up along twisted tree trunks, withered and gray, waiting for one good rainfall. That's when the fern would bounce back full and green, proving that life springs eternal. It was then I realized exactly where I was.

South Harrington is an old black community hidden off the main road—a place filled with history, magic, and beauty. It's remained much the way the island originally looked hundreds of years ago. The reason being, it was deeded to emancipated slaves after the Civil War and the land has been passed down through each succeeding generation. These direct descendents continue to live on South Harrington today, even as the rest of St. Simons is snapped up and developed for the gentry.

Brightly painted bungalows, with torn mesh windows and

tattered screen doors, sat back off the road; the structures so old that some are original slave cabins. Word had it this area was one of the last holdouts in the island against developers and big money.

I continued on past a little girl skipping barefoot in a yard of sandy loam. Her hair was pulled back into braids and decorated with bright red ribbons. The child stared at me through big, brown eyes as I drove by, paying little heed to the puppy that playfully nipped at her heels. It made me feel all the more an intruder slinking through a place to which time had now come knocking.

That perception was further strengthened as another row of shacks came into view. Old women kept watch from dilapidated porches, dressed in raggedy housecoats and plastic shower caps. They all rocked in syncopated time, like a senior citizen chorus line, anchored to wooden chairs that squeaked in perfect unison. But what truly united the women were the handpainted signs that stood diligent as armed guards on each front lawn, bellowing the same angry proclamation.

DON'T ASK/WON'T SELL!

It was South Harrington's version of an outraged scream. Little detective work was required to discover exactly what they were protesting.

An old house had been razed on a lot across the street, while the tract next to it showed obvious signs of a building in progress. The groundwork for a yuppie McMansion was being laid. But it was the billboard springing up from the ground like a weed that caused me to slam on my brakes.

FUTURE SITE OF MARSH MEADOWS
LUXURY HOMES AND CONDOMINIUMS
A GOLDEN DREAMS DEVELOPMENT!

Evidently, Clark Williams wasn't restricting himself to just the north end of the island, but also planned to go full steam ahead in this area.

I could feel the old women bristling like angry porcupines, wrongly assuming that I was a prospective buyer. I threw the Ford into gear and moved on, not stopping until the road dead-ended at Village Creek Landing. This was where Eight-Ball had said I would find him.

Grabbing a six-pack, I got out of my vehicle and began to walk along the marsh. The surroundings were so quiet I literally heard oysters popping in their beds, while gnats droned in discordant harmony around my ears.

Plop!

I turned in time to catch sight of an otter "belly whopping" down a mudbank on its stomach of rich brown fur. The critter propelled itself even faster with the help of its twelve-inch tail, while chattering away in glee. Had I still been a child, I would gladly have joined him, happily oblivious to the problems of dead critters and sad manatees.

A moment later, I spotted Eight-Ball and noticed something tied onto his wrist—a cord attached to a cast net. I watched as he lifted the finely woven mesh in both calloused hands and twisted his body ever so slightly. Then casting forward, he propelled the net over the water with a quick snap of his wrist. The task was executed in one fluid motion, displaying the grace of a ballet dancer and the precision of an Olympic discus thrower. The net swirled through the air, billowing into a wide circle before landing upon the water. Then it slowly sank, pulled down by tiny lead weights attached to its hem. A snowy egret stood patiently waiting nearby, solemn as an undertaker, as if hoping to partake of the catch.

I pulled a can of beer from its plastic ring and handed it to Eight-Ball, after which I opened one for myself. I took a sip and my body began to relax as a buzz settled in, lightly vibrating from my toes to the tops of my ears.

"What are you catching?" I asked, looking down at the water.

The liquid was dark as Eight-Ball's skin. A fish jumped, shattering the serene surface, which broke into thousands of viscous splinters. They slowly reconverged into a fairy's ring of concentric circles.

"Shrimp for tonight's dinner."

The words whistled between what few front teeth he had left, and his watery eyes looked tired and red.

He slowly drew the net up from the water, pulling on its cord so that the web closed tight as a drawstring purse around its prey. Water dripped off the plastic filament to land on my feet, as an array of fish and shrimp futilely flopped about inside the mesh. Eight-Ball transferred the contents into a blue ice chest, and then threw the net into the air once more. This time, it resembled a petticoat that flew through the sky with an effortless *whooosh*, as if tossed by a bride eager to shed her garments.

"I want to thank you for calling me with that tip about Purvis Creek," I said, as the net disappeared under the water. "I went out this morning and took some samples. We should know soon enough if there's a problem."

"Oh, there's a problem, all right," Eight-Ball confirmed. "I know cause there ain't nearly as many blue crab, whiting, and redfish as there used to be. I just kept going there anyways cause it was easy to get to, and ya gotta fish if ya wanna eat. Which is why I'm real glad to be back home again on St. Simons. There ain't any dead critters or birds floatin' around in these waters."

Eight-Ball discreetly glanced my way, probably to see if I was disappointed.

"But there's lotsa dead things in other spots around Purvis that I can take you to," he eagerly offered. His lips continuously moved over his gums, as though trying hard to dislodge something.

Eight-Ball filled a moment of silence by polishing off his beer. I promptly opened a second and gave it to him. It was then I noticed the tremors running through both his hands, as he lifted the can and took a sip. Though I tried my best not to stare, I couldn't help but be curious. I wondered if Eight-Ball possibly had Parkinson's. A relative of mine had contracted the disease and, to this day, I remembered the way she would shake. I decided not to ask anything too personal yet, but to stick with more routine questions.

"So tell me. How did you and Clark Williams first meet?"

"Mr. Williams? Well, he comes around a lot where I work. You know, he's friends with my boss and all. In fact, it was Mr. Drapkin introduced us. He told Mr. Williams how I know lots about fishing and the marsh. And it's true, I surely do. Pretty much like the back of my hand," Eight-Ball said with pride.

I believed him. He'd probably grown up in this area and had explored every creek and stream as a child.

"There's only one place on this island where I never did fish," he added.

"Really? Where's that?" Maybe there *was* something bad on St. Simons, after all.

"Ebo Landing right close to here, down along Dunbar Creek."

"Why? What's the problem?"

Eight-Ball's eyes wandered over the water and he cocked his head, as if listening to a sound I couldn't hear. "Africans snatched from the Ebo Tribe drowned themselves there, every last one of 'em, rather than become slaves when they were shipped over here to Georgia."

My limbs turned icy cold, and I shoved my hands deep into my pockets.

"You can't fish there no more anyway, even if you wanted. Not since they built all those big fancy houses with private docks. But it don't matter none. Truth be told, you couldn't pay me to go there no way, no how. I ain't lyin' to you when I say that Ebo Landing surely is haunted."

I didn't feel the need to respond after my own experience last night. Instead, I wanted to get off the topic as quickly as possible.

"You never told me exactly what it is that you do at DRG," I said, deftly changing the subject.

"Oh, you know. A little of this, a little of that. Whatever's needed." But his eyes kept drifting back over the water. "Just general handyman stuff to keep the place running."

Then I asked a question I'd been curious about ever since we'd first met.

"Why are you called Eight-Ball?"

A bittersweet smile flitted across his face. "It's 'cause I got a knack for telling the future. Turns out it's both a blessing and a curse. Sometimes even those in the spirit world get jealous of me. That's why I'm so tired today. The hag came and rode me last night."

I almost hated to ask. "A hag?"

"Why, it's a spirit that every man can expect to meet at least once in his life. She comes to the door, takes off her skin, leaves it on the floor, and then rides you through the night, returning you to your bed in the morning."

Uh-huh. What it sounded like was one too many evenings spent watching the Playboy Channel.

"You may think you're hollerin', but you can't even speak. She'll do it till you get so tired you're barely alive. But I took care of it last night, alright. She won't be comin' back and botherin' me no more."

"What did you do?" I asked, against my better judgment.

"I hung a colander on the doorknob and sprinkled salt on the floor. That way, she won't be able to get back into her skin."

Okay. Who was *I* to judge, when I slept with a TV on to keep my demons at bay?

"So tell me. What do you see in *my* future?" I lightly questioned, having always had a weakness when it came to fortune-telling.

Eight-Ball studied me with wizened eyes. "What I see is a whole lotta pain, and that you're gonna be alone for a while. You're also gonna find out what's killin' those critters in Purvis Creek. 'Course, there's a good chance that you'll wind up dead yourself while working out in the marsh."

So much for any humdrum prophecy of marriage, kids, and a house with a white picket fence.

A bell jar of absolute silence descended upon us, and I imagined this was how it felt to be encased in a coffin. The spell was broken when a bird's piercing cry shattered the invisible dome. It also jostled Eight-Ball into action. Pulling up the net, he dumped its contents into the ice chest, which was nearly brimming with shrimp.

"Well, I see you still got beer, and I got fish. So why don't I cook us up a Lowcountry Boil for supper?"

Fresh shrimp for supper? He's cooking? Sounded good to me.

"Sure. I'll follow you back to your place. I'm in that black Explorer over there, so you don't lose me."

"It would be hard to do that even if I wanted," Eight-Ball chuckled. "I'm stayin' with my cousin these days, and she lives just down the road."

This time I drove back along South Harrington not as an intruder, but an invited guest. No matter. The old women in their shower caps still gave me the evil eye. I followed Eight-Ball onto a tiny dirt path marked Mamalou Lane, near where yet another old shack was being torn down.

No longer was I surrounded by rustic forest, but a near impenetrable jungle. The area was rife with Tarzanlike vines, palmettos, and live oaks weeping tears of Spanish lace. I could have used a machete just to cut my way through the place.

Eight-Ball came to a stop in front of a tiny house that looked as though a vat of cotton candy had exploded all over it. The exterior color nearly pulsated, so vibrant was its coat of shocking pink. All except for the door and window frames, which were painted an unusual shade of blue.

Eight-Ball parked next to a lime-green Chevy Caprice, while I pulled up behind an old Pontiac Catalina topped with a red velour roof. Gold tassels hung gaily from the Pontiac's rear window, but it was the sticker plastered on its bumper that I loved best: *Bitch Goddess*.

Equally apparent was that Eight-Ball's cousin had joined forces with the rest of the neighborhood by the sign on the lawn that declared, DON'T ASK/WON'T SELL.

Owww ooooh, came a deep howl from around the back of the house.

Owww ooooh! The call sounded again, only this time much closer.

Owww ooooh! The yowl morphed into a hairy critter with four legs and a tail.

I almost thought it was a spectral version of Elvis's Hound Dog, as a mangy mutt that was greatly in need of a bath came trotting toward us. Eight-Ball bent down and the hound went to work licking his face, followed by another round of baying.

"It's okay, boy. I'm home now," Eight-Ball reassured the lovesick pup. "This is my dog, Jake. I swear the day I die is when he'll finally stop howling."

Funny about that. The day *I* died was when I wanted *my* Jake to begin crying bloody murder. I took a closer look at Eight-Ball's dog and decided that both Jakes shared almost the same exact nose. Only mine had much better breath.

"Did Venus leave you outside again? Well, we're just gonna have to do somethin' about that," Eight-Ball said, and gave the pooch a loving pat. "You come on in with me."

I followed along, figuring that he was probably talking to both of us.

We walked into a house that literally took my breath away. I'd never before seen a place that looked as though Tammy Faye Bakker and Hugh Hefner had joined forces to decorate. The color scheme in the living room was bright pink and burgundy red, with accentuating touches of black and gold. Tammy Faye's influence was in all the frills, velvet pillows, lace curtains, and bows, while Hef held sway over the abundance of nudes that filled the room, from porcelain figurines to lamps and paintings. I began to wonder if Eight-Ball's cousin might not be running a bordello. In fact, it made me curious as to what all those women wearing shower caps had in *their* homes.

However, if I'd been expecting someone in a raggedy housecoat, I was in for a big surprise. A vision in pink satin pajamas and a blond Shirley Temple wig floated into the room. Only this was no petite girl, but one heck of a lot of woman. She wasn't alone.

Accompanying her was an equally large man dressed in a brown pinstriped suit, and flaunting a gold medallion around his neck. Each of his steps held the heft of a tractor trailer, causing the nude figurines to quiver.

Eight-Ball's cousin headed directly for me, shaking her curly head so hard that the rest of her body followed suit.

"You see that sign out front, girl? That says it all. Don't ask, cause I ain't gonna sell. Now if you're smart, you'll get outta my house while the going is good!"

Jake protested for me by emitting a loud howl.

"And what's *that* ugly mutt doing back in here?" she demanded of Eight-Ball, placing an ornery fist on each hip.

"First off, this is Rachel Porter," Eight-Ball retorted. "You remember? She's that Fish and Wildlife agent who didn't give me a ticket."

His cousin's demeanor abruptly changed, as she now turned to me with a broad smile.

"Why, Eight-Ball told me all about you. I'm Venus Monroe. In that case, come on in and sit yourself down."

I was led to an overstuffed sofa that was missing its springs. I sank into the cushions and was nearly suffocated in velvet.

"And this is my good friend, Reverend Bayliss," she said, introducing the man beside her.

The Reverend's teeth gleamed like polished pieces of

ivory. "God blesses those that fight for the helpless," he said by way of greeting.

"But that still doesn't explain what this damn dog's doing in here," Venus remarked with a scowl.

"Now, Venus. Jake's one of God's creatures, too," the Reverend tried to reason.

"So is a snake," she snapped. "That thing can come into this house on one condition only. You gotta give it a bath."

I had to admit, she had a point.

"Okay, but I'll do it later," Eight-Ball grudgingly consented. "First I wanna tend to dinner. After all, we gotta eat."

Venus and the Reverend vigorously nodded in agreement.

"Why don't we all join him in the kitchen where we can talk?" she suggested.

The Reverend helped to pull me up from my velvet crypt, and I followed them down the hallway. The decor slowly changed until the house looked like any other, without the slightest hint of erotica. In fact, the kitchen was downright homey. Things got even cozier as Venus and the Reverend helped themselves to beer while Eight-Ball prepared dinner.

"Do you mind telling me why everyone has those signs posted in their yards? I inquired.

"Why, that's to keep the vultures away," the Reverend explained. "There's a land grab going on in these parts that's like a damn shark feeding frenzy."

I was momentarily taken aback to hear him curse. "Is this something that's fairly recent?"

"No, it started about four years ago. Developers kept themselves busy before then with the southern part of the island. But that's all been built up, so now they're beginning to move here. They figure it's time to target large tracts of land owned by poor black folks. Next thing you know, they're sending letters, calling all the time and knocking on doors. Generally doing whatever they can to harass our senior citizens into accepting their offers."

"I guess the developers are getting tired of waitin' for us all to die off," Venus sniffed.

"It seems there's no longer any room for those folks who've been here for generations. All that matters these days is the almighty dollar." The Reverend's voice rose in an angry throb.

"Apparently, some people *have* decided to take the money and run," I remarked. "I noticed that a few new houses are already under construction."

It was as though I'd lit the fuse on a powder keg as the Reverend turned to me, full of hellfire and brimstone.

"Let me tell you a little something about those people that sold. We're talking old folks who were preyed upon and worn down, until their spirit finally broke. Developers came in here offering them what seemed like a whole lot of money. But they soon discovered it didn't go very far. Not after they paid their lawyers and had to find another place to live. Where they wound up was over in the projects in Brunswick. Now those folks are worse off than before. Their land is gone and they'll never get it back."

"Not only that, but what do you think it does to the rest of us who are trying to hang on?" Venus chimed in. "You got these big fancy-ass mansions being built next door. That means our property values soar. My taxes just went up forty percent. *Forty percent!* We're all low income. None of us can afford to pay that kind of money. Soon, we'll have no choice but to sell. That's when all the wealthy white folk will move in."

"Meanwhile, you know how much those damn lots are going for? Anywhere from three hundred thousand to one million dollars, depending on their size and access to the Frederica River. And this is happening right here, in the last bastion of historic black-owned property in these United States. It's economic genocide, I'm telling you!" the Reverend indignantly exploded. "How are we supposed to preserve our heritage on this island when we're losing out to golf courses and resort developments? I'll be damned if we aren't getting shafted all over again!"

The community was clearly under siege.

"But worst of all is that people are being strong-armed to sell," he asserted. "You just ask sister Venus here."

Venus strenuously nodded, sending the curls on her wig bobbing like a clutch of hungry chicks.

"Reverend's speaking the truth. I worked as a maid for a family of rich folk over on Sea Island only to be fired because I refused to sell my house."

Sea Island was connected to St. Simons by flyway. Locally referred to as La La Land, the place fully lived up to the name. A drive along Millionaire's Row showcased a succession of houses with each one larger than the next.

A profusion of Mercedes, Jaguars, Ferraris, and Porsches sat like motorized jewels in the driveways, while the guy mowing the lawn raked in a cool two hundred grand a year. Residents spent their days either jogging, playing tennis, or shooting a game of golf. And why not? They wanted to stay healthy and live forever, in order to enjoy their money for as long as they could.

Maybe if I was a good girl in this lifetime, I'd be born wealthy in the next. As it was, I felt lucky just to be able to pay my bills.

"Why would your former employer have cared whether or not you sold your home?" I asked Venus.

"Beats the hell outta me. But the good Lord provides in the most amazing ways. Would you believe I'm getting back at him, and he don't even know it?" she revealed with a mischievous grin. "Praise the Lord is all I can say!"

"Amen, sister," intoned Reverend Bayliss.

I wouldn't have been surprised if a gospel choir had materialized, singing and clapping their hands.

"I got my own business now. Well, it's a school actually," Venus divulged. "What Mr. Howard *damn-the-man* Drapkin don't know is that his wife comes here twice a week to study with me. Hell, she pays double what I used to make, and I ain't cleaning no toilets or scrubbing no floors. Glory be to God!"

"Shout it out loud, sister!" the Reverend encouraged.

I now realized who Bayliss reminded me of, with his pomaded hair and bombastic voice. The good Reverend was a cross between the Godfather of soul, James Brown, and that guerilla politician and PR machine extraordinaire, Al Sharpton.

I was musing on that, when the name Venus had just mentioned penetrated my consciousness.

"Howard Drapkin? Is that the same Mr. Drapkin that *you* work for, Eight-Ball?"

"Sure enough," he chuckled. "Funny thing is, he don't realize that Venus is my cousin."

"That's right. It's cause we don't have the same last name. Not that he ever gave me much thought, anyway," she said, making a face. "Why don't you tell Miss Rachel what Drapkin did to *you*, Eight-Ball, and see what she has to say."

Eight-Ball grew somber. "That old house we passed around the corner that's being torn down? It's where I used to live."

"It's a helluva lot more than just that. Not only was Eight-Ball born there, but also his mama, and Grandma Lulu before her," Venus interjected.

Eight-Ball's expression became pained as he continued on, almost as if guilt were eating him up. "I didn't wanna sell, but Mr. Drapkin, he badgered me something awful. Then he got me that extra job taking Mr. Williams out in the marsh. After a while, he offered to set me up in a place near DRG. Said it would be real nice and I could even walk to work. Soon, I didn't have no choice but do what he wanted."

"What do you mean?" I questioned. "Did he threaten you?"

"Not in so many words. But Mr. Drapkin, he let me know that people might be laid off, and he'd only keep those who were loyal. So, I went ahead and did as he asked."

Drapkin sounded like a real piece of work. But then again, he was a businessman who knew how to get what he wanted.

Eight-Ball fell silent as he tended to the mixture of unpeeled shrimp, sausage, crab, onions, rutabagas, white and sweet potatoes, turnips, carrots, and corncobs all simmering together in a big stainless steel pot. He expelled a deep sigh while stirring the contents with a wire scoop.

"Turns out selling my house was the worst thing I ever done. That nice new home Mr. Drapkin had all set up for me? It's in the Brunswick projects, not a place fit for man or dog. Ain't that right, Jake?" Eight-Ball shook his head and a bitter laugh escaped his lips. "Sometimes I hate that man for what he done. *Hunnuh ain gwine kno wey hunnuh duh gwine ef hunnuh ain kno wey hunnuh dey frum.*"

"What's that?" I asked, never having heard the language before.

"It's an old Gullah saying Grandma Lulu used that means you won't know where you're going, if you don't know where you're from. Ain't that the truth? Our West African ancestors knew it was important not to lose their roots. That's what my home was to me. Course on the other hand, I still got a job."

"And you'll always have a home and roots here with me." Venus gave Eight-Ball a hug, as the man wiped a tear from his cheek.

"That's enough of that. Let's eat," Eight-Ball gruffly announced, ladling the stew into four big bowls.

We sat down at a pink Formica table and began to eat.

"So, why do you think Drapkin pressured you to move?" I asked him.

"Most likely 'cause I inherited five acres of waterfront property along South Harrington Road."

Eight-Ball's metal spoon clinked against his teeth, as I tried to figure out how much money that would amount to.

Ka-ching! Ka-ching! the spoon responded, tallying it up to millions of dollars.

"Besides like I told you, Mr. Williams and my boss are friends. I figure he's just helping Mr. Williams get land for his Golden Dreams Development company."

"And probably getting a hefty kickback in the process," Venus cynically snorted.

"It's obvious that Golden Dreams Development and your boss, Mr. Drapkin, are linked in some way," I responded, having no doubt that she was correct.

"You want to know what's *really* going on? I'll be happy to tell you," the Reverend pompously interjected. "Drapkin and his kind have ruined Brunswick with all their damn dirty industry, and don't want to live there anymore. Instead they've decided to come here to St. Simons where everything's nice and clean. But first they gotta move us poor folk out of the way to make room for their big fancy houses. I'm telling you, they're planning to make St. Simons their own private resort. Hell, it wouldn't surprise me none if they even gated this place to keep others out, just like those folks on Sea Island are trying to do." Bayliss stabbed a finger in the air, punctuating each point.

"I think you're getting a little carried away," I offered, dipping a piece of bread into the stew. "There are lots of shops here on St. Simons. No one's about to close those off to the general public and shut down a good source of revenue. Besides, putting a stop to commercial development would only be counterproductive to someone like Williams."

The Lowcountry boil was terrific. I got up to get some more, only to have Jake nail me for the easy mark I was. He waited until I'd lowered the ladle into the pot, and then began to whine as though he hadn't eaten for days. I slipped a spoonful into his dish to quiet him down.

"Which brings us around to Clark Williams and his damn Golden Dreams Development Corporation. Golden Dreams my ass! Golden Dollars is more like it," the Reverend irately huffed. "You can't tell me that Williams and Drapkin aren't somehow washing each other's hands. Hell, we don't stand a chance, what with Williams now running for Congress. You can bet your bootie he'll get all sorts of legislation passed that'll end up helping the 'haves' and screwing the 'have nots.' I've got a good mind to run against him, myself."

Bayliss was reminding me more of Al Sharpton with each passing minute.

"As far as I'm concerned, we got us a case of environmental injustice going on here, what with rich folks messing up their own backyard and then thinking we're all gonna swap places." The Reverend stopped speaking long enough to shovel a spoonful of stew into his mouth.

Bayliss obviously viewed the world in black-and-white terms. But then, Clark Williams had accused me of exactly the same thing. It might prove interesting to snoop around and see what other business dealings he and Drapkin were involved in. However, right now I was eager to learn more about the woman sitting beside me wearing the Harpo Marx wig. I turned to find Venus downing her third bowl of stew with gusto.

"You mentioned having started some kind of school. What is it that you teach?"

Venus sucked the meat from a shrimp tail before turning to me with a crafty smile. "I help women feel good about themselves. I show them how to be more like J-Lo, and go out there and shake their booties. But even more important, I teach them how to gain power over their men."

Hmm. I wouldn't mind picking up a few pointers when it came to that myself.

"Fact is, Mrs. Drapkin was my first student. Mrs. D spread the word since then, and damn if my school hasn't caught on like wildfire. Now there's a wait list of wealthy women dying to plant their fannies in my living room twice a week."

"Does your school have a name?" I inquired, becoming increasingly curious.

"Sure does. *The Venus School of Woman Power.*"

Catchy title.

"What sort of courses do you teach?"

"Well, there's Learning to Make Your Man a Good Lover, Woman Thang Power, and How to Become a Goddess."

So far, so good.

"And also, The Art of Root."

"What's that?" I asked, hoping it had nothing to do with cooking.

"Why it's using herbs and roots to cast spells, in order to get what you want. I make up individual potions for my students, depending on what kinda trouble they got. But it always boils down to the same damn thing. No good, cheating husbands who are keeping firm young things on the side."

"Is that Mrs. Drapkin's problem?" I brazenly questioned.

"If it walks like a duck, talks like a duck, and has tailfeathers, then it's probably not a mink," Venus sagely replied.

What the hell did *that* mean?

"Of course he's cheatin' on her! Trouble is she's so much in love with that man, she can't see straight. Though for the life of me, I don't know why. You ever seen that skinny ass of his?"

"I can't say that I have."

Venus rolled her eyes. "Well, he's playin' around with some crazy white bitch who's got him wrapped tight as a virgin's legs around her little finger. Meanwhile, *that* girl's got a thing for big ol' ugly manatees. I hear she runs around calling herself some kinda scientist, when she's nothin' but a cheap piece of white trash. So, I'm helping Mrs. D get back her man. After that, I'll give her some root to make his life a holy living hell. That'll be my ultimate revenge, along with the fact that I'm getting paid for the pleasure of doing it."

My brain spun into overdrive at this new piece of information. Apparently, Candi had dumped a dud Spud for her very own sugar daddy—one who didn't need to strip the sid-

ing off her mobile home in order to make a few extra bucks.
Hmm. I wondered if Drapkin's friend Clark Williams had
gotten her the job at Manatee Mania Water Park. It seemed
one hand *was* washing the other in the most interesting
ways.

Venus now fingered a polished bone, which hung from a
red string around her neck. Long and curved, it had a knob
on one end.

"What kind of bone is that?" I inquired, having noticed it
earlier.

"Why, it's a coon dong," the Reverend answered.

"Come again?" I asked, not certain I'd heard him correctly.

"A raccoon penis bone," Venus explained.

"Now you know what happens to roadkill around here,"
Bayliss added with a chuckle.

"You stop that," Venus responded, giving him a playful
pat.

"Why in the world would you wear something like that?"

"Cause it's a love charm, of course. All the women attending my school buy them from me. Slip it under your
mattress, and that man of yours will perform better, harder,
stronger, and longer."

I had to hand it to Venus. She was turning out to be a hell
of a shrewd businesswoman.

"Herbs and charms? Doesn't superstition go against what
you preach?" I asked, turning to Bayliss.

"Why should it? Root is part of our West African culture
dating back thousands of years. Truth is, root only has power
over you if you believe in it. For instance, you take Venus's
front door. It's painted haint blue. Lotsa folks believe that'll
keep bad spirits away, and it makes them feel better. Same

reason why houses around here are painted bright colors—
for luck. Ain't nothing wrong with that. Besides, sister
Venus ain't hurtin' nobody with what she's doing."

"Listen darlin', the truth is I help women get back their
power; power that they should never have given away to
those husbands of theirs in the first place."

She'd innately hit upon one of my own fears—lowering
my defenses, only to end up being hurt. My mother had done
so, and I'd sworn I'd never let it happen to me. The problem
was, Santou and I had arrived at an emotional crossroad. I
needed to know how to move forward without giving any of
my power away.

"Women gotta reclaim their sassiness by doing what
makes them look and feel good. See now, I think you should
dress a little more like Mariah Carey, myself. You've got a
nice body. So, what are you hiding it for? You'd be amazed
how good it makes you feel to reclaim your power as a
woman. Not only that, but I guarantee your man will enjoy
it, as well."

"Amen to that," the Reverend chortled, and gave Venus
what looked to be a love pat. She reciprocated with a throaty
purr.

It was time to call it a night, and Eight-Ball walked me
outside. I said my good-byes and was heading for my Ford,
only to stop and look back at the haint-blue door.

"Do you really believe in spirits, Eight-Ball?" I softly inquired, not wanting to disturb the night.

"Course I do. They're everywhere around us. Fact is,
they're whispering to me right now."

I stared hard into the darkness, trying to put a face on
whatever it was that he heard.

"Spirits are real as any flesh-and-blood person. That's

what makes them so powerful. It's just a natural fact. Same as a rooster crowing on your doorstep is a sign of death; or knowing that the rain washes away a person's last footsteps before they're buried, removing all traces they ever walked the face of this earth."

Though I still couldn't hear anything, a cold breeze began to caress my neck, moving slowly down my arms, legs, and back. I jumped in my vehicle and took off as a light rain began to fall. It pitter-pattered on the landscape of rooftops as I turned off Mamalou Lane and onto South Harrington Road, aware that this place was a tinderbox just waiting to explode.

The rain came down harder now, its pellets erupting with the power of live bullets as they hit each metal roof. DON'T ASK/WON'T SELL, the signs roared, their echoes chasing my Ford, as they followed me all the way home.

The rain had stopped by the time I reached Tybee. Having part of a six-pack left, I made my way to the east end of the island to hang out on the beach. Jake was still away. I'd turned into an FBI widow without the benefit of being married. But then I suppose Santou had the same complaint about me.

I drove down Butler Avenue, through the small commercial district that was fast asleep. For once, there were no lines in front of The Breakfast Club, hungry for their pecan waffles and chorizo con huevos. I passed IGA, the only grocery store in town, and headed for Doc's Bar on Tybresa. A buck will buy you a beer, making its location very convenient. Nearby was T. S. Chu's, which calls itself a department store, though it's clearly unlike any other. Dimly lit, the place sells tourist schlock in the front, with hammers, lightbulbs, and dishpans for sale in the rear.

There was no question that Tybee was a poor man's land when compared to its ritzier brethren, Sea Island and St. Simons. But I also knew of no other place that celebrates with both a Mutt Strut and a Beach Bum Parade each year. That alone wouldn't have made me trade my new home for anywhere else in the world.

I passed the Mity Tidy Laundromat and turned toward the beach, where I parked in an empty lot. Then kicking off my shoes, I grabbed the beer and slipped past dunes, their mounds interwoven with lengths of railroad vine. The sinewy strands snaked through the sand like twisting channels of veins. Feathery sea oats grew wild among them, flaunting golden seeds atop chest-high, elegant stalks. They swayed in the ocean breeze like willowy showgirls, holding fans to keep their essentials modestly covered.

The wet sand squished between my toes, leaving a series of footprints upon the beach. But they were far from being the only ones there. They mingled with an eclectic traffic pattern formed by crabs, raccoons, and birds in an interspecies mosaic. Their tracks ran up and down the shoreline, gradually disappearing off into the distance. Large pieces of gnarled driftwood added to the mood, creating a boneyard of the dead.

A moon so full that it was ready to burst threw light across the shore, its beams dancing upon the waves in a dainty minuet. Saucer-shaped moon jellies rhythmically joined in the waltz, while moon snails watched from where they were safely tucked away in their shells. Long-legged ghost crabs became part of the dance as they sped along the beach. I glanced away for a second, and when I looked back, they'd already morphed into phantoms of the night.

I laid down on the beach and the wet sand accepted me as

one of its own, the grains conforming to my extremities so that I was slowly turned into a dune. The transformation was complete as the particles found their way into my scalp, my nose, and my mouth. I remained still as a mouse, not daring to move, an invisible wave having entered my body.

Ba bump, ba bump, ba bump.

It was the ocean relentlessly pounding the sand like a telltale, beating heart. I wanted the tide to wash everything away—the all-too-tempting offer Clark Williams had made to help me with my climb up the career ladder, along with the insidious doubts about my boss that were eating their way through my brain. I yearned to live in a black-and-white world like the Reverend Bayliss, so that I could easily distinguish the good guys from the bad.

My hand wrapped around something solid by my side. I brought it close to my eyes to find it was a living, breathing sand dollar. Its message couldn't have been any more clear.

Wake up and smell the salt water, Porter. The world revolves around money.

It was then that I began to hear the whispers, though I couldn't decipher what the spirits were trying to tell me. I finally gave up and heeded my own inner voice by polishing off the last of the six-pack.

Twelve

My car phone began to ring early the next morning as I was on my way to the office. At least that's what I assumed it was through the lingering remnants of my beer haze. This was one of those days when even the smell of coffee made me feel nauseous. Or, maybe it was just the aftereffect of my own homemade brew. That along with the fact that I had yet to clean out the coffeepot, my reasoning being that adding fresh java to yesterday's dregs would give it a more robust flavor. Naturally, Santou had a different way of looking at it. He simply called me lazy.

The irritating ring of the phone continued to boomerang inside my vehicle. There are times when you just don't want to pick up the damn thing. This happened to be one of them. But there was only one way to end the insistent jingling that worked on my nerves like a jackhammer. My finger hit the talk button.

"Good morning there, Pepper. Who woulda thunk that I'd be hanging out with a celebrity?"

"What are you talking about?" I groused, not in the mood for games.

"Just the fact that you made the front-page news of our local paper."

159

Oh shit! That was right. I now remembered Lowell had warned me about this yesterday, though he'd refused to reveal the contents.

"Would you like me to read the beginning to you?"

"Oh God, no." How was I supposed to handle this, when I couldn't even deal with my morning coffee?

Gary read it aloud anyway. *"The U.S. Fish and Wildlife Service places manatees above jobs and the economic needs of our community."*

Just great.

"It goes on to say what a monumental bitch you are for trying to shut down Manatee Mania Water Park. I'm paraphrasing, of course. Oh yeah. And that Manatee Mania, along with Golden Dreams Development, is generously donating ten acres of wetlands to the Georgia Department of Natural Resources to show their goodwill."

How clever of them.

"Well, it's not something the community has to worry about anymore, since I no longer have a case," I informed him.

There was a moment of stunned silence before Gary responded.

"What in the hell happened?"

"Some good old boy networking was undertaken by the indomitable Clark Williams. As a result, Manatee Mania has been granted an emergency permit to operate. It also so happens that both Williams and Wendell knew about it in advance, while my boss, Lowell, never bothered to mention it to me."

"Ooh, now that's nasty."

"No kidding. I've reached a whole new level of frustration, what with this and that DeLorean defense stunt. What's the sense of trying to make cases if Fish and Wildlife keeps cutting my legs out from under me?"

"Hey, none of that, Pepper. Buck up, 'cause I have just the thing for you. This could be your ticket to spelling R-E-L-I-E-F."

"You mean someone has finally performed surgery and given the paper pushers at Fish and Wildlife an actual backbone?" I sniped.

"Don't expect miracles," Gary laughed. "But this is damn near close to being as good. You know the sampling we did in the marsh yesterday? Well, it paid off. What I've discovered is pure dynamite."

My beer haze vanished in a flash, replaced by a surge of adrenaline that shot through me. "Why? What did you find?"

"It's no wonder things are dying out in that creek. The grass, the water, fish, birds, animals, even the mud, are loaded with high levels of mercury, along with some PCBs. An industrial plant in the area must be illegally discharging one hell of a lot of heavy metals into the water. For chrissakes, just thinking about it gives me the heebie-jeebies. The ramifications of it are almost too mind-boggling to be believed."

I hated when Gary clicked into his scientific mode, and automatically assumed that I knew what he was talking about.

"Would you mind explaining this to me?"

"It would be my pleasure. With PCBs, you've got a toxic pollutant that never breaks down. Instead it remains part of the food chain, eventually harming your stomach, liver, kidneys, and thyroid. Kids are particularly susceptible to the stuff. They stand a good chance of developing 'thinking' problems, stemming from a diminished IQ. PCBs can also lead to cancer, which is the main reason the EPA banned their use altogether a few years ago. Not for nothing, but this area has a pretty high cancer rate."

This wasn't something that I really wanted to know. Every part of me started to feel a little bit weird, as though cancer cells were already eating away at my body.

"As for mercury, it's so highly toxic that it plays havoc with your nervous, renal, and reproductive systems. Not to mention the permanent damage it can do to the brain, lungs, colon, and heart. And remember, when brain cells die, that's it—they don't regenerate."

Gary was one hundred percent correct. This information had the potential of being an enormous bombshell.

"Are there any obvious symptoms that someone might have?" I asked, secretly wanting to see if any of them applied to me.

"You mean as a result of accumulating too much mercury in your system?"

"Uh-huh."

"Sure. You ever hear the phrase, *mad as a hatter*?"

"Of course. It's from the Lewis Carroll book, *Alice in Wonderland*," I responded, making an immediate connection. Thank God, at least my memory still worked.

"Well, it refers to the effect mercury had on laborers in the hatmaking industry during the nineteenth century."

"You're joking. I never would have dreamt of putting the two together."

"Well, it's true. A mercury compound was used to remove the fur from beaver and rabbit pelts, and turn them into felt. The hatters spent their days breathing in the fumes. Eventually, they wound up with the shakes, loss of coordination, memory loss, even slurred speech and loose teeth. Oh yeah, and also irritability and depression."

That last part was a no-brainer. If I lost my teeth and memory, I'd be irritable and depressed, too.

"Mercury is potent as hell. Doctors even found holes the size of quarters inside hatter's brains during postmortem autopsies."

I must have begun to daydream, allowing my vehicle to drift into the next lane. A passing car angrily blew its horn, and I hastily jerked the Explorer back into place, causing my heart to race. Taking a deep breath, I glanced down at where my hands now shook on the steering wheel as though an electrical current were running through them. It was then I remembered the tremors that had gripped Eight-Ball's hands as he'd lifted the beer can. Could it be that what I'd thought was Parkinson's might actually be something else?

"Would a chlor-alkali plant use mercury?" I asked, on a hunch.

Gary thought for a moment. "Let's see. A chlor-alkali plant produces caustic soda, hydrochloric acid, and sodium chloride, used by paper mills for bleaching. That's manufactured through the Solvay process, which requires liquid mercury for its electrolytic cells. So, the answer to your question would be yes."

We were both quiet for a moment.

"Okay Pepper, spill the beans. What do you know?"

"I'm not sure yet. But the old man who was running Clark Williams's boat? Well, he works over at DRG, the chlor-alkali plant in Brunswick. Anyway, I spent some time with him yesterday, and noticed that his hands shook. I figured it was either the beginnings of Parkinson's, or that maybe he had the DTs from drinking too much. Now I'm beginning to wonder if there could be a deeper connection."

"Good observation, Rach," Gary noted. "Not for nothing, but DRG's fairly close to Purvis Creek."

"Are you thinking what I'm thinking?" I asked.

"You mean that we're gonna have a greasy barbecue lunch today, seeing that you'll be heading back down this way?"

"You always read my mind so well." I laughed. "Yeah, I think we should pay DRG a visit. Besides, I want to meet the owner, Howard Drapkin."

"Why? Is he supposed to be good-looking, or something?" Gary inquired.

Was that a tinge of jealousy in his voice?

"Not so far as I've heard. But remember Candi Collins? The babe who's passing herself off as a marine biologist over at the water park?"

"How can I forget?" he asked with a sigh.

"Whoa, down boy. She's already spoken for. It turns out that Candi is Drapkin's mistress."

"Don't you love these towns where everybody seems to be sleeping with everybody else? So how come I'm always left out of the action?"

"Probably because you're a gentleman, and an all-around nice guy."

"Oh yeah, that's right. I keep forgetting. I have to work on that," he drolly responded. "I'm off to practice my charms on Lucille right now. She needs a good grooming this morning. I'll meet you at the office afterward."

Gary was waiting when I got there, and we quickly headed out.

We again drove through the industrial heart of Brunswick,

which struck me as having the ingredients of a bad sci-fi flick. Smokestacks rose out of the marsh like mutant stalks of spartina grass, while a caustic odor filled the air. I rolled up my car window and Gary laughed.

"You know that song, "On A Clear Day, You Can See Forever?" Well on a clear day in Brunswick, you can see a fine chemical mist filling the sky."

"How could a place so beautiful have been turned into such a dumping ground?" I wondered aloud.

"What, are you kidding? Let's be real here. This is rural Georgia. You've got cheap labor, very little oversight, no workplace controls and, in case you haven't noticed, there aren't a whole lot of environmental activists around. What Brunswick *does* have is access to raw materials, along with good rail and sea passage. Add it all up, and you've got the makings for one hell of an industrial hub in the South. In other words, it's the perfect place for people like you and me to make cases," he said with a grin.

"Yeah, I only wish that we were allowed," I grumbled.

"Let's look at it another way," Gary reasoned. "You must have hit one helluva nerve to make those boys scramble as fast as they did. So, when those cardboard matadors who we work for try to knock us off a case, we just have to be clever enough to get around it by taking a different route."

No wonder I was so fond of Gary.

"Your boss is doing his damnedest to checkmate you. The trick is not to let him break your spirit."

"So what's your secret? How have *you* managed to stay so upbeat?"

"Easy. I found out that they 'proud cut' the old biologist who worked in this office before me. I vowed then and there never to give them that much power."

"Proud cut? What's that?" I asked.

"It's what they do to a horse when they geld it. Except sometimes they don't quite get everything, so this gelded horse runs around thinking he's still a stud. Then when a stallion comes on the scene, the gelded horse gets his ass kicked. That's what happened to Harry Phillips after he had some big run-in with the head honchos over a case down here that he wanted to make. He'd let them whittle away his power until he no longer had any left. Old Harry became so disgusted that he gave up and retired around the Okefenokee. I decided that would never happen to me."

I was about to ask what made him think that it hadn't already when DRG, with its twin smokestacks wreathed in a plume of emissions, came into view.

"Hi ho, here we go," Gary quipped, and drove in through the gate. Even with the windows closed, the air nipped at my throat.

We parked in the lot and entered the main building, where our footsteps echoed on the linoleum floor. Large color photographs of the marsh were mounted on the walls, displaying the Georgia coastline in all its glory. Funny, but none showed an industrial plant or smokestack in sight.

Everything appeared to be pristinely clean as we strode down the hallway. The ventilation system must have been working overtime, for there was nary a whiff of an unpleasant odor. It was either that, or I was already getting used to the stench that hung over the grounds.

We made a beeline for the first door, where a matronly woman sat behind a clutter-free desk. She smiled, making her cheeks so round that they swelled into chipmunk's pouches.

"Good day. What can I do for ya'll?" she inquired in a

singsong voice, her head rhythmically bobbing from side to side.

"We'd like to speak with Mr. Drapkin," I informed her.

Her ten pudgy fingers lay entwined on the desk like little pork sausage links. Breaking apart, they fiddled with the nameplate that announced her identity in bright gold letters.

"I'm afraid he's an awfully busy man. I'll have to ask what this is in regard to."

"It's official business, Mrs. Miller," I replied, and pulled out my badge.

"Oh dear, I hope nothing is wrong," she responded, her smile collapsing as quickly as air escaping a balloon.

"No, we just have a few questions is all," Gary reassured her.

"Oh, that's good. Then why don't you wait here and I'll be back in just a minute?" Mrs. Miller graciously suggested.

She waddled down the hall toward a closed door. My guess was that either Candi Collins or Mrs. Drapkin had hired her, preferring not to deal with any unnecessary competition. She soon returned, smiling as broadly as before.

"Like I said, Mr. Drapkin's a busy man but he'll be glad to spend a few minutes with you."

Smart move. It wouldn't have looked very good had he refused.

"Just go to that first door and walk right on in," she advised.

We did as instructed, only I knocked first. A courtly gentleman stood from behind his desk and approached to greet us.

"Please, come in and sit down."

Drapkin wasn't at all the brash industrialist that I'd expected. Rather, the man couldn't have been more cordial.

Appearing to be in his late fifties, Drapkin was tall and fit with a shock of white hair that was moussed and blown dry to perfection. It gave him a striking resemblance to the old game-show-host-turned-animal-activist Bob Barker. His clothes were as expensive and finely tailored as those of Clark Williams, making me wonder if the two men shopped together.

"Mr. Drapkin, I'm Special Agent Rachel Porter, and this is Dr. Gary Fletcher, a contaminants expert. We're with the U.S. Fish and Wildlife Service."

I was caught by surprise as he took hold of my arm and guided me across the floor, as though I were eighty years old.

"Why don't you sit here? This is a comfortable chair," Drapkin courteously suggested, helping me into my seat.

Yikes! I didn't know whether to thank the guy or punch his lights out. I looked over at Gary to find he was smiling away like a loon.

Sitting down, I discovered that Drapkin was right. The chair molded itself to my every contour. All I needed was a cat in my lap, a martini, and I'd be all set. Gary took the chair next to me.

"Thanks. This one's pretty comfortable too," he joked.

Drapkin ignored the remark as he sat back down behind his desk. "Now, what is it that I can do for you?" he asked, flashing a smile that was neither too big nor too small, but just right.

Even his pearly whites were perfect. A fitting nickname popped into my mind, *The Silver Fox.*

"We've discovered a large number of dead animals and birds in the surrounding marsh. Whenever something like that happens, I'm asked to investigate," I began.

Drapkin opened his mouth as if to protest, only to decide against it. Instead, he nodded his head and then murmured, "Of course."

"That led us to do some testing to try and discover the cause."

"And what we found were amazingly high levels of mercury, not only in the water and environs, but also in animals, fish, and birds," Gary added.

"Really? Well, that's disturbing," Drapkin remarked, with what appeared to be genuine concern. "I hate to think that something's harming our marsh. Maybe it's just some sort of natural die-off. The area looks the same to me as it always has. But then of course, I'm no scientist."

"No, you're not," Gary bluntly remarked.

Drapkin's expression rapidly changed from one of concern to alarm. "Surely you're not suggesting that DRG is in any way involved."

"Well, you do use liquid mercury in your electrolytic cells," Gary pointed out.

"For which I have all the necessary permits, I assure you," Drapkin firmly responded.

"Would you mind showing them to us?" I asked, glad to have Gary along. Otherwise, I'd only have a general idea of what I was looking for.

"Not at all. You'll find that everything is in order," Drapkin asserted.

However, his impeccably tan complexion now held a reddish hue, as if a fire had begun to burn beneath its surface.

Opening the small filing cabinet next to his desk, he pulled out a folder.

"Here, see for yourself."

Though Drapkin pushed the papers toward me, I chose to

get up from my chair. A number of picture frames were on his desk and I wanted to see the photos. I was curious if they were of Candi, his wife, or both. I walked around to find that each frame held a formal "beauty" shot of only one person—Howard Drapkin, himself. Talk about being creepy. I suddenly saw the man in an entirely new light.

His hair was perfectly coiffed in each photo, while his tan and smile struck me as chic accessories. Gary joined me to catch a glimpse of the pictures and silently raised an eyebrow. Then we proceeded to examine the paperwork.

Drapkin was correct. DRG had all the necessary permits. In addition, he presented us with a slew of reports that were prepared and sent into the Georgia Environmental Protection Division each month. They revealed the plant was well within the legal limit of the amount of mercury discharged each day. The levels were low enough not to have a harmful effect on the marsh.

"I understand you're only doing your job, and I appreciate that. But as you see, DRG is operating within permitted boundaries. Perhaps the marsh is just experiencing one of those phenomenons of nature that happen every now and again," Drapkin affably proposed.

"Yeah, right. The marsh is turning around and biting itself in the ass just for the hell of it," Gary caustically retorted.

Even I was taken aback by the vehemence of his reaction.

"Sorry to have bothered you, Mr. Drapkin," I offered, hoping to smooth any ruffled feathers.

However, it was clear that Drapkin was annoyed. He pursed his lips and glared at Gary before addressing me.

"Not at all. Let me know if there's anything else I can do to help," he responded, beginning to usher us out of the room.

"Well, it would be nice if you did something about the odor in the area. Is it possible to fix that?" I joked.

But Drapkin wasn't amused. He turned on me as though I'd accused him of not wearing enough deodorant.

"We've got industrial plants around here and when the wind is right, you're going to smell them. That doesn't make it a damn health emergency," he defensively snapped.

This time, it was Drapkin's response that took me by surprise. What the hell was he so touchy about? I decided it would be prudent to find out.

"Actually, there *is* one more thing you can do," I said, digging in my heels before he pushed me out the door. "I'd like to take a quick look inside the plant."

"Absolutely not," Drapkin brusquely rejoined and then quickly backtracked, as though realizing just how bad that sounded. "No one's available to show you around at the moment. Besides, we don't allow people to traipse through here unless absolutely necessary, what with the penchant for lawsuits these days. Heaven forbid, you so much as stub your toe. I'd never hear the end of it from my insurance company."

"Except that I'm not John Q Public. I'm a federal agent," I reminded him. "And I'm not here to hit you with a lawsuit. I'm only asking to check out the plant."

"I'm sorry, but not without the proper authorization. Nothing personal, Agent Porter, but I've heard far too many horror stories when it comes to dealing with the U.S. Fish and Wildlife Service. For all I know, you're planning to drop an endangered mouse on the grounds as an excuse to shut me down, all because you don't like the smell. Too many employees depend on DRG for their livelihood. Come back with the proper paperwork, and then we'll take it from there.

After all, I showed you mine. I think it only fitting that you now show me yours," he said, and closed the door behind us.

Talk about your slick customers. Drapkin was good. Almost as good as Clark Williams, himself.

"What do you suppose that was all about?" I asked, as we walked outside.

"I don't know, but there's something definitely ghoulish about the guy. He's slippery enough to work for the Feds. So, what do you propose we do, Pepper?"

"Well, we can't get inside the plant right now. However, Drapkin didn't say that we weren't allowed on the grounds. So why don't we take a stroll around and see what we can find?"

"You're a woman after my own heart," Gary replied, and took hold of my arm. "You want me to help you there, grandma?"

He was lucky I didn't deck him.

"Wait here," he said and ran back to the vehicle. Gary returned with his sampling bag.

I looked at him in surprise.

"It's a compulsion," he admitted. "I like to live up to my motto. *Have Bag Will Travel.* Besides, you never know what we might find."

We began our trek.

"Do you have any idea how much property DRG has?" I asked, curious as to its size.

"Yeah. I checked it out at the office right before we left. They've got about six hundred acres, two hundred and fifty of which are tidal marshlands."

He wasn't kidding. The view from the back of the main building took my breath away. The marsh spread out before us like a giant hula skirt, its golden grasses swaying in a thick layer of fringe. It drove home the point that no matter where you are in this area, you're never far from the marsh.

"See over there?" Gary pointed north to south. "You've got residential housing, while the marsh, Purvis Creek, and the Turtle River border us to the west."

Then I looked at the other buildings, as Gary pointed them out. "My guess is those are treatment and disposal units, along with tank storage facilities. And then of course, you've got railroad spurs by those tracks. Let's head this way first," he suggested, and we began to work our way toward the marsh.

My feet grew increasingly damp with each step, until I felt like one more swamp creature.

"You're clearly going to owe me a new pair of shoes," I remarked.

Gary turned, looked at my feet, and laughed. "That's because you're doing it all wrong. How long have you been down here, anyway?"

"That's beside the point," I retorted. "Just tell me what you're talking about."

"Observe and learn," he instructed.

I watched as Gary swept the marsh grass over and down with every step.

"See? As long as you lay the grass down with your feet, you won't sink into all that crap. It places a fibrous layer of material between yourself and the mud. The other thing to be aware of is that this will leave a track for a day or two. It's one way to tell if someone has been in the area before you."

I proceeded to keep my eyes plastered to the ground. Though I didn't spot any tracks, I did see something else.

"What's that?" I asked, pointing off to my left.

Gary followed my finger. "Interesting. There appears to

be some kind of drainage canal coming from the plant. Not only that, but there's plenty of stressed vegetation all around. What say we take a water sample?"

"Sounds good to me," I agreed.

Gary pulled out a jar, filled it with liquid, and screwed the lid on tight.

"Okay, Pepper. What do you want to do now? Keep walking into the marsh, or head back?"

I scrutinized the area and carefully weighed my options. Now that I knew what I was looking for, I could spot stressed vegetation everywhere. There was a good chance that I could always get back out into this marsh if I so chose. However, I didn't know when I'd be able to nose around the buildings again.

"Let's see what we can find around the plant. Only why don't we head in that direction?" I pointed toward a group of buildings that we hadn't spotted before.

The first thing we hit were a couple of abandoned railroad cars. Not far from those were an outfall pond and a weir. But what grabbed my attention were two large buildings that lay off to our right.

"What do you suppose those are?"

Gary gazed at them and then nodded in recognition. "Why, that's the heart and soul of any chlor-alkali facility. Those are the generating plants. It's where processing takes place and the electrolytic cells are housed."

The words were said almost with reverence.

"Then that's what I want to check out."

"Be my guest," Gary complied, with a wave of his hand.

As we headed toward them, a worker in coveralls and boots appeared from around one of the buildings. He stopped short upon catching sight of us.

"Sorry, but you need permission to be in this area," he called out.

"There's no problem. Mr. Drapkin said it would be all right," I boldly lied, with what I hoped passed for a charming smile.

The workman waved and continued on his way.

"I suggest you take a quick look, because my gut tells me that guy is about to rat us out," Gary warned.

He was probably right. We hurried on, only to stumble upon what appeared to be a manmade lake just south of the second building.

"Now you can see why I bring this bag wherever I go," Gary remarked, while removing a jar. "Personally, I think I deserve a medal for diligence above and beyond the call of duty."

"Would you settle for a brownie?" I proposed, secretly glad that Gary was such an obsessive maniac.

"That'll do."

Gary bent down, filled the container with a liquid sample, and then slapped a sticker on its surface. "Body of water south of cell building two," he said aloud, writing the information on its label.

We continued toward the buildings when Gary flung out an arm, blocking my advance. I gazed down at where I'd been about to step.

"Well, lookee here," he said, pointing to what could have been prehistoric bubbles preserved in a pool of dried mud. They looked like the metallic remnants of some dying creature's last breath.

"Call me crazy, but I could almost swear that was mercury," he observed. "Wouldn't that just be ducky?"

"Oh God, I certainly hope not," I said, unwilling to part

with any brain cells. "But I suppose you better take a sample just in case."

Gary pulled a clean jar from his bag and scraped a portion of mud and bubbles inside, carefully preserving the specimen.

"You've gotta wonder why mercury would be out here, if that's really what it is," Gary pondered, zipping his bag. "That stuff is expensive."

"I don't know, but let's continue on," I proposed, anxious to get closer to the buildings.

We'd scarcely made a move when an angry voice stopped us dead in our tracks.

"Just what the hell do the two of you think you're doing?"

Drapkin came flying toward us so fast that his feet barely touched the ground. "Unless you leave this instant, I intend to call the police and have you arrested on charges of trespassing."

"That won't be necessary," I assured him, holding up my hands in surrender. "Sorry, I didn't think you'd mind if we simply walked around. Besides, I swear that I didn't drop an endangered mouse anywhere." The last thing I wanted was to have the Brunswick cops on my tail, especially since Drapkin had every right to order us off DRG property.

But Gary refused to let the matter drop.

"So what's your problem, anyway?" Gary asked, scuffing his feet on the ground like a rebellious kid itching for a fight. "It's not as if you've got something to hide, right?"

I glanced down and saw that he was kicking dirt toward the puddle of silver bubbles. Drapkin picked up on it as well, and the color rapidly drained from his face.

"I want you both out of here immediately," he spat between clenched teeth.

"Okay, okay. Take it easy," Gary pretended to placate him, all the while continuing to grind his feet into the dirt. "Otherwise, you're gonna give yourself a heart attack."

"Now!" Drapkin hissed, nearly apoplectic.

"Come on, let's go. We got what we need," I urged, beginning to feel uneasy about the game being played.

Much more of this and I'd be forced to kick ass and break up a fight.

I grabbed Gary's arm and began to pull him away. Drapkin followed along like a crazed watchdog as we made our way to the pickup. He even trailed us halfway down the drive as we drove toward the gate.

"Now there's a guy who's just a wee bit uptight, wouldn't you say?" Gary snickered, peering into the rearview mirror.

"Yeah. But why did you have to go and bait him like that? It doesn't help our case any."

"It's because those kind of guys drive me crazy. He thinks his money buys him the right to do whatever the hell he wants, while the rest of us poor slobs just have to deal with it. Wendell, Drapkin, Williams—they're all alike. I'm checking out something in Florida right now that's potentially so hot it would make your skin sizzle. Naturally, it involves another of these fat cats."

"In other words, you're making new friends wherever you go." That's what I loved about Gary. He was as popular as I was. "Do tell me about it," I said, settling down for a good story as we headed toward DRG's gates.

But Gary shook his head. "Uh-uh. The time's not right yet. Besides, our plate's already full at the moment."

"Well, in that case, you better get cracking on whatever it is that we've got in those vials. I'll be damned if you're going to start on something else without me."

"Aye, aye Pepper. Your wish is my command," he laughed, as we turned onto Highway 17.

A warm breeze tumbled into the cab. Surfing on its current were a bunch of ragtag gnats that voraciously zeroed in on my skin. I swatted at my neck and arms, knocking the pesky little suckers off one by one, until they'd finally been decimated. Then pulling back my hand, I stared at the drops of blood as the realization hit me. There had been no bugs on DRG's grounds.

We'd been so preoccupied that neither Gary nor I had given it much thought. But there hadn't been a sound. No birds, no insects, nothing had been around. I hadn't seen one mink running past us on the grounds, nor had any blackbirds crowed. There'd been no sign of life at all. The silence had been so complete, we could have been buried six feet underground.

A cold sweat broke out on my skin, even though the day was warm. I jumped as a squeak pierced the air. It was Gary shifting about in his seat. But the sound I'd heard was a coffin lid being closed. It came along with the growing awareness that we'd been inside a dead zone.

Thirteen

Gary went into his office to begin testing as I got in my vehicle and took off. My pulse picked up its beat, until it was in direct competition with my tires, as they sped round and round. It wasn't a wildlife case that had my heart revving, with every cell in my body primed. Rather, it was the message that had been left on my answering machine. Santou would be home tonight.

I ran into a fancy excuse for a deli and grabbed my version of survival gear—a couple of prepared meals. My philosophy has always been, *Why cook if you don't have to?* Especially when somebody has already gone to the trouble of placing gourmet fare in conveniently frozen packages?

My next stop was the wine store, where I carefully chose a couple of bottles based solely on their labels. Why stop there? I stocked up on vodka and bourbon while I was at it. A quick detour for candles and I was in the homestretch.

That is until I flew by a dress shop and Venus Monroc's School of Woman Power popped into my mind. The next thing I knew, I was inside the store trying on outfits like Goldilocks on a shopping craze. But this was where Venus and I parted ways. I wasn't looking for anything too short, skimpy, or tight. Nor did I have any desire to pretend I was

Mariah Carey or Jennifer Lopez tonight. Instead, I simply wanted to be myself, with all that it implied. But for one exception—I planned to wear something that would drive Santou totally wild.

I found the perfect dress. Sheer and off-the-shoulder, the fabric draped itself against my every curve. Equally captivating was the color, nicely contrasting with my skin, hair, and eyes. I gazed at myself in the mirror and knew it would do the trick. Only while driving home did I realize that I'd seen the same shade of blue on Venus Monroe's house.

I put it out of my mind as I pulled in the drive, rushed up the steps, and unlocked the front door. I quickly showered and slipped into my new frock. Then turning on the oven, I set the table, lit the candles, and uncorked the wine. Everything was in perfect seduction order. Whoever said that watching *Sex in the City* had no redeeming value? Hell, I even switched on those little lobster lights that Santou liked so much. Then I curled up on the couch, hiking my dress up along my legs just so.

I've always wanted to be a bad girl with eyes that smolder, a deep throaty voice, and lips that look permanently wet. Lauren Bacall and Kathleen Turner move over. I longed to be the type of woman that men adore, a sexy siren who magically made their blood pressure soar. But tonight especially, I wanted to make Jake's heart ache with desire. So much so that he'd stop dead in his tracks at the very sight of me.

A vehicle pulled up, and my pulse began to race as a car door opened and closed. Footsteps hit the ground like fireworks exploding in the night. Then Santou walked into the house.

The man was a study in contradiction as he looked around, his eyes lighting up in surprise. Yet, I could tell something was eating away at him. The tip-off was the frown that tugged at his mouth. Then his eyes landed on me, and I knew that things weren't all right. By now, he should have swept me off my feet and into his arms in delight.

"Hey, *chère*. What's the occasion?" he asked, his lips barely brushed against mine. "You're all dressed up tonight."

I shrugged, not wanting to show my disappointment. "I just felt like a change, is all."

"Great. Now if you'd only apply that same philosophy to other areas in your life," he quipped.

I walked to the table and poured myself a large glass of wine. "And what's that supposed to mean?"

"Just that I'd like to know what it is you've gotten yourself involved in this time."

This always happened when Jake found out I was working on a case that he didn't like. It had nearly broken us up in the past. Though Santou tried to be enlightened about things, he still couldn't seem to keep his nose out of my business.

I looked at the candles, smelled our dinner in the oven, and tried not to destroy the night. Instead, I took a deep breath and swallowed my annoyance.

"I already told you. I gave this guy, Clark Williams, a ticket on a game violation, and then learned that he'd once been an Interior Department bigwig."

But Santou wasn't buying it. "Uh-uh. Something else is going on," he insisted.

Shit! "Okay. It happened while you were away. I had another run-in with Williams over some crazy water park on St. Simons. The place not only has endangered manatees, which must have been illegally obtained, but they're also being used as amusement rides. Williams has a stake in the place, along with his front man, Wendell Holmes. Anyway, I tried to have the park closed down and the manatees removed. But Williams beat me to the punch; endangered species be damned. Evidently, he still has plenty of friends and influence back in D.C. Before I could say *boo*, Manatee Mania was granted an emergency permit to stay open."

Clark Williams's warning once again came back to taunt me. *Learn to run with the big boys, or get crushed.*

I almost mentioned it to Santou, but was afraid that he might agree. Which is why I was surprised when Jake nodded, as if he knew all too well what I was talking about. However rather than empathize, he proceeded to drill me with yet another question.

"What else are you digging into?"

I was tempted to tell him about my meeting with Drapkin at DRG, along with the excessive amount of mercury in the marsh, but quickly decided against it. Knowing Jake, he'd insist that I play it safe and pass the case on to Georgia's Environmental Protection Division. That was the last thing I intended to do. Especially since I was now aware that Drapkin and Williams were friends. Politics had already proved itself to have far-reaching tentacles. Who knew just how deeply the old boy network here was connected? Speaking of which, Santou seemed to have one of his own going when it came to knowing way too much about what I was up to.

"That's it. Nada. Nothing more," came my snappy response. "So, now do you want to tell me what's up with all the questions?"

I received my answer as Jake reached into his jacket and handed me a piece of paper.

Unfolding it, I quickly scanned the contents. The first

thing I noticed was that this wasn't the original document, but a Xeroxed copy. The second was that it had been stamped CONFIDENTIAL. Then my eyes lit upon the salutation and I realized I was in very deep shit. The letter was addressed to Bob Montgomery, Fish and Wildlife's Regional Director for the Southeast. In essence, it warned that something had to be done about Rachel Porter.

"For chrissakes Bob, can't you keep control over your own agents? That woman is running amuck down here."

Of equal interest were that the letters *m.f.* preceded each mention of my name. But the real shocker was when I reached the end and discovered the identity of its author—Clark Williams. Damn, but that man had one hell of a big Rolodex!

"It's just a wild guess, but I'm betting those letters *m.f.* don't stand for 'my friend' Rachel Porter," Jake wryly noted.

"How did you manage to get this?" I asked, beginning to feel ill, even as the first stirrings of exhilaration raced through my veins.

"Let's just say it was passed on by a friend."

Santou pulled a toothpick from his pocket, placed it between his teeth, and began to chew on it.

Better a toothpick than me, I thought, resolutely keeping my mouth shut.

"Cut the crap Rachel, and tell me what's really going on."

I gave my hair a nonchalant toss, going for my best Kathleen Turner imitation. "I'd be happy to, if I had any idea."

Then I held my breath and waited.

Santou continued to skewer me with his eyes, but I could tell that he was beginning to waver. Reaching over, he took the wine glass from my hand and polished off its contents.

"Let me give you a word of advice then. Clark Williams is a very powerful man. Back off while you still can," he warned, his fingers rubbing a furrow into his brow. "Whatever you're digging into, it's not worth it."

You don't know, you don't know, you don't know, I silently thought.

That message branded itself in my brain, along with the rush that always comes with starting out on a high-stakes case. I could already feel the thrill tunneling its way deep into my bones. This was the one that would kick me up the career ladder where I belonged. I was suddenly giddy with excitement—until I took another look at Santou and realized that something was still wrong.

"Okay, it's my turn. What's going on with you?"

He shrugged and a renegade curl tumbled down onto his forehead.

"Oh, come on. You just gave me the third degree. I deserve some information in return," I cajoled.

Santou didn't say a word, but I could sense the darkness coursing through him, as dangerous as an undertow. This was precisely what had attracted me to the man in the first place. His eyes settled upon me with their predatory gaze, as though he knew it as well.

"I'm doing some undercover work and think I might have been made."

My stomach twisted into a sickening knot. How could I have been such a jerk as to assume that all his worries had to do with me? I should have known there were other issues at play.

"Then you have to pull out of the case right away," I flatly stated.

But Santou stubbornly shook his head. "I can't. I'm not

absolutely certain, and it would only destroy all our hard work."

"Isn't that going to happen anyway if your cover is blown?" I edgily questioned. "Not to mention that you could be killed."

"You know perfectly well that's what comes with the territory," Santou reminded me. "Besides, aren't you the woman who loves to take risks?"

He held my eyes until I blinked and looked away.

"So, who is this guy who might have recognized you?" I finally asked, the words sticking like cardboard in my throat.

Santou's hand crash-coursed through his hair, and the lines in his face deepened. "Someone from my old drinking days."

There it was—the tantalizing hint of a past that had still barely been revealed. I was tempted to ask if it was a man or a woman, when the realization hit me.

"You wouldn't be dealing with any of this if you'd taken that job offer in D.C."

This must have been why the FBI had never wanted him in Savannah. Santou knew too many people around the area for his own good.

"But then I wouldn't be here with you," Jake said, and flashed a lopsided grin. "Don't worry. It'll all work out."

Santou had sacrificed more than I'd imagined by coming along to Georgia. A layer of guilt snuck up from behind and firmly grabbed hold of me. My way of working it out was to get some more wine. But Santou gripped my arm and pulled me against him.

"Hey, you haven't yet given me a proper welcome home."

The words merged with the pounding of my adrenaline.

"And just what do you think this dress was for?" I retorted, my voice resonating so deep that it could have made Lauren Bacall sound like a soprano.

"It's what's under the dress that I'm interested in."

Santou proved it as his hands now played hide-and-seek, causing the garment to fall from my breasts to my feet. I twined my fingers in his hair, and held on for dear life, as the career ladder I'd begun to climb was swiftly kicked out from under me, swept away in a wave of passion. All that mattered at this moment was satiating the hunger that ravaged me. That, and letting Santou know just how much I loved him.

I wrapped my legs around the man and slipped ever closer to the edge of the abyss. Then gathering all my courage, I released control and let go, knowing that Santou was more than just my soulmate. He'd become part of my very soul.

The room was black when I awoke, and the bed felt cold beside me. I tried to roll over to see if Santou was there, but found I couldn't move a muscle. I lay flat on my back, beginning to realize that my arms and legs were paralyzed. I broke into a cold sweat, feeling more frightened than I'd ever been in my life.

Thank God for Santou. He'd know what to do. I began to call his name, only to discover that I had no voice. My fear now turned to panic.

It was then I remembered Eight-Ball's story about the hag who had ridden him through the night. Either that's what this was, or I was experiencing a full-blown panic attack.

An invisible weight began to cut off my breath, as the implication of Clark Williams's letter now fully registered. If Williams and Fish and Wildlife's Regional Director were in cahoots, then I was completely on my own except for Gary.

The two of us would have to uncover whatever was going on together. That was, if I didn't suffocate here tonight.

I struggled for air as the weight continued to press down upon me. The blackness receded into an ethereal mist as my body started to cave. I gasped, taking a jagged breath, afraid I'd reached the end of the battle. It was then that a jarring sound pierced the night, abruptly breaking the spell.

I bolted upright and a searing pain rushed down into my lungs. It was a flood of fresh air. The shrill din rattled the night again, and I felt Santou roll toward me.

"Aren't you going to answer that damn thing, *chère*?"

My hand trembled as I reached for the phone, glad for the cover of darkness.

"Hello?" I hoarsely croaked.

For a moment, there was nothing but silence. Then a voice slithered over the wire that made my every hair stand on end. Insidious and low, it was one that I didn't know.

"Stay the hell away from DRG. Otherwise, you might find it's not beneficial to your health."

I held onto the receiver, wondering if this might not all be a dream, when the dial tone peevishly buzzed in my ear.

Damn! I hate when that happens. Quickly gathering my wits, I pressed star 69, determined to ID my caller and nail the sucker. Instead, I found that my call had been blocked. I hung up and unplugged the phone, having battled enough ghosts for one night.

"Who was that? A prank caller?" Santou drowsily asked as I nestled against him for refuge.

His arms folded around me like a pair of wings that were safe and strong in the night.

"Yes. That's all it was," I replied.

But I knew it was much more than that. The voice had belonged to neither Drapkin nor Williams, making me terribly
wary. Someone was out to get me. It was coming from up
top, and most frightening of all was that I wasn't merely being paranoid.

Fourteen

I awoke, wondering if last night's call had been nothing more than a bad dream. Rolling over, I turned to ask Santou, but he was already gone for the day. My tip-off was the phone cord that lay limp as a dead body on the floor, while the telephone sat unplugged on the nightstand. Last night's experience now came rushing back to me in gruesome Technicolor. No wonder my throat felt so sore.

I hooked the phone back up, took a shower, and got dressed. Then heading into the kitchen, I began a search-and-destroy, rampaging through cupboards and drawers, intent on finding my prey. No, I wasn't on a crazed quest for a box of Cap'n Crunch, or a few derelict Pop-Tarts. Rather, I was on a mission to unearth a colander. The damn thing had to be around here someplace.

Where would I store a colander if I were Santou? I wondered.

The question seemed reasonable enough, since he was the only one of us who ever cooked. Checking under the sink, I then rummaged through the pantry, before stumbling upon where the pots and pans were kept beneath the stove. I pulled out the colander and headed back into the bedroom, taking along a container of salt.

This better work, I silently thought, knowing that other-wise I'd be forced to call in Marie and her dead husband for help.

I proceeded to do exactly as I'd heard Eight-Ball describe. Only rather than merely sprinkle salt on the floor, I liberally tossed it around by the handful. By the time I was through, my bedroom resembled the beach after a storm. The *pièce de resistance* was to hang the colander on the doorknob.

There! Take that, I challenged any hag that dared try to cross my threshold.

Finally, I dug a *mezuzah* out of my drawer and nailed it on the door for an extra dose of good luck. Then I dragged my tired rear end to work, feeling rather like a hag myself, this morning.

Unlocking my office, I stepped inside, where all appeared to be quiet on the Southern front. Wow. Even the answering machine seemed to have taken the morning off. Not a single call was recorded on it.

I made myself a crappy mug of joe, knowing that a good cup of coffee would simply shock my system. Then I sat down to sort through the mail, intent on losing myself in busywork. But I couldn't turn my mind off. I finally gave up even trying.

Threatening phone calls be damned. I had no intention of backing off from DRG. Truth be told, the fact that someone wanted me to only further whet my appetite. However, I also knew that nothing more could be done until Gary finished his testing.

With that in mind, I decided to refocus my energy on the manatee case again. Williams and Wendell, along with all the bureaucratic hotshots in D.C., could take a flying leap if they didn't like it.

I knew that Manatee Mania's critters must have been illegally obtained. The question was, how? I turned on my computer, typed in the word *manatee*, and began to surf the Internet, hoping for an educational ride.

One by one, a series of articles popped onto the screen. Most dealt with manatees in Florida and told of how speedboats were knocking them off. It was old news that never changed from year to year. The only difference was in the revolving cast of intellectually challenged characters manning the boats. I continued my search, until I finally began to get bored.

Whoa, hold on there! A story flashed by that unexpectedly caught my eye.

Manatees Seek Warmth As Water Temperature Falls Below Sixty-Eight Degrees

A Florida power company was making PR hay off the fact that manatees were attracted to the warm waters of its thermal discharge.

"The animals like to think of this spot as their own personal health spa," a company official was quoted as saying. "And we certainly enjoy hosting the gentle giants. They're just like most Florida residents, who are spoiled when it comes to dealing with cold weather."

I stared at the story as I now thought about manatees and their migration routes. It's well known that they like to swim up along the Georgia coastline in the summer. But what about those mammals that decided to extend their stay? I, myself, was a sucker when it came to soaking in a hot tub. So, it seemed natural that manatees would also be attracted to places with plenty of warm water.

Thermal discharges and power plants.

Yeah, okay. That made sense. But there were other indus-

tries as well that used water in the course of their daily oper-
ations—certainly plenty of which were located in Brunswick.
The only question was, how easy would it be for manatees to
reach them?

I pulled out a map and began to mark the location of all
those plants that seemed like good bets. Let's see. A gas and
light company, along with a paint manufacturing plant,
could be reached via the Turtle River, while a resin factory's
warm water outlet was readily accessible by traveling up
Terry Creek. Then there was the pulp mill that sat right
along Purvis. That place discharged tons of warm water, creating a man-made waterfall through an enormous tube.

Finally there was DRG. I again remembered how the
chlor-alkali facility fronted hundreds of acres of marsh, and
undoubtedly had a discharge.

My stomach now flip-flopped as I realized what I had discovered. Most likely, manatees were being exposed to
deadly mercury. Not only had Gary found toxins in the vegetation, mud, and water, but the next steps up the food chain
were fish, birds, and manatees.

My mind became a topsy-turvy whirling dervish, jumping
first to Spud before careening over to Candi Collins and the
water park. Hadn't I stopped by and seen a manatee swimming lopsided just the other day? The coffee churned sickly
inside me and I pushed the cup away.

Perhaps the creature hadn't been affected by undue stress
after all, but was reacting to an overload of mercury in its
system. The loss of balance could very well be a symptom—
a form of Mad Hatter's syndrome in marine mammals.

If that were true, then it would also be a clue as to where
Wendell was nabbing the animals. But I still needed rock-
solid proof on which to base my case. Nothing less than one

hundred percent ironclad evidence would do. Otherwise, Williams and Wendell might very well wriggle out of the charges. Something like an eyewitness confession from Candi would help. If nothing else, I could then set up a sting operation.

If Candi truly cared about manatees as she claimed, maybe she'd finally listen to reason. Hopefully, she'd spill whatever information she knew. If not, I still intended to do everything in my power to bring Williams and Wendell to justice. I'd just have to come up with a different approach.

I no longer cared about my boss Jim Lowell and his angry warnings, or last night's threatening phone call. I'd be damned if I'd close my eyes and allow this matter to slide any further along. No way would I let a species edge one step closer to extinction. Certainly not so I could climb another rung up the ladder in my career.

Maybe it wasn't a black-and-white world, as Williams maintained. But I wasn't yet willing to sell my soul and settle for gray. My philosophy had always been to charge ahead, do what's right, and to hell with the consequences. I intended to discover what was going on and, in the process, make somebody pay.

With that in mind, I picked up the phone and dialed the one person I knew who also refused to compromise. Which was probably why we were both stuck in steamy south Georgia in the first place.

"Fletcher here," Gary fumed into the phone, sounding distinctly pissed off.

"What the matter with you?"

"Plenty," he barked. "Where do you want me to start?"

"Wherever you want. I've got nothing but time, a cold cup of coffee, and a kick-ass attitude. Let me just zap my cup in the microwave, put my feet on the desk, and then you can begin."

Gary chuckled in spite of himself. "That's what I like about you, Porter. You always keep your priorities straight, no matter what."

"Okay. So, what's up?" I asked, after heating the coffee.

"I got home last night to find a message on the answering machine from my boss. Damn if Drapkin didn't manage to go and blow the whistle on us. Anyway, the old coot warned that I had no business poking around DRG's grounds, and to stay the hell away from the place. His exact words were that I hadn't been authorized to work any such case, and was on the verge of finding myself in big trouble. It seems we've been blocked yet again."

Boy, was *that* ever fast! Drapkin must have rushed back inside his office and speed-dialed some power broker's number on the double. I wondered if he'd called his friend Clark Williams for help. That seemed to be the only plausible explanation. It also revealed just how much of an old boy's club was actually going on down here.

"You know what really sucks?" Gary continued, just beginning to warm up. "I always figured that no one could force me to back off from a case. You know why? Because I'm with the federal government, and we're the good guys. Who'd have guessed that the people we'd be fighting most would be our own bosses? It's a miracle we ever get anything accomplished, at all."

"I had a phone call last night, as well."

"Oh yeah? Who from? Lead-ass Lowell?"

I laughed at Gary's nickname for my boss. "No name was given. He just warned me to stay away from DRG, and then inquired after my health."

"How thoughtful," Gary dryly commented. "Gee. You'd almost think they knew we were onto something."

That was enough to kick-start my heart. "Does that mean we really are?"

"Only if you consider mercury up the wazoo to be a major problem. You remember that drainage canal you pointed out on DRG's grounds?"

"Yes."

"Then you also remember that I took a water sample from it."

"Enough with testing my memory already. Just tell me what you found!"

Gary chortled at my impatience. "Let me preface it by saying that the maximum safety level for mercury is considered to be two parts per million. Well, there were *twelve thousand, five hundred parts per million* in that water sample. And it ain't nothing when compared to the amount of mercury that's floating in the man-made lake we stopped at just outside the second cell building. No wonder Drapkin had a shit fit when he saw us there."

"Then there's no doubt that DRG is illegally discharging mercury?"

"Not so far as I can tell," Gary confirmed. "In the process, that plant is poisoning the marsh, the water, and the wildlife, to say nothing of what it's probably doing to a bunch of sorry-ass people. And the amazing thing is that I've been ordered to keep my mouth shut and sit on all this information."

"I suspect there's probably even more going on than we know about."

"What makes you say that?" Gary asked.

"Just call it women's intuition for now," I said, thinking again of Eight-Ball's jitters.

"That's good enough for me. But it still doesn't make sense as to why so much mercury is being discharged. I guess Drapkin thinks of the marsh as his own personal toilet, into which he can flush a smorgasbord of contaminants, and just hope that it all disappears. But even so, this is pretty damn excessive."

"The other question is, what are we going to do about it? And how much proof do you actually have?"

"Enough to kick this puppy up to the next level of investigation. That's why I disregarded instructions, wrote up a report on our findings, and faxed it off to my boss early this morning."

"Great. There's no way he can choose to ignore solid evidence. Fish and Wildlife is going to have to let us move forward on this, whether they like it or not. I'll get to work and shoot off my own report concerning all the mercury in those wildlife carcasses around Purvis Creek."

"You might want to hold off on that, Pepper."

"What for?" It wasn't like Gary to want to hog the limelight.

"Because I haven't finished my story yet. I received a second phone call shortly after faxing my report, once again telling me to back off in no uncertain terms. Only this time, the order came straight from the Regional Director's office. It seems that Bob Montgomery has taken a sudden interest in my activities."

Holy shit. First there was the letter Santou had shown me, and now this. Clark Williams's tentacles appeared to be spreading everywhere. The thing was, why should he care about DRG?

Then I realized. Drapkin was probably contributing money to Williams's congressional war chest. If so, he'd expect a favor in return. Still, there were things that didn't add up.

"I don't get it. Why would Fish and Wildlife first want to stop us from investigating Manatee Mania, and now DRG?" I questioned. "Especially if DRG really *is* dumping contaminants into the marsh and creating a potential health hazard?"

"That's easy," Gary responded. "It all comes down to money and politics. Do you have any idea how many people visit the Golden Isles each year? About two million tourists responsible for generating more than two billion dollars along the Georgia coast, and tourism only keeps growing. Now imagine that word leaks out as to what's going on down here. What do you think is going to happen? Not only that, but politicians are trying to attract more business to the area, while also making this a desirable place for wealthy senior citizens to retire. They don't want people knowing about polluted water. Instead, they're doing everything they can to keep a lid on it."

"Who's this great universal 'they' that you keep referring to?"

"The county, the state, anyone with a vested interest. My guess is they've put pressure on Montgomery to force us to back off."

This was all beginning to make sense. "Listen, I found out Williams sent Montgomery a note complaining of my activities and demanding that I be controlled," I revealed.

"Should I even ask how you managed to unearth such a tasty tidbit?"

"The information was passed on to Santou."

"Unbelievable. This just keeps getting better and better."

"I feel as though we're being derailed at every turn," I groused.

"That's because we are," Gary agreed. "Which is why drastic measures are called for. It's time that someone took a stand. And seeing as how I'm sick of all the crap, I figure it might as well be me."

"What are you talking about?" I cautiously asked, made wary by Gary's tone. It sounded as though he were preparing himself to be some sort of sacrificial lamb.

"I phoned my boss fifteen minutes ago and informed him that, under the circumstances, I had no other choice but to turn whistleblower."

Whistleblower. The very word set my nerves on edge. I'd always wondered if I'd have the courage to take that step. Gary had just proved himself a man of conviction, signaling that he strongly believed his superiors to be caving in to political pressure.

The Whistleblower Protection Act of 1989 prohibits any form of reprisal against employees who expose waste, fraud, and abuse—in theory, at least. But there was bound to be a backlash.

"Fuck 'em all. I'm tired of being told by Fish and Wildlife to play nice and work well with others. If Montgomery and his crew don't have the guts to take on big business in this region, then I'm sure that some hard-hitting environmental groups in D.C. will. That ought to blow the top off this whole house of cards. Then maybe there'll be an honest-to-God investigation."

"How did your boss take the news?" I asked, my nerves turning into sparks of excitement.

There was a pause, during which I heard Gary take a drink. I wondered if it was coffee, or something stronger this early in the day.

"Just as you'd suspect. He pooh-poohed it as a shallow

threat. I assured him it wasn't, and told him that at least one of us still has balls. But then we've been butting heads for years. As for Montgomery, he's always hated me with a passion. Probably because I see him for what he is—a political ass-kisser."

I took a deep breath and plunged in. "Okay. So, where do we take it from here?"

"Whoa! Hold on there, Pepper. You'd do better to keep your distance and stay out of this one. It's bound to get nasty."

"Like hell I will," I retorted, not about to be left out of what was shaping up to be a heavyweight championship fight. "We're in on this together, right?"

I could feel Gary grinning straight through the phone wire.

"Besides, I think I figured out where Wendell is getting his manatees from."

"Spill the goods, Rach."

"I stopped by the water park a few days ago and had a chat with Candi."

"Be still my heart," Gary teased.

"Yeah, yeah. Anyway, I noticed that one of the manatees was swimming rather funny."

"How so?"

"Lopsided. At first, I thought it was because a kid was trying to ride the animal. Then I figured maybe it had something to do with stress. But I've been digging around since and learned that manatees like to hang out near industrial plants with heated effluents."

"I think I see where you're going with this," Gary said. "The only problem is that DRG's water discharge isn't heated."

Damn! So much for my theory.

"However, the one at the pulp mill certainly is, and that's only a hop, skip, and swim away. Which means that manatees would still be traveling up the Turtle River and into that area of Purvis where the vegetation is chock full of mercury, regards of DRG. And they'd obviously be munching on it."

A note of disgust rose in Gary's voice as he continued to speak.

"Good work, Rach. I may make a top-notch scientist out of you yet."

"Thanks. I'll keep that in mind in case I get sacked. By the way, I'm planning to take another spin over to Manatee Mania and see if I can twist more information out of Candi. Care to come along?"

"You do know how to tempt me, don't you?" Gary chortled. "But I'm afraid that I'm going to be busy today running all those test results once more. After that, I have to summarize the results and make a bunch of copies to send off to environmental groups. Being a whistleblower is a full-time occupation, you know," he joked. "But let me give you a few more clues to look for while you're out there. See if you can spot a manatee that any won't eat anything, or if one of the mothers seems unable to feed her young. That'll be a tip-off that something is wrong, which might possibly be tied into mercury poisoning."

"Will do," I promised.

"Remember I told you that there's always more than one way to crack a case wide open? Well, if manatees really *are* being affected by mercury, then you've just found a whole new angle of attack. We may still be able to put both DRG and Manatee Mania out of business by the time we're through."

"You sure know how to make a girl feel good," I teased.

"In that case, how about stopping by at the end of the day? I'll give you a copy of the test results, and we can celebrate with dinner."

I didn't want to turn down Gary's invitation after having done so just the other night. Especially not with all that he was going through right now.

"We may not have a smoking gun here, Rach. But there sure are a hell of a lot of bullets on the floor," he offered as further inducement.

"How can I refuse?" I laughed. "See you later on."

"Love ya, partner," he added and hung up.

Part of me wondered if he actually meant it. I began to head for the door when the phone rang again.

"Hey, *chère*. How you feeling this morning?"

Santou's voice wrapped itself around me like a warm cocoon. Each of my pulse points sprang to life at the memory of what had taken place after he'd removed my dress last night.

"Fine. But then why wouldn't I?"

"Because you packed away quite a few drinks before bed. You're beginning to make *me* look like a rank amateur."

The sparks were instantly doused, and I felt myself begin to bristle.

"I don't drink more than I can handle," I curtly retorted.

"Well, it's sure beginning to seem like a helluva lot these days."

"Did you call to scold? Or is there something you actually wanted?" I coldly responded, and immediately felt guilty. For chrissakes, this was the man who'd put his own career on hold to be with me in Georgia.

"Take it easy, *chère*. It's just an observation, is all. Believe me, I've been there. I know what I'm talking about."

"For chrissake, it's not like I'm drinking during the day," I gruffly responded, determined to fight the guilt.

I wasn't about to mention the few beers I'd had the other afternoon on my way to meet Eight-Ball. As far as I was concerned, those didn't count.

"Listen, I don't want to fight. In fact, just the opposite. I made reservations for us to have a fancy dinner tonight in Savannah. I thought we'd live it up and go to Elizabeth's on Thirty-seventh Street. What do you say?"

Either Santou had come into money, or he was also feeling bad about something. That was both a fancy, and an expensive restaurant.

"I wish you'd told me sooner. I'm afraid I already have other plans."

My response was met with a moment of frosty silence. Damn! What was going on that was so special tonight? My head began to pound. Maybe Santou was right. Perhaps I *did* have a little too much to drink last night. I rummaged through my drawer, pulled out a bottle of aspirin, and knocked two back with the last of my coffee.

"What's going on that you're not telling me about?" Jake asked, his tone now tinged with suspicion.

"Nothing. There's just a bunch of paperwork piled up, and Lowell is on my back."

"Don't bullshit me, Rachel," Santou responded, his voice becoming tense and low. "You never gave two hoots about that before. So what gives?" He paused and I held my breath, wondering what he would ask next. "Are you seeing another man?"

Oh God. That was it. Santou was jealous. He still didn't trust me. The last thing I wanted was for him to worry about that again.

"Of course not. Look, something *is* going on. I can't talk about it yet, but things have gotten rather crazy around here. Gary just turned whistleblower this morning." I realized too late that I should have kept my big mouth shut.

"Goddammit, Rachel! Then why did you lie to me last night when I showed you that letter?"

"Precisely because of the way you're reacting right now. I didn't want to deal with it."

The silence between us deepened.

"When are you ever going to learn that I'm just trying to help you?" Santou finally asked.

"And when are you going to learn that I don't need your help?" I stubbornly retorted. "Besides, you're one to talk. I didn't see you taking *my* advice last night."

The silence now turned prickly around the edges.

"I'm sorry about dinner, Jake. But I have to go through a bunch of test results and reports. Please trust me. It's important. Can't we go out tomorrow, instead?"

"No. I'm catching a red-eye late tonight and will be gone for a few days."

"Then, why did you even want to go out to dinner in the first place? You'll only end up feeling rushed," I tried to reason.

"Forget it, okay? It's nothing. I just thought you'd like to celebrate the anniversary of when we first met."

I inwardly groaned, feeling more guilty than ever. That had been five years ago. It could have been a lifetime, considering everything we'd been through since then. The fact that I'd forgotten the date was yet another black mark against me, one that I'd have to work hard to erase.

"I'm sorry, Santou. My mind's been a sieve lately. I promise I'll make it up to you."

Santou must have sensed how badly I felt. He immediately softened. "It's not a big deal, *chère*. We've got plenty of years left to celebrate."

The fact that he forgave me so easily only made it that much worse.

"Where are you going?" I asked, already beginning to worry. "Does this have anything to do with the case that you mentioned last night?"

But Santou only partially answered my question. "Down around Miami. I'll call tomorrow morning if I'm gone by the time you get home. I'll also leave my cell phone on so that you can reach me."

"I love you, Jake," I said, wanting things to work out between us more than ever.

"I love you too, Rachel. Please take care of yourself."

"Don't I always?" I joked, though my heart wasn't in it. I was too concerned for Santou's safety. I waited until I heard him hang up, and then ran out the door.

Fifteen

I played leapfrog all the way south along Highway 17, practically mowing down cars that drove too slow. Okay, so I should have opted to travel on I-95. But then, how could I have enjoyed this great scenery—even if it *was* rushing by at record speed? Instead, I reveled in the beauty of the Georgia coastline, made all the more bittersweet since I now knew that hidden beneath lay a dirty little secret. Perhaps someday people would realize that man and nature are integrally intertwined, rivers and oceans are one, and no place is totally immune.

I swung left onto the F. J. Torras Causeway, which rose and fell in a series of humps like a roller coaster ride. It provided a bird's-eye view of the land as it melted into the marsh, before joining with the sea. Lowering the Ford's window, I stuck out my hand, certain that if I stretched hard enough I could pluck a bird from the sky, so close was I to the firmament that hung above me like a freshly starched sheet.

Laurel, sweet gum, and live oak filled the air with their heady perfume as I landed on St. Simons and hurried along the winding road. Light filtered down, turning palmetto fronds into gleaming stars beneath the thick foliage canopy. But the only thing on my mind was how best to approach

Candi in hope of saving the manatees. Unless I could do that, all my work was for naught. My thoughts wandered once more to Williams and Drapkin, as well as Fish and Wildlife's dynamic duo, Montgomery and Lowell.

You're the naïve stooge in all of this, Rachel.

Maybe so, in that I was unwilling to play the game. But then fighting for wildlife seemed to be imprinted in my DNA. How could I allow creatures so unique to disappear while I stood by and did nothing? There was no question but that I was in a race. No longer did it matter if I won every meet, only that I stayed the course. What other choice did I have when the world was losing over three species an hour, eighty a day, thirty thousand a year?

Soon the water park came into view. The plastic manatees standing guard seemed to wink at me as I drove through. I heard them whisper, *Good luck! The joke's on you.*

We'll just see about that, I cockily retorted.

I was more determined than ever to twist Candi, no matter what I had to do.

I hurried through the park, paying little heed to kids colliding in bumper boats, and screaming on the Ferris wheel ride. Instead, I followed the raucous notes of Aerosmith belting out "Dude Looks Like a Lady" straight to Manatee Lagoon. Flashing my badge, I stepped inside and looked around, but Candi Collins was nowhere in sight.

Damn, damn, damn!

The lopsided manatee was also AWOL.

"Any idea where Candi might be?" I asked the ticket taker, who sat prettily perched on her stool.

The babe summoned up a noncommittal shrug. The next marine biologist in training finally got the message that I wasn't about to go anywhere until she gave me an answer.

"Why don't you try the aquarium?" she wearily suggested.

I rushed over and entered the building. Just as before, none of the manatees were chowing down in the tank. Jeez. When did Wendell give these animals a meal break, anyway? Not that any of the food floating around inside looked all that appealing.

Candi had to be somewhere on the grounds. The question was, where to find her? Going back outside, I walked toward the corral where tourists paid to pose with manatees. Perhaps she was doing a photo shoot. I opened the gate and peeked inside.

There was Candi in the pool, attempting to bottle feed a young calf that was struggling to get away. A lock of long blond hair obscured her view, so that she didn't notice as I walked over and knelt down behind her.

"Hey, Candi. What are you doing?"

She jumped and the manatee escaped her grip, quickly swimming back to its mother.

"What the hell's the matter with you?" she angrily demanded, turning to face me. "Can't you see that I was trying to feed the poor thing?"

"Don't you think its mother should be doing that?"

"Of course. For chrissake, I'm not dumb about this stuff, you know," Candi snapped in frustration. "Except that she's refusing to nurse her baby. So, what else am I supposed to do?"

"How about helping to get these manatees transferred to a facility that actually knows how to care for them?" I suggested.

"Wendell says hands-on experience is the best teacher there is, and I have plenty of that," she defiantly responded.

"And you believe him? Come on, Candi. You know better

than that. Wendell's a greedy man who doesn't want to spend a penny more than is absolutely necessary. As far as he's concerned, these creatures are disposable. After all, he can always get more of them, right?"

"I have no idea what you're talking about," Candi obstinately retorted, thrusting out her jaw like a bulldog squaring off for a fight.

"Okay then. At least tell me this. Where's the manatee that was swimming on its side the other day?"

Candi looked away as her lips began to tremble.

"I know you love these animals, Candi. I'm also aware you're doing everything that you can for them. So why won't you let me help save them?" I gently asked, trying to reel her in.

She looked back at me, and her eyes welled up with tears.

"Why not speak with someone who's been doing this a bit longer? Experts consult each other all the time. You never know. You might learn something useful."

But she firmly shook her head. "No, it's too late for that. Nothing will help now." A sob wracked her voice. "Dasher's already dead."

Candi wrapped her arms around her bare midriff, as if that would help contain the sorrow. But a renegade sob escaped, skillfully penetrating my veneer so that I also had to wipe away a tear. Maybe it still wasn't too late for something good to come from all this.

"Where is Dasher's carcass stored?"

Candi looked at me as though I were crazy. "What are you talking about?"

"I have a friend—a doctor—who can perform an autopsy on Dasher. That way we'll find out what caused her death,

and maybe prevent it from happening to the other manatees," I explained, suspecting it would provide further evidence of mercury poisoning.

"She's gone," Candi replied, wiping her nose with her
hand.

I pulled a tattered tissue from my pocket and gave it to
her. "What do you mean, she's gone?"

"Wendell had her cremated. He always does that. I think it
has something to do with his religious belief," Candi revealed, while blowing her nose.

Why that wily old coot. Yeah, the philosophy of *his* religion was, *let me keep raking in the bucks and make sure that
my ass stays out of jail, oh dear Lord.* It was time to unmask
Wendell for who he really was.

"Let me tell you a little something that I've learned,
Candi. The Turtle River and Purvis Creek are badly contam-
inated with mercury. If that's where Wendell is getting his
manatees from, then there's a good chance that all of the animals here have been affected. Should I clue you in as to
what the symptoms are?"

It was clear that Candi was listening, even though she refused to meet my eyes.

"Manatees lose their balance so that they can't swim
straight. They also suffer from a loss of appetite and aren't
able to feed their young."

Candi now looked at me without a word.

"But there's more. I've learned that mercury is purposely
being dumped in the water."

"Why would anyone ever do that, even if it were true?"
she asked in alarm, curiosity having gotten the better of her.

"Probably to save money in the long run. Why else?" I

disclosed, dangling the bait. "But of course, that's all part of doing business, right? Who knows? Maybe the culprit will eventually be caught and forced to pay a small fine."

"That's ridiculous! Scum like that should be locked up and the key thrown away," Candi vehemently insisted. "Otherwise they'll just do it all over again."

"You're absolutely right," I agreed. "But it's not always easy to obtain the kind of solid evidence we need. That is, unless someone who knows about it decides to come forward and talk."

"Well, you're some kind of cop, aren't you? How hard can that be?"

"I don't know. Let's find out. I've been able to pinpoint the plant that's responsible. The mercury is coming from DRG."

Candi looked as though she'd just been slapped in the face.

"But that's impossible! Howard would never do anything to hurt manatees. Not when he knows how much I love them. In fact, he said his plant is like a spa with all the water that's released. And the place next door even discharges it hot. That's what attracts them! Besides, he got me this job. Why would Howard do that if he were going to hurt manatees?"

My pulse boogie boarded through my veins as fast as greased lightning. Candi had as much as admitted that the water park's manatees were coming from Purvis Creek. Now all I had to do was to bring it on home.

"It's true that manatees love warm water, Candi. And there's nothing wrong with them hanging out near heated effluents. The problem has to do with the spartina grass that they're foraging on. Just think about it. What's the closest creek in which they can feed in that area? Purvis, of course."

Tears now began to stream down Candi's cheeks as she watched the two manatees in the pool beside her. The mother clearly tilted to one side, even as she tried to care for her calf.

"How many more manatees are you going to let this happen to?"

"I'm not doing anything to hurt them!" Candi sobbed, as though she, herself, had been wounded.

"Yes you are, by not telling the truth," I roughly insisted. "Wendell is obviously nabbing manatees from somewhere around here. For chrissakes, none of the animals show signs of recent scars, and they're clearly not being rehabbed."

What would it take to finally get through to this girl? I decided to plant one more seed, even if it was a lie.

"You must also know that Drapkin never intends to leave his wife. She'll always live in their big fancy house on Sea Island, while you remain stuck in some lousy trailer. The most you can ever hope for is that you won't lose the aluminum siding on your mobile home again. Meanwhile, Drapkin will expect you to be grateful for whatever crumbs he throws your way."

"Oh, yeah? Well they may be living under the same roof, but they're as good as separated. It's just a matter of time," Candi lamely tried to defend herself.

I started to walk away, but then turned back around. "That's the other thing, Candi. I heard some news that you might find of interest. Drapkin and his wife have patched things up and are getting back together—on one condition. I'm afraid you're about to be dumped."

"That's a damn lie!" Candi hissed, looking like an alley cat ready to pounce.

"Believe whatever you want. But maybe that's why Drapkin doesn't care about the manatees anymore."

Candi looked as confused as if she'd just ingested too much mercury, herself.

I walked out the gate, knowing that my work with her was done. If nothing else, I'd given Candi something to think about. All I could do now was hope that it would pay off.

I headed next for Wendell's office, determined to see what kind of trouble I could stir up there. It must have been a quiet day inside the brain trust. There was no message lodged in the cardboard manatee's fins. I didn't bother to knock, but simply opened the door and walked in.

Wendell was chowing down on his lunch, with half a manatee burger stuck in his mouth. Damn! This place would wind up being closed before I ever even got a chance to try one.

"Well, well Miss Rachel. Back again so soon?" Wendell inquired, spraying a bit of burger, bacon, and mayo my way.

Jeez, that smelled good!

"Come on in and sit down. How about letting me buy you some lunch?"

The idea was tempting. I wondered what Miss Manners would say? What *was* the etiquette anyway, when it came to accepting lunch from a scoundrel who you planned to throw in jail?

"If I were you, I'd take advantage of all the free food I could get. From what I hear, you may not have a job all that much longer," Wendell snickered.

Whadda ya know? The man was trying to pull the same number on me as I'd just pulled on Candi. Someone should

have told him that intimidation is an art form not to be practiced by amateurs.

"No thanks. I'd hate to find out that the food in this place
is as tainted as your manatees."

Wendell's face immediately darkened. "What in the hell
are you talking about?"

I leaned over his desk, picked up a French fry, and twirled
it between my fingers. "My goodness, Wendell. You should
have more regard for your health. Haven't you heard that
these things can cause cancer?"

"I ain't scared of no lil ol' French fry," Wendell scoffed
and stuffed a handful into his mouth.

"I guess not. Especially when you've got much bigger
problems on your plate to worry about."

"Aw, I get it. You're here to play a round of *my balls are
bigger than your balls*. Well, I'm afraid I've gotcha beat
hands down on that one, Miss Rachel."

That's what *he* thought.

"Listen, Wendell. I know that you're nabbing manatees,
and where it is that you're getting them from. And to tell you
the truth, I'm a bit surprised."

"I have no idea what you're talking about. But why would
that be?" Wendell asked, continuing to play coy.

"Because I had expected that you would be smarter.
What happens when your supply of manatees finally runs
out?"

"Now you're just talking plain ridiculous and not making
a damn bit of sense," Wendell snapped, looking annoyed.

"Okay, then let me put it another way. What do you think
your manatees are dying from?"

"Old age, parasites, disease. The same as people, of
course. What else?"

Wendell stated it so matter-of-factly that I knew he must truly believe what he said. It was *my* turn to be surprised.

"You mean that you really don't know? Then why are you cremating the manatees that die?"

Wendell's eyes narrowed, and he pushed his French fries out of the way. "What I'm about to say is purely hypothetical, of course. But it would be one way to make sure that nosy Feds like yourself couldn't get hold of 'em and do any of that hocus-pocus DNA crap to try and figure out where they came from. Now why don't you just cut to the chase, and tell me what you're getting at?"

"In that case, I've got bad news for you, Wendell. We've been doing some testing in Purvis Creek and found that the marsh along there is dangerously poisoned."

Wendell rocketed out of his seat. "Poisoned? Why didn't you say so in the first place? What, is some foreign terrorist throwing strychnine in the water and trying to kill us all?"

"I don't know what you're getting so upset about, unless you're drinking the water from there," I calmly observed.

He quickly sat back down. "I just care about our local environment, is all."

Uh-huh.

His fingers nervously rap-tap-tapped on the desktop. "So, are you gonna fill me in as to what's going on, or not?"

"Sure. A local company is discharging mercury straight into the marsh. Anything swimming around, and eating spartina grass in the area, is bound to end up being affected."

"And just who might this lunatic be who's doing this?" Wendell asked, his voice turning noticeably ominous.

"Oddly enough, it's someone you know. Howard Drapkin of DRG."

Wendell's fingers stopped drumming, and his mouth fell open.

"Just how long do you suppose tourists are going to keep coming to see a bunch of sick manatees?" I asked, adding fuel to the fire so that his anger would grow. "It seems your emergency permit isn't really going to help matters, after all. Funny, isn't it?"

I didn't stay for further conversation, but left Wendell stewing behind his desk. Everything had been set in place. Now all I had to do was wait. It shouldn't take long for the fireworks to begin.

I felt so good that I wanted to celebrate. And I knew just where to go in order to do so. I flew out of Manatee Mania and raced back across the bridge.

My Ford knew the way, navigating straight for the U.S. Fish and Wildlife office in Brunswick. Though I was earlier than expected, I didn't think Gary would mind. I parked in the lot, got out of my vehicle, and tried to enter the building. Huh. That was odd. The place was locked with no one around. But then again, it was lunchtime—albeit a late one, at two o'clock. Knowing Gary, he'd probably run home to brush his horse. I decided to head over there now and surprise him, being that his place was only a fifteen-minute drive away.

Gary's house was the last one on a dead-end road. A contemporary ranch, it had fallen into disrepair after the death of his wife. A once-beautiful flower garden was now choked with weeds, and the grass badly needed to be cut.

Gary felt pretty much the way I did when it came to gardening. We both preferred to let Nature do her own handiwork. But even I had to admit that she needed a certain amount of help every now and then. I was beginning to wonder if Gary might not be a little more depressed that I'd originally thought.

I pulled in next to where his pickup sat parked. Skipping past the house, I headed straight for the barn, knowing that was where I'd probably find him. His horse was the one sure thing Gary would never neglect.

Lucille whinnied softly from her stall and pawed the ground as I entered. I understood the mare well enough to know this was her way of demanding attention.

"Gary, are you in here?" I called.

But the only response came again from Lucille, who impatiently flicked her tail.

"How you doing, girl?" I asked, and walked over to pet her.

I slipped my hand into a bucket of oats, and let the horse nibble them from my palm. I must have been wrong. Gary was probably in the house eating lunch.

I turned to join him, when I spied Lucille's curry brush thrown on the ground. Gary really *was* becoming a bit too lackadaisical. I bent down, planning to pick it up, only to have my attention drawn to a gallon-sized bottle of DMSO. The liniment lay facedown with the cap off. Whatever liquid had been inside was now gone, soaked up by the surrounding straw.

I stuck the bottle near the barn door. That way, he'd remember to buy more for Lucille's sore joints. I knew Gary used it on his own aches and pains, as well.

Walking to the house, I rang the bell. Gary finally answered on the third ring. I gasped before I could stop myself. His complexion was gray and his skin held a clammy sheen.

"What's going on?" I asked. "You don't look very good."

"Thanks a lot. You always know just the right thing to say. How come I never hear, 'Wow, Gary. What a sexy hunk you are.' Huh?" he joked, with a wan smile. "Yeah, okay. I *do* feel like crap. I must have caught a twenty-four-hour bug or something."

"When did this begin?" I asked, putting my celebration plans on hold.

"Not long ago. I came home for lunch, had a bowl of soup, and then began to curry Lucille. I was in the barn brushing her when a killer headache started. I took a couple aspirin, waited for it to pass, and then went back to work. Shortly after that is when it really kicked in. I became so dizzy that I was barely able to make it home again. Right now, I plan to stay here and just rest a while. I'd invite you inside. Only I'm afraid whatever I've got could be contagious, and you don't need to get sick."

"Who? Me? You don't know who you're dealing with. No stinking bug is going to take *me* on."

"Oh yeah. That's right. You're the woman with the incredible cast-iron stomach."

"And don't forget it. Now go sit down and I'll make you some tea," I instructed.

So there! Whoever said I wasn't maternal? I thought, giving myself a mental pat.

I went into the kitchen and began to root around. *Oy vey.* It quickly became clear that Gary's eating habits were even worse than my own—something I'd thought was an impossibility up until now. His mainstay appeared to be cans of soup that were jam-packed with sodium. Always a wise choice for a guy with high blood pressure. The remainder of his cupboard was filled with an array of chocolate desserts—none of which had the slightest whiff of Weight Watchers about them.

"Would you like some soup?" I called out to him.

"No thanks. I'm not hungry," came his reply.

Gary must have been sick. He usually ate twenty-four hours a day. Maybe I *should* try to catch what he had. God knows, I could stand to lose a few pounds.

I filled the kettle, placed it on the stove, and turned on the burner. A previously used teabag sat slumped nearby on the counter, as if waiting to be recycled. Though I checked everywhere, it seemed to be the only one around.

"Hey, Gary. Do you have any more tea stashed away in here?"

A muffled sound was the only response.

"What's that?" I asked, and walked back into the living room.

I stopped dead in my tracks. Gary looked even worse than before.

"Some sort of muscle tremors are traveling up my arms," he revealed, with a note of concern.

However, much more was going on than just that. His entire body was visibly shaking.

"I'm taking you to the emergency room right now. You need to be examined and given antibiotics," I declared, trying to hide my alarm.

"Don't be such a drama queen, Pepper. I'm on a new blood pressure medication. It's probably just some kind of reaction," he retorted.

But I could tell that he was afraid.

"Where's that medication?" I asked, intending to take it with us.

"In the bathroom cabinet."

Bottles of Tenormin and Cozaar sat side by side on the shelf. I grabbed them both and hurried back out, to discover that Gary was now drenched in a layer of heavy sweat.

"That does it. We're going to the hospital. Don't give me any argument," I commanded. Gary wasn't the only one who was scared.

"Yeah, I think you're probably right," he weakly agreed, and began to push himself up from the chair.

"Wait, let me help you."

But it was already too late. I watched in horror as Gary swayed and clutched at his chest. Doubling over in pain, he toppled onto the floor, shattering the air around us. Its slivers pricked at my skin like tiny, sharp pins, prompting me to instantly jump into action.

"Gary, are you all right?" I cried and rushed to his side, where I frantically searched for a pulse. It beat faintly beneath my fingertips, and his skin felt sticky and cold.

Running for the phone, I dialed 911 and barked out directions for an ambulance. Then I dashed back to where Gary lay, his prostrate form already resembling a clay mold more than that of the man I knew.

For chrissakes, get a grip! Now's not the time to panic, I harshly chided myself. I'd dealt with plenty of emergencies before, but it's always different when it involves someone who's close to you.

Kneeling down, I began to give him CPR. A strong whiff of garlic emanated from within Gary as I pressed on his chest. I took a breath, placed my mouth over his, and exhaled hard.

It was then that I felt something else in the room. The floor creaked, shooting a squall of shivers throughout my body, and an icy film stroked the length of my skin like an attentive lover's caress.

My head jerked up and my eyes swept the area, to confirm that I was alone—all except for the whisper of a wail. It kept rhythm with my breathing as I continued to give CPR to Gary. I did my best to ignore it, knowing there was nothing I could do. It seemed to know it too, and deliberately toyed with my fear. But I no longer cared about anything other than my friend.

The cry slowly intensified, until it filled my entire body. Only then did it transform into the incessant howl of a siren's scream. I breathed a sigh of relief. The ambulance was finally here!

I kept guard over whatever it was that hovered around us. It watched from behind my shoulder with unseen eyes, as the paramedics arrived. Only when Gary was safely inside the ambulance did I jump in my vehicle and follow toward the hospital.

I raced down Highway 17, past a funeral home where a coffin was being loaded into a hearse. My fingers touched the St. Christopher's medal around my neck, hoping that it wasn't a sign. Anywhere U.S.A. sped by in a blur of fast-food stops, drug marts, and retail clothing stores as my Ford brazenly sped through a red light playing pin-the-tail-on-the-ambulance.

My attention was momentarily drawn to where a school had been torn down and rebuilt upon discovery that it was sitting on toxic soil. Rolling up my window, I cut off the stench wafting from the wood chemical plant that stood next to it. I let my mind wander, grateful for any distraction, not yet willing to deal with the fact that something awful had happened to Gary.

The ambulance turned at a doc-in-the-box health clinic and I breathed a sigh of relief. The hospital was just down the road where a stretcher stood waiting, and an attending physician was already on hand.

"My friend thinks he's having a reaction to his new blood pressure medication," I quickly informed him. "Except that muscle tremors shot up both his arms, and his body was shaking before he passed out."

"Heart attack," the doctor muttered.

And suddenly, I wanted to scream, *NO!* Only I couldn't get the word out. Instead, I mutely watched as Gary was wheeled into the operating room.

I don't know how much time passed as I waited. It seemed like forever. Possibly, it was as brief as the flutter of a hummingbird's wings. I couldn't tell, having drifted into a different dimension. It was one in which such notions as time and space didn't exist. All I was aware of was the rapid beating of my heart as images began to flow through my mind: muscle tremors, dizziness, loss of appetite, headaches, cold, clammy skin. I stared at the floor, not daring to say what I knew out loud, yet certain that it added up to only one thing. Soon, the doctor's shoes appeared within my line of vision.

"Agent Porter?"

He could have been speaking to me from a distant planet, his voice echoing hollow in my ears.

"I'm afraid I have to tell you that your friend didn't make it."

I struggled to decipher the words, certain that I hadn't heard them correctly.

"However, his death was quick and painless, if that's any consolation."

If I'd had a burning poker, I would have stuck him with it and then inquired how quick and painless *that* had been.

Instead I asked, "What did he die from?"

"Why, a heart attack, of course."

"You're wrong," I brusquely blurted out.

The doctor stared at me as though I were crazy. "I know this must come as a shock. But we performed an EKG, and I can assure you that his heart rhythms were aberrant. Dr. Fletcher had health issues that exacerbated his condition. There's no question but that he died of a heart attack."

I shook my head, refusing to listen. "I want you to test for an elevated level of mercury in his system."

"You're really not taking this very well. Why don't we sit down and I'll prescribe a sedative for you?"

"Just do the test," I ordered, gritting my teeth. "I know exactly what I'm talking about!"

Our eyes locked together in a showdown.

"If you refuse, I'll get a court order," I warned. "It's your choice, doctor. Either do it now, or I swear I'll arrest you for refusing to cooperate with a federal agent."

He continued to study me, as if wondering how far to push.

"Got any dietary restrictions, doc? 'Cause, I hear the food in jail is really lousy."

He blinked, and then nodded his head. "All right. I'll do a tox test."

"Good. How long will it take?"

"It's a simple procedure. A couple of syringe stabs are all that's needed to collect cardiac blood and urine. Then I'll take a quick look. You can wait if you like."

"You'll find me right here."

The doctor thrust his hands into his jacket pockets, as

though they were punching bags. "But you should know that you're wasting my time. Also, you've got a real issue with anger that needs to be addressed."

I kept my mouth shut as he walked away. He was right. I was mad that Gary had died, pissed off with physicians who'd become callous from dealing with illness, and angry at hospitals for making too many mistakes. But most of all, I hated death.

Right now, what I could use was a good, stiff drink. However, that would have to wait. I didn't want to miss the look on *this* doctor's face when he had to admit he'd been wrong.

I didn't wait long. His footsteps soon rang back down the hall, each tread confirming, *You were right. I was wrong*.

"Here are the test results, Agent Porter. As you can see, they confirm my initial findings. Dr. Fletcher died as the result of a heart attack." His brittle voice clipped the end of each word with the precision of a surgical instrument. "There are no traces whatsoever of mercury poisoning."

How can that be? I wanted to shriek.

Instead, I bit my tongue. I bit it all the way home, not yet willing to concede defeat.

I pulled into the carport, surprised to find Santou's vehicle still in the drive. Then I walked inside and poured myself a glass of vodka, drank it straight down, and waited for its magic to work. My body began to tingle. However, that wasn't enough to do the trick.

I now tore through the kitchen cabinets as though possessed, driven by the urge to find junk food to eat. Blinking back tears, I savagely flung items off shelves, feeling more desperate with each passing moment, until I finally found what I'd been searching for—something in which to drown my pain. My therapy came in the form of Hostess Twinkies and cupcakes.

I swiftly gathered up all thc boxes. But why stop there? I also grabbed ancient packs that had long been stale, as well as my hidden stash of Snickers and Mars bars. Balancing them all in my arms, I seized the bottle of vodka and went back outside, where I climbed the stairs to Marie's deck. Once there, I proceeded to binge to my heart's content.

I popped one Twinkie after another and inhaled the cupcakes. I didn't even taste the candy bars as they effortlessly went down. Instead, I thought about what the doctor had insinuated—that Gary's death had been partially brought on from being overweight. The good doctor could go to hell. I didn't believe that for one frigging minute. In my heart, I knew the man had been poisoned.

I ate for Gary and myself until I thought I would burst, but still I didn't stop.

What the hell. Someday when my metabolism gives out, I'll start a regimen of throwing up. This is my memorial to you, Gary, I toasted, and washed down the last remnants of my two-week supply with a hefty swig of vodka. The combination tasted better than I would have thought.

I quickly passed the threshold of feeling sick to enter new, uncharted territory. Though none of this would bring Gary back, it did wonders for helping to numb my pain. The sun began to set as I poured myself yet another drink. Then I heard the crunch of Santou's footsteps on the gravel, and guiltily hid all evidence of junk food wrappers and boxes under the bench, covered by a wayward tarp.

"Hey, *chère*. What are you doing home so early?" he asked while climbing up to sit beside me, where he caught a glimpse of my face. "What in the hell's wrong?"

I polished off my drink. "It's Gary. He's dead."

There. I'd said it. But what I hadn't expected was the cascade of tears that now came bursting forth.

"Oh God. I was there when he died, Jake. The hospital insists it was a heart attack. But I know that it wasn't! Somehow, someone infused mercury into his system."

Santou's hand gripped my arm so hard that his fingers dug into my skin. "What are you talking about, Rachel? Does this have anything to do with a case that you're working on?"

My head began to spin, as I remembered that I'd decided not to tell him. Now there was no choice.

"We were looking into a plant that we thought was dumping mercury into the marsh. But we were ordered to stop."

"And did you?"

"Yes," I lied.

"Good, because that's EPA's jurisdiction." He slowly relaxed his hold. "All right then, what are you saying? That there were needle marks in Gary's arm? That he was injected without being aware of it?"

I suddenly realized just how ridiculous that sounded. "No, but all the symptoms were there. The shakes, sweating, dizziness."

"Which are also indications of a heart attack," Jake reasoned. "Not everything's a conspiracy, Rachel. Come on. You know Gary wasn't in the best of health. He had high blood pressure, was overweight, and drank too much."

"I guess you should know about that last one," I snapped, refilling my glass and swallowing my tears.

"You're absolutely right," Santou agreed, removing the drink from my hand.

"Hey! Give that back," I sputtered, reaching for the tumbler.

"Uh-uh. I'm sorry about Gary. But I'm not going to watch you follow in his footsteps. I don't expect you to become a teetotaler, but you've got to learn to put on the brakes. It's time you acknowledged that you've got a drinking problem."

"Not only is that totally ludicrous, but I need this right now like a hole in the head," I argued, fighting to grab my glass.

"Oh yeah? Well your friend is dead, and all you can think about is having another drink. What's wrong with *that* picture?"

My face began to burn, as more tears welled up in my eyes. Could Santou be right? Or was he enough of a bastard to turn his own problem around on me at a time like this?

"For chrissakes, Rachel. Let yourself mourn. Don't drown your emotions in a bottle of vodka."

He wrapped me in his arms and my protective armor cracked, so that I now sobbed as though my world had come to an end. I wept for Gary, and for the fact that Santou just might be correct.

Jake placed a finger beneath my chin and lifted my face to his. "Why do you drive yourself so hard, *chère*? What are you trying to prove, anyway? That you're better than any other agent?"

"No. That I'm just as good."

That was it in a nutshell. I'd been running as hard as I could all my life, hoping to justify my worth.

Jake pressed his lips to my forehead, and then directed my eyes to where a flock of wood stork flew silhouetted against the setting sun, their wings enormous white sails, their legs trailing like long, slender ribbons. The sight was so heart-stoppingly beautiful that it turned into a bittersweet ache.

"That's where you draw your strength from, Rachel. It's the one constant in your life that will never change. Always remember to take shelter in nature when things become tough."

Though I said nothing, I knew that Santou was wrong. My ultimate refuge was in the man sitting next to me. He'd become my best definition of home.

We continued to watch the birds until they disappeared from sight. Then his lips softly brushed against mine.

"I have to get to the airport, *chère*. I've got a plane to catch. But I'll call you first thing in the morning."

"Don't go!" I said, suddenly filled with an irrational sense of dread, even while mortified to hear the words spill from my mouth.

Santou looked at me in surprise.

Oh, Christ! What was happening, anyway? I took a deep breath and tried to exhale all the insecurity that was starting to pile up inside. Gary's death was hitting me even harder than I'd imagined.

"Of course I have to go," Santou gently responded. "Why? Is there something else you want to tell me?"

I shook my head. "I just don't want to lose you, is all."

"You never will," Jake promised. "Always remember that I love you."

"I love you, too," I replied. And then he was gone.

I went back into the house as a soft rain started to fall. Soon it turned into a downpour, its pellets beating on the tin roof like the rat-tat-tat of a snare drum. Once again, I felt the urge for a drink. Instead, I decided to do without one and prove Santou wrong.

Walking into the bathroom, I began to wash up. I'd splashed water on my face and lathered my hands, when I caught a whiff of something that made me feel sick. It was the same scent that had emanated from Gary as he lay dying.

What's wrong with this picture? I once again heard Santou ask.

Only this time, it had nothing to do with vodka, but with garlic. Gary hated the stuff and would never have eaten anything containing it.

The odor wafted through the air, where it wrapped itself around me like a cat's tail. I now realized that the scent had been lingering on my hands, and on my breath, for the past several hours. Either I was beginning to hallucinate much like my friend, the Mad Hatter—or this was Gary's way of letting me know that he was still hanging around.

Sixteen

I woke up the next morning before daybreak. Actually, I'd never fallen asleep last night. I knew that I had plenty to do today. The most important of which was to force myself out of bed, so that I could take the first step. After that, everything else would be a piece of cake.

It was still dark as I climbed into the Ford and headed toward the office. Night and dawn lay entwined above me in a sensual embrace. It wouldn't be long before the sun rose to send the night clouds scurrying away. I'd heard Eight-Ball refer to this moment as *dayclean*, when the world is made fresh and new again. Maybe so. But that no longer seemed the case. Not after the events of yesterday. One more life that I cared about had been taken away, and the world would never again be the same.

I unlocked my office and turned on the lights. Then I sat down and made all the necessary phone calls. It didn't take long to notify Fish and Wildlife, along with what few distant relatives constituted Gary's remaining family. After that, I made arrangements for a friend to take his horse. Plans for a funeral were simple. Gary's will stated that he wanted no service, but merely to be cremated.

With all that out of the way, I next turned my attention to

other matters at hand—like making sure that Gary's death hadn't been in vain. It's while driving that I tend to think best. I got back in my vehicle and began to do so now, as I headed for points south.

I was still unwilling to admit that Gary had died of a heart attack. The question then was, what else could have caused his death? There were certainly enough people who'd be glad to know that he was gone—from Wendell all the way up to Gary's boss.

I parked in front of the Fish and Wildlife office in Brunswick, and pulled out a ring of keys. They'd been part of Gary's possessions, which the hospital had released to me yesterday. Trying each one, I eventually unlocked the building and opened his door. His office looked pretty much the same as before. Still, something felt the slightest bit off. Probably the fact that Gary wasn't around.

I stepped over piles of books on the floor, marveling at the organized chaos. Fortunately, I knew exactly what I was looking for—the test results from DRG. His desk seemed like the natural place for them to be. I inspected the heap of documents that lay neatly stacked beneath his *Crisis de Jour* paperweight. However, no written reports concerning DRG were there. After that, I checked inside the drawers and scoured the desktop, but still found nothing. It was as if they'd vanished into thin air.

I'd had a slightly creepy feeling ever since entering this place. Now I realized what was wrong. It hit me like the proverbial ton of books on the floor. Gary's office was just a little too neat. My skin began to crawl as I grew suspicious that someone had been here before me, probably looking for the very same thing.

I knew that Gary sometimes taped conversations on his

answering machine. Maybe that would help provide some kind of clue. I rushed over, and pressed the play button.

Click, click. Click, click.

Wouldn't you know? The tape was gone, too.

For chrissakes, think! I admonished myself.

Okay. There was one last place to look. Locking the office, I drove down the road, straight to Gary's home. But first, I ran into the barn. Lucille was already gone. I made a mental note to visit her as soon as I could. Then I beelined it directly for his house.

Unlocking the door, I stepped inside. A lamp lay on the living room floor. It had been knocked over when Gary had fallen. I picked it up and put it back in place. Then I set about ripping the house apart. Or, in this case, actually making it neater. No matter. I still couldn't find anything of importance. Forget about documents relating to DRG. There wasn't even the slightest shred of evidence to suggest that Gary had ever planned to turn whistleblower.

Next I snooped around in his bedroom. Laying on the nightstand was a book that he must have been reading. How apropos—*Alice in Wonderland*. I felt as though I had also passed through the looking glass, and was now struggling to find my way back to reality.

As I picked up the book, something fell out from between its pages—a Rolodex card that had marked Gary's place.

Harry Phillips
232 Cypress Road
Waycross, Georgia 31501

The name sounded familiar. Then I realized why. Phillips was the biologist who Gary had mentioned—the one who'd

quit Fish and Wildlife in disgust, and retired to the Okefenokee.

Gary must have had this card out for a reason. My mind
jumped to a dozen different conclusions, each of which
made sense. But the important thing was that Harry Phillips
might know something I didn't. It was enough to make me
drop everything and hightail it out to his place.

The Okefenokee was a good hour's drive away, which
gave me plenty more time to think. I used those sixty minutes well, recounting the fate of biologists who'd butted
heads with the Service and lost. Their offices had been
raided and important data seized, after which it had an un-
canny tendency to disappear. The universal response had
been for victims to either transfer out of Fish and Wildlife,
or quit—all except for one biologist who'd committed suicide under the most suspicious circumstances.

I leaned forward over the steering wheel, urging my vehicle to fly even faster. We sped past mile after mile of bristly
pine trees guarding a black ribbon of road that was slowly
being swallowed by encroaching vegetation. It was while
careening toward the swamp that I realized Santou hadn't
yet called. Damn the man. I should have heard from him by
now. Not that I had anything important to relay. I just wanted
to hear his voice again.

I punched his number into my car phone, only to receive
no answer. Santou had promised to leave his cell on, knowing that this drives me crazy. However, I had little choice but
to try again later. A dirt path that led to Harry Phillips's
house now came into view.

I drove toward a log cabin, which sat on the edge of a
swamp composed of meat-eating pitcher plants, mating gators,

and unstable peat bogs—the reason this place is nicknamed "Land of the Trembling Earth." The door opened, and a man in jeans, rubber boots, and a denim shirt appeared. Bulky and dour, he could have passed as the bouncer at the local Swamp-A-Rama bar. A silver ponytail that looked as though it had been doused in eau de motor oil hung down his back. Phillips warily eyed me as I got out of the Ford and approached.

"Hi. I'm Rachel Porter, the U.S. Fish and Wildlife agent here in Georgia."

I instantly regretted opening my mouth. For all I knew, Phillips was still pissed enough at the Service to take a potshot at me. Instead he gazed at the Ford, as though expecting someone else to emerge.

"There's no one with me, if that's what you're wondering."

"I figured Gary Fletcher might have come along."

"Why? Did you know him?" I asked, a chill settling deep into my bones.

"No, but he called yesterday morning. Said the two of you were working on a case, and that he wanted to run some figures by me. Something to do with mercury, right? I've been expecting him to drop those numbers off. So, do you have them with you?"

I was about to answer when Phillips cocked his head and stared at me. "Hey, wait a minute. What do you mean, *did* I know him? What happened? Did he go and quit already?"

Maybe it was the sun beating down so strong that made me break into a sweat. "I'm afraid Gary died of a heart attack yesterday afternoon."

But it was more than the heat, as my body began to swoon. The next thing I knew, Phillips was helping me onto the porch and into a rocking chair. A glass of lemonade was placed in my hand a moment later.

"Drink this. It'll make you feel better," Phillips gruffly instructed.

I took a sip. Mmm. He was right. The lemonade had a definite kick to it. Santou had said that one glass a day was acceptable. This would just have to count toward my daily allotment.

Phillips sat in the rocker next to mine, where the two of us squeaked together in harmony, blending in with the cacophony of cicadas and frogs that surrounded us.

Harry waited until I'd regained my color before he spoke. "There's obviously more to this case than I've been told. So, why don't you fill me in from the beginning?"

"It's actually two different cases that seem to have become entwined," I began, trying to keep it simple. "A place called Manatee Mania is charging tourists to swim with manatees. The pretense is that they're being rehabbed. Only the animals aren't injured and the facility isn't licensed. The second case involves mercury that's being dumped in the marsh. We suspect a chlor-alkali plant, DRG, to be the culprit. Linking them is a former Interior Department bigwig and lobbyist, Clark Williams, who's now a developer in the area. He's not only financially connected to Manatee Mania, but is also a close friend of DRG's owner, Howard Drapkin. However, what makes all this truly diabolical is that Gary and I independently had our cases squashed on both counts."

Harry folded his hands over his belly, emitting a low rumble that sounded like water gurgling up from deep within a well. It took a moment before I realized that it was laughter.

"You think your only enemies are poachers and smugglers of wildlife? Take a better look around you, girl. The enemy is much more insidious than that. It's politics and the damn Service, itself."

He wasn't telling me anything I didn't already know.

"What did Gary say when he contacted you?" I questioned, curious as to what they'd spoken about.

Harry sipped his lemonade. "Just that he wanted advice. The problem was, he called too late. Your friend had already faxed his report and test results in to his boss. That was a big mistake. Anything with political overtones is immediately brought to the attention of the Regional Director."

"Then what should he have done?" I asked, knowing I would have made the same mistake.

"Simple. The first lesson is never write anything down. Always memorize your information until you're fully ready to make your case. That way, the Service is caught by surprise and doesn't have time to sabotage you."

I had to admit, it was sound advice.

"Wait here," Harry said.

Getting up, he walked into the house. A few minutes pased before he emerged with a large manila envelope. Harry handed it to me and I saw that it bore Gary's address. I took a deep breath, and ripped the package open.

Inside were copies of reports that Phillips had submitted while working for the U.S. Fish and Wildlife Service. The records dated back over a period of ten years. They dealt with mercury contamination, and the buildup of PCBs in Purvis Creek. Included were a list of animals, fish, and birds that had been affected.

Harry nodded as I finished reviewing his notes. "I can only imagine how much mercury must be in that marsh by now. People shouldn't be eating *any* fish coming out of there. My guess is that women are probably producing a greater number of babies with birth defects, while kids are more prone to developing leukemia and brain cancer. As for DRG, you can bet your ass there's a definite tie-in."

"What makes you say that?" I questioned, my heart beginning to thump.

"The fact that I told my boss as much. Funny thing, but my report was squashed, much like your own, by the very same Director—Bob *Don't-Rock-The-Boat* Montgomery."

I wanted to jump in with both feet, but something stopped me. For all I knew, Phillips was just one more conspiracy nut.

"I still don't understand what Montgomery's interest is in all of this. Why should he care about protecting a chloralkali company?"

"I asked myself that very same question for years. One of the benefits of early retirement is that you have plenty of time to dig around," Phillips dryly noted. "And it paid off. Let me show you what I found."

Harry removed a piece of paper from his wallet and gently unfolded the sheet. Its battered edges and frayed creases revealed how long he'd been carrying it around. Then he handed it to me as carefully as if it were the Holy Grail.

I held the photocopied page lightly between my fingers and began to read. The cherished document was a list of alumni from Holton University's graduating class of 1968. Circled in red were two names—Howard Drapkin and Bob Montgomery.

"Okay. So they attended the same school together," I remarked, though I couldn't help but be surprised. However, I still wasn't ready to make a rush to judgment.

But Phillips slyly grinned, as he shook his head. "Uh-uh. You don't get it yet. Montgomery and Drapkin were college roommates."

There was no question but that Phillips had made his point, as my mind began to whirl.

"If there's something I've learned over the years, it's that old friends remain tight, no matter who they are."

"Are you saying that Montgomery is involved in whatever is going on?" I cautiously questioned.

The Okefenokee began to stealthily close in around me, as I found myself gasping for air.

But rather than reply, Harry simply chose to shrug, a response that I found to be maddening. Now I knew how Alice must have felt when she'd dealt with the Cheshire Cat.

"Some things are better left unsaid until you have the evidence to back them up," he finally offered.

Damn! If Phillips had something on Montgomery, I sure as hell wanted to know about it. I decided to tackle it from another angle.

"Okay. Then what's your take on Clark Williams and how he fits into all this?"

"Ah! Therein lies the rub." Harry smirked, turning Shakespearean on me. "That bastard is my old nemesis. He worked in Interior when I was a government employee. Let's just say, we rarely had a meeting of the minds. Williams is a political animal who'll do whatever it takes to get what he wants. And right now, he wants to be elected to Congress. That takes a whole lotta money."

"Then I can already guess what Williams's stand on chemical plants and pollution standards will be," I concurred.

"Now you're on the right track!" Harry enthused, beginning to knead his hands. "DRG is a hell of a large company, and wants to remain that way."

"Which is why Drapkin must be funneling big bucks into Williams's campaign," I surmised.

"When in doubt, always follow the money trail," Harry gleefully agreed. "Hell, chemical manufacturers have given over five million dollars to presidential and congressional candidates since nineteen-ninety-nine."

"Still, the Regional Director can't be turning a blind eye to all this merely out of friendship," I reasoned, bringing the subject back around. "Surely he must want something in return."

That's when the fog finally cleared.

"Ohmigod, now I get it!" I nearly shouted, feeling as though I'd just won the Indy 500. "Williams must have promised to help Montgomery become Director of Fish and Wildlife if he's elected."

Harry sagely nodded his head. "It wouldn't surprise me one bit. Ambition will do funny things to a man."

To a woman too, for that matter. After this, any hope I'd had of moving up the career ladder was pretty much doomed. The feeling was bittersweet. Yet it would have been far worse had I been seduced into becoming one more blind cog in a daisy chain of corruption.

"You've gotta hand it to Glynn County. They've done one hell of a job of keeping the lid on DRG."

A mosquito skidded into a pool of sweat on Harry's forehead, and he flicked it off.

"Do you really think they know what the company's been doing?" I asked.

Harry's head bobbed around like a spring-loaded dashboard ornament. "Yes and no. Let's face it, they haven't wanted to look too deep. The bottom line is to keep the money flowing. Hell, they'd have to change the name of the area from the Golden Isles to the Mercury Isles, if word ever got out. We can't have that now, can we?"

I wondered if Harry wasn't being just a tad too cynical. But then again, maybe not.

"Why do you think DRG is discharging mercury into the marsh, anyway? It can't just be that Drapkin is out to screw up the environment," I reflected, trying to give him the benefit of the doubt.

"Oh, Lord. There could be any number of reasons. First off, mercury-contaminated wastewater is normally pumped into a settling tank and treated. Maybe they didn't build a tank large enough to begin with, and now don't want to cough up the money for a new one. So instead, it's being flushed down pipes and directly into the creek."

Harry poured himself another glass of lemonade.

"Or maybe the plant isn't being maintained properly. DRG has giant electrolytic cells on the top floor of both cell buildings. Liquid mercury could be leaking from them. Say it mixes with other chemicals. If so, they'd eat through the cement floor, allowing mercury to sink into the groundwater.

I remembered the man-made lake that Gary and I had stumbled upon near DRG's second cell building.

"Could that cause a body of water to form, which would need to be contained?"

"Anything's possible. Especially if wastewater's in the mix."

No wonder Drapkin had a conniption upon finding us

there. We'd been standing right next to the mother lode. It was also where Gary had taken his last sample.

"The other thing to consider is what's happening to the poor bastards who work in that place. Breathing in mercury vapors is bound to create a certain amount of brain and neurological damage."

"Something else is bothering me," I now admitted. "I'm not convinced that Gary died of a heart attack."

Harry's eyes narrowed, and his rocker came to an abrupt halt. "Exactly what is it that you're saying?"

"It's just a gut feeling, but his symptoms progressed over a period of several hours."

"What were they?"

"Headache, dizziness, loss of appetite, and then there were tremors. They didn't just shoot through his arms, but seemed to grip his entire body."

Harry pulled a pint of bourbon from his back pocket, and splashed some into his lemonade, after which he offered me a refill. I thought of Santou, and turned it down.

"That's exactly why I got the hell out of the Service when I did," he confided. "Eliminate the biologist and nobody can say for certain that DRG is causing any harm. It makes perfect sense to remove the man who's doing the research."

"I was suspicious enough to make the hospital do a postmortem test for mercury poisoning. But it came back negative," I disclosed. "So a heart attack remains the official cause of death."

"Sure. Unless there's a knife's sticking out of you, or a gaping bullet hole, death is always written off as resulting from natural causes down here."

"Then what else could have caused those tremors?"

Harry homed in on me as if I were a bug he was about to dissect. "Are you asking what *really* killed him?"

I silently nodded.

He mulled it over while sucking on his bourbon-laced lemonade. "My guess is some kind of organo-phosphate."

"Come again?"

"A pesticide. Who knows? It might have been added to something he ate. Or maybe applied to his skin."

Right. Like Gary wouldn't be able to tell if someone had sprinkled ant poison into his soup, or sprayed him with a can of Raid while his back was turned. For chrissakes, the guy had been a contaminants expert! I stood up to leave.

"Just remember, choose your target carefully before you go running off half-cocked and get yourself blown to high hell," Harry cautioned.

"Thanks," I drolly replied.

"And if worse comes to worst, you can always hightail it back here. There's plenty of room in the swamp to hide."

A gator bellowed as if on cue, sounding like an outboard motor on the fritz.

Harry nodded in the critter's direction. "They may sound ominous, but gators are a whole lot less dangerous than the folks you're dealing with."

"Which ones in particular might you be talking about?" I inquired, hoping he'd help narrow the list.

"All of 'em."

Terrific. "I'll keep that in mind."

Then I got in my vehicle and began to pull out. I glanced in the rearview mirror to spy Harry looking more morose than when I'd arrived. He must have known I was watching, because he slowly raised his hand and waved good-bye.

A band of crickets joined in the farewell, rubbing their legs together in a frenzy. I felt as if I were being sent off on my first day of school. Only the crickets knew better, and tried to warn me.

Beware! they seemed to cry. *For tonight is a good time to die.*

Seventeen

I couldn't shake the feeling of gloom that had settled upon me. It hugged tight as cellophane stretched across my skin. To top it off, Jake hadn't yet called. It wasn't like him to say he'd ring and then forget. Because of that, I did something I rarely do. I buzzed his boss, John Guidry, in the Savannah office.

"Agent Guidry speaking," he answered in that dry, clipped monotone that all FBI agents love to use.

I secretly suspected recruits were forced to watch hours of *Dragnet* reruns before they could graduate.

"Hey, John. It's Rachel. I'm trying to track down Santou." There was a pause before he responded. "Why?"

Why? Because I'm his significant other, you tight-assed suit!

"He said he'd call and I haven't heard from him. I'm just checking in to make sure everything's okay."

"I'll have to get back to you on that," Guidry replied and quickly hung up.

What in hell was that all about? Had Santou gone off to the Caribbean with some hot babe for a few days? Hmm. What would the gals on *Sex in the City* do in such a situation? Probably hop a plane, track him down, and torture Jake until he finally confessed.

Tempting as that might be, I still had a job to do. I put Santou out of my mind and focused on the matter at hand. The one thing I cared about more than anything else right now was discovering what had really happened to Gary.

Follow the money, Harry had said.

As I thought about that, Reverend Bayliss sprang to mind. He'd accused Drapkin and Williams of washing each other's hands. I now wondered if he knew more than he'd originally told me. This seemed as good a time as any to find out. With that in mind, I made tracks for Venus Monroe's house. If the Reverend wasn't there, she'd surely know where he might be.

Once again, the live oaks reached out to me as I drove onto St. Simons Island. Only this time, they weren't so benign. Their limbs raked against my Ford as a ghostly wind picked up and bent them toward me. Their leaves ominously whispered, *it's a good time to die.*

Though I told myself not to listen, the words parked themselves in my vehicle, snapped on a seatbelt, and came along for the ride. I swung onto South Harrington Road, jostling them so hard that they angrily murmured, *You'll die tonight, you'll die tonight.*

Flooring the accelerator, I flew toward Mamalou Lane, fully determined to outrun their warning. It was soon replaced by the flurry of signs in front of each house that screamed out, DON'T ASK/WON'T SELL!

I arrived at Venus Monroe's, where I slammed on the brakes, surprised to find a flotilla of luxury vehicles parked out front. Every kind of dream car was there, from a gold Mercedes to a forest-green Jaguar to a little black Porsche. Eight-Ball's dog gave each his stamp of approval by running around and peeing on their tires. Either Venus was selling hot autos on the sly, or one of her classes was in progress.

I received my answer as I was swept up by a chorus of loud voices. This was no gospel choir, but a glee club with a common cause. Their pledge of allegiance was none other than Aretha Franklin's anthem for downtrodden women—that kick-ass soul tune, "Respect."

I approached the blue door and entered, to find a group of middle-aged women wildly dancing around inside. Each matron was toned, bronzed, and blow-dried to perfection. This was clearly the sort of crowd that religiously played tennis, had personal trainers, and ate their meals at exclusive country clubs. Dressed in designer outfits, every woman wore a coon dong around her neck.

The curls on Venus's wig shimmied like animated cubes of Jell-O as she scurried over to greet me. "You here to join us today, honey?"

I'd always wondered what it must feel like to be that rich, that thin, and that pampered. Unfortunately, I was too stressed, broke, and hungry to find out right now.

"No, thanks. Maybe another time. I stopped by to ask where I can find the Reverend," I shouted, attempting to be heard above the music.

Venus took hold of my arm and quickly pulled me aside. "Heaven help us. If it's not one thing it's another," she bemoaned, anxiously clucking her tongue. "Something awful happened today. Eight-Ball went and got himself injured on the job. All I can say is thank the good Lord for the Reverend. He went over in his Chevy and picked Eight-Ball up from work."

"Is he badly hurt?" I asked, starting to worry. Whatever had happened, it couldn't be good.

"Nothing the Reverend can't fix. I tell you, that man's got the touch of an angel. He and Eight-Ball are holed up in the kitchen until these women leave. But why don't you head on back and pay them a visit?"

I found Eight-Ball seated in a chair with his pant leg rolled up. Angry welts ran down the length of one leg, as though his dark chocolate skin had been crying bloody tears. Only these teardrops were burn marks. Jagged and red, the streaks were curled and puckered around the edges, like sheets of parchment singed by hot flames.

The Reverend knelt beside him, applying salve to each burn. Then he lightly wrapped Eight-Ball's leg in a protective layer of gauze.

"Oh my God! What happened, Eight-Ball?"

The man looked up through eyes that were rheumy from pain. "Oh, I just had a run of bad luck, is all."

"Bad luck, my ass. That plant is nothing but a damn booby trap," the Reverend angrily huffed.

"And what makes you say that?" I asked, zeroing in on Bayliss.

The Reverend became momentarily flustered. "'Cause that's what Eight-Ball told me."

But I had the feeling that Bayliss was covering his tracks.

"It ain't that bad, really. There've been worse accidents over there," Eight-Ball offered. "I was just doing a little repair work on a motor in cell building two, when some water splashed up over the top of my boots."

"*That's* what caused those burns?" I asked in astonishment.

"What he's *not* telling you is that caustic soda is in the water. That stuff will melt the skin off a man faster than the devil stoking a fire around him."

I wasn't sure why, but the Reverend was beginning to get on my nerves.

"Eight-Ball's just plain lucky he didn't get electrocuted," Bayliss continued to grouse.

"And how is it that you know so much about DRG?" I questioned the good reverend. "Have you ever been there?"

Bayliss didn't answer, but kept his mouth firmly closed.

I turned my attention back to Eight-Ball. "There's caustic soda on the floor of the cell building?"

"Yeah, along with a lotta other bad stuff," he confirmed. "You gotta watch out for the puddles, is all. Especially when something goes wrong and there's a flood. All you can do then is hold your breath and pray. That's why I was glad when the nurse bandaged my leg, gave me some pills, and told me to go home for the rest of the day."

"And a damn lousy job she did of fixing him up. Why do you think I had to rewrap his leg?" the Reverend haughtily interjected.

But something Eight-Ball had said caught my attention. "DRG has a plant nurse?"

"Sure. Verena Harper."

He grimaced, and the Reverend gave him a pill, along with a shot of whisky. Eight-Ball's hand seemed to shake more than usual as he downed them both. Then he slowly began to relax.

"That poor woman. Seems Verena's always having to take a sample of somebody's urine."

"What for?"

Eight-Ball stared into space, as though searching for the answer. "I believe they told us once. But for the life of me, I can't remember no more."

Maybe they were keeping track of the mercury level in each worker's body to see how much they could withstand.

I now focused on Bayliss. "The other day, you said that Williams and Drapkin were washing each other's hands. What did you mean?"

The Reverend's chest swelled, as if taken with his own self-importance. "Just that. Each is helping the other out."

"But how? Do you think DRG is giving money to fund Clark Williams's upcoming campaign?"

"Of course! Big time. Any fool should know that," he pompously imparted.

"Maybe so. Still, how do *you* know?" I countered, determined to pin him down. "And exactly what sort of proof do you have?"

Bayliss and Eight-Ball nervously exchanged glances.

"My cousin works as the cleaning woman at Williams's campaign office. Damn if she didn't see a piece of paper with all the contributions from DRG toted up."

"Really? I'd like to speak to her."

Bayliss began to fidget. "I'm afraid that won't be possible. She just went up north to visit my aunt."

I looked over at Eight-Ball, who immediately glanced away, leaving no doubt that the Reverend was lying.

"No problem. You can give me the phone number then."

Both men remained silent.

"Why don't you just tell me what's really going on? Otherwise, this information might find its way to the local newspapers, along with your name as a source. Maybe you'd prefer to speak to a bunch of reporters," I warned the Reverend, beginning to apply the screws.

"Don't do that," Bayliss hurriedly replied. "It won't do none of us no good."

Eight-Ball shook his head like an old hound dog who knew when the jig was up. "I think you better tell her, Reverend. She did right by me. And it's not like she's after you."

I grabbed my cue and ran with it. "That's true. The only ones I'm interested in are Drapkin and Williams."

"So that means you're not out to make a scandal of me or my church?" the Reverend asked.

"Are you doing anything to hurt wildlife?"

The Reverend shook his head so vigorously that his jowls joined in the dance.

"Then absolutely not," I assured him.

"And you swear you won't bring me into this?" he nervously questioned. His fingers latched onto the gold medallion around his neck, as if for reassurance.

"I'll keep you out of it," I vowed, hoping I'd be able to live up to my word.

"All right then. Drapkin called me a while back, and we had a meeting in his office about a business proposition. He promised to make large donations to my church if I worked to deliver the black vote for Clark Williams."

The very air around me began to quake.

"And you agreed to it?"

"Well, that old building of ours is falling apart and I figured, what's the harm? It doesn't seem to matter who gets in. They never do nothing for us anyway. Besides, he said that Williams would sweeten the deal. Golden Dreams owns the lot the church is sitting on. Drapkin promised the land was ours if Williams got elected."

"But all I've ever heard you do is bad-mouth those two," I replied in surprise.

"The Lord has shown me the error of my ways since then, and my soul has been saved!" Bayliss roared, as if preaching to his congregation.

"Amen," Eight-Ball concurred.

Uh-huh. More likely, Bayliss had learned that the donations weren't going to be quite as large as he'd expected.

"That still doesn't explain how it is you know that DRG is funneling money into Williams's campaign," I pressed.

"I know lots of things I haven't yet told you," Bayliss advised, with a dangerous gleam in his eye.

"Such as?" I skeptically inquired, hoping to rattle his pride.

"Such as that Golden Dreams is nothing more than the real-estate development arm of DRG. Drapkin is the real owner. Here's a little something else you probably don't know. Fish and Wildlife is planning to buy swampland from Golden Dreams for a hefty price tag. Gonna make it into a wildlife refuge, though I don't know why. The place is as polluted as Purvis Creek."

That was all it took—just that simple piece of information to bring the world raining down upon my head. I now knew that Regional Director Montgomery and Drapkin were far more than just old friends. They were involved in a lucrative deal for which Montgomery was bound to receive a hefty kickback.

"Are you sure about this?" I asked, barely able to catch my breath.

"Absolutely. I spotted the proposal among a bunch of papers on Drapkin's desk, at the same time that I saw the sheet listing DRG's contributions to Clark Williams. Drapkin has given that man over a quarter million dollars! Can you imagine?"

I believed Bayliss. He should know. After all, the good Reverend had also been washing his hands in dirty money. I began to feel sick, remembering how I'd nearly been seduced by blind ambition myself—until reality kicked in and I realized what Bayliss had just said.

"Wait a minute. There's no way Drapkin would have left you alone in his office to rummage around."

"You're right. He didn't," The Reverend revealed, and grew quiet.

"Hell, we've gone this far. You might as well tell her the rest," Eight-Ball prompted.

Bayliss nodded in agreement. "Eight-Ball snuck me in one night while he was working late. That's when I saw the conditions in that place. It's also when I realized that Drapkin was stringing me along for pennies."

"So you're blackmailing him?" I asked, taking it the next logical step.

"No, we came to a stalemate. I promised not to reveal what I knew, in exchange for Drapkin's silence about the few payoffs I'd received. Up till now, everything's remained that way."

"Then what's changed?"

"The land grab here on St. Simons for one. Besides, Eight-Ball's not the first man to get hurt on the job. Someone's got to put a stop to what Drapkin is doing. And that means also derailing Clark Williams. Otherwise, he'll become Georgia's next congressman and nothing ever *will* change."

I now knew what I had to do. "Eight-Ball, can you tell me exactly where the nurse's office is located?"

"Why? Ain't you feeling so good?" he asked, looking at me strangely.

"Let's just say I'm trying to figure out how to make Drapkin clean up his act. And the best way for me to do that is to get hold of the employee medical records."

I needed them now more than ever, since Gary's test results had been swiped.

"Mr. Drapkin ain't never gonna let you in there to poke around," Eight-Ball warned.

"I don't believe Agent Porter plans to get Howard Drapkin's permission. Do you, Agent Porter?" Bayliss asked with a chuckle.

Maybe the Reverend was wiser than I'd thought.

"Actually, I intend to find a way into DRG tonight," I revealed, secure in the knowledge that neither man would betray me.

Eight-Ball carefully rolled down his pant leg. "Not alone, you're not. I'm coming along."

I looked at the shriveled figure, and knew the man had long ago paid his dues. "Sorry, Eight-Ball, but you're in no shape to go running around. What I'm planning is far too dangerous."

"Ain't nothing more dangerous than what I do every day in that place," he maintained, thrusting out his bottom lip. "There's an awful lotta widows whose husbands worked at DRG. Seems to me most of them died before their time. The way I figure it, Mr. Drapkin owes us a lot more than we owe him, and there ain't never gonna be enough money to pay us all back."

Eight-Ball had once again said something that piqued my interest. "Can you tell me how these men died?"

"Some of them got real bad shocks. I'm not sure what happened to the rest."

"Do you remember any of their names?"

Eight-Ball's forehead puckered into a nest of wrinkles as he tried to think. "Let's see. There was Joe Fellows, Ralph Moore, and Bill Norris. There've been plenty of others. I can see their faces plain as day. But for the life of me, I just can't recall who they were."

"That's all right," I assured him, and wrote down those three.

"I'm coming along, Miss Rachel," Eight-Ball stubbornly insisted. "DRG's taken too many lives and there are ghosts with no names who need to be repaid."

"Are you sure about this?" I asked, still having my doubts.

"As sure as I need to be. Besides, you're gonna want me around," he slyly added. "You see, I got the keys to the kingdom, and that's the easiest way to get into DRG."

He jingled a set of shiny keys before me, like precious pieces of Blackbeard's gold.

"How did you get those?" I asked in amazement.

"You forget. I gotta be able to get in there night and day to do maintenance work."

"But you said you only did a little of this and that," I responded, beginning to regard Eight-Ball with newfound respect.

"Sure, cause that's exactly what Mr. Drapkin and his foreman tell me to do. Fix things the best I can, doing a little of this and a little of that. That man don't wanna spend a plug nickel on any repairs."

"I had me a daddy like that," the Reverend mused, shoving his way back into the limelight. "He held on to a nickel for so long that the buffalo shit on the Indian."

I purposely ignored Bayliss just to drive him crazy.

"Okay, Eight-Ball. You can come," I relented. "But you have to promise to take it easy and rest whenever your leg hurts."

"It's a deal," he agreed and glanced impatiently toward the living room. "When are those women ever gonna leave, anyway? Don't they know they got men waiting for them at home? Besides, I want Venus to come in here and whip us up some dinner. We might as well eat a good meal, seeing as how there's plenty of time to kill."

"What do you mean?" I asked, already raring to go.

"Just that it won't be safe to head over until after ten o'clock."

I began to realize it was a good thing that Eight-Ball was coming along. He'd be able to save me time, frustration, and possibly, unexpected trouble. I just hoped he was up to it. The last thing I wanted was for his leg to get any worse.

The class wrapped up as the ladies broke into a rousing rendition of "I Am Woman" that very nearly shook the roof. Venus came into the kitchen shortly after, looking positively radiant in a pair of satin fuchsia pajamas.

"Damn, if I don't feel empowered just knowing those women are gonna go home and kick them some butt," she declared, throwing on an apron. "Now ya'll get out of my way while I cook a meal that'll make Eight-Ball feel better. And I expect you to stay, Rachel. Seems to me, you could use some meat on those bones."

I liked this woman better and better. But then the way to my heart was easy. Just say I look thin, and don't call me *ma'am*.

We sat down to a hearty meal of macaroni and cheese, collard greens, and spoonbread. I didn't even want to think about the calories. But then Venus had said that a gal shouldn't look too thin. I was on my second helping when a cell phone rang. I looked up to find everyone staring at me.

"For chrissakes, Rachel. You're the only one in here with one of those damn things," the Reverend reprimanded.

"Oops. Sorry about that." I said, and flipped open my cell phone. "Agent Porter," I mumbled through a mouthful of macaroni and cheese.

"You were right! Happy now?" a weepy voice wailed in my ear.

"Candi? Is that you?" I asked, washing down my food with sweet ice tea.

"I can't believe I've been such a fool all this time! Stupid, stupid, stupid!" she bawled, while smacking what sounded like her palm to her forehead.

"You're not stupid, Candi. Whatever it is, you've probably just been misled. Now what are you talking about?"

"Wendell and I *have* been nabbing manatees over near DRG," she revealed, with a loud sniffle.

"How?" I asked, barely able to contain my excitement over the fact that Candi had cracked.

"Howard said all we had to do was stretch a net across the area at high tide to catch them. And he was right. The manatees always leave DRG and the pulp mill as the tide rolls out, and that's when we'd snatch one. Then we'd just pull in the net."

"You and Wendell did that all by yourselves?" I questioned in disbelief.

"Along with four of his other workers. Then Wendell would give the critter a tranquilizer shot, and we'd roll the manatee on its side, slip a stretcher underneath, and slide it into the van."

I now remembered the yellow truck that had been sitting outside Wendell's office. No wonder its interior had been padded with foam rubber. I could only imagine what manatees must have thought as they were immobilized in slings and transported in the dark inside a coffinlike trailer.

Candi started to sob even harder. "I always felt real bad about that part. But it seemed they'd have a better life, not having to worry about where to get food or sleep at night. I even stayed in the back with them during the ride, putting water on their skin to keep it moist."

It's amazing what we do, under the guise of trying to help Mother Nature.

"I'm glad you called, Candi. You're doing the right thing," I said, hoping to pump her for more information. "What made you decide to finally tell me?"

Candi's wails grew even more distraught. "You know that little baby I was trying to feed yesterday? Well now *she's* sick and I'm afraid she's going to die! I don't know what to do. I've never felt so helpless in my life."

I would gladly have reached through the phone and throttled her, if I'd been able.

"I told Howard about it. But he said it was no big deal—to just go out and catch a few more. He even joked that we should make *real* manatee burgers out of those that are dead. At least then we could make a few extra bucks. I can't believe *this* is the man that I thought I loved."

She paused, as if waiting to be consoled. What could I

say, other than that she was one more woman who'd made a bad choice?

"I wasn't gonna tell you this, but another two manatees started to swim kinda funny a few hours ago. Not only that, but now Wendell is missing."

"What do you mean, he's missing?" I asked, hearing alarm bells go off. Perhaps he'd taken the money and fled the country, realizing that things were starting to fall apart.

"All I know is that he went to see Howard this morning and never came back," Candi revealed. "Wendell got all upset after your visit yesterday. He started thinking maybe you're right. Maybe people *will* stop coming to the water park if manatees keep getting sick. So, I told him exactly what you said. That Howard's been dumping mercury into the marsh and it's killing all our manatees."

"You mean, Wendell really didn't know?"

"Not until he spoke to you. His life savings are invested in this place. Maybe it's silly, but I'm beginning to worry. He was really angry when he left. I'm afraid he might have decided to drive off the road, or kill himself or something. I called Howard a little while ago, but he said that he hadn't seen Wendell all day."

I was starting to have a bad feeling about this, myself. It was just possible that the fireworks I'd so carefully put in place had erupted in a major explosion.

"I'll make some calls and see what I can find out," I promised. "I'll also arrange for an expert to come and care for the manatees." Bureaucracy and red tape be damned. I only hoped it wasn't too late. "Just do the best you can for them tonight."

Candi began to sob once more, as though her heart would break.

"Are you going to be all right?" I asked, softening against my better judgment. What I really wanted to scream was, *why didn't you listen to me before this?* Only I knew the reason all too well. She was another woman trying to please a man while attempting to claw her way up the career ladder.

Candi took a moment to blow her nose. "I'll be fine. Spud called a while ago, and he's here with me now."

Wouldn't you know? Spud had a lot in common with lowlife vermin. He instinctively sensed when it was safe to crawl out of his hole. Even worse, he now got on the phone.

"Hey, Porter. So are you gonna kick Drapkin's crummy ass, or do I have to do it for you? Nobody's gonna hurt *my* girl. Right, sugar?"

The last part was delivered in baby talk. I presumed he'd been speaking to Candi, since I now heard heavy smooching on the other end of the wire. That's another problem we women have. We tend to repeat the same mistakes, being all too eager to give men the benefit of the doubt.

"Stay out of this, Spud! Or I swear the only time you'll see Candi is when she visits you in jail," I warned.

"Yeah, yeah. Just get out there and do something about Drapkin. I'll be checking up on you, Porter," Spud cockily retorted.

I didn't bother to respond, but simply hung up. Then I placed a call to a friend with Sea World in Florida. He immediately agreed to hop on a plane and fly to Georgia. At least I knew that the manatees would be taken care of. The toughest thing now was waiting until ten o'clock. Finally, it reached the magic hour.

The Reverend broke into a blessing while Venus gave us each a small bag of root.

"Here. This will keep you safe," she said, pressing the packets into our hands.

Even the dog, Jake, got into the act, howling at the top of his lungs when we walked outside. A raspy chuckle rose from within Eight-Ball, as if stoked by the fire still sizzling inside his burns.

"I swear that dog'll stop howling the day I die," he uttered, which seemed to be his favorite expression.

I just prayed the dog didn't stop howling tonight.

Eighteen

Soon we were underway, winding past expensive new homes, built on land once owned by former slaves. Eight-Ball tilted his head while lowering the passenger window, once again listening to something I couldn't hear. That was all right. My mind was otherwise engaged as we raced beneath a sky darker than death.

We were flying across the causeway toward Brunswick when the moon slipped from behind a bank of clouds as if it had been playing hide-and-seek. I gazed down to where its golden rays formed a mystical pool on the still black water.

Lo and behold, floating on its mirrored surface was a manatee! The mammal stood upright, seductively basking in the moon's milky light, like legendary sirens of old. An aquatic Mae West, she beckoned to me while swaying to a silent melody, and I knew I'd never seen such a magnificent creature in all my life. I vowed to do everything in my power to make sure that the species never died. Then the manatee slowly sank from sight, into the watery depths below.

I shivered in the warmth of the night, nearly jumping out of my skin as my phone suddenly rang.

It better not be Spud, I swore. *One wrong move, and I'll kick his ass straight across Georgia.*

"Agent Porter," I snapped.

"Rachel? Don't you ever check your machine at home? I've been trying to reach you all evening."

It was Santou's boss. He couldn't have been trying terribly hard. All he had to do was dial my cell phone.

"Why? What's up?" I asked, fully prepared to hear some lame excuse as to why Santou hadn't called.

"I've got some news. It's not great. But we also don't know everything yet, so don't go jumping to any conclusions."

The headlights around me blurred into a large fireball and my heart began to pound. It's always a bad sign whenever the first words out of someone's mouth are to stay calm. I immediately steered off the road, knowing that something was wrong.

"Why are we stopping?" Eight-Ball inquired.

But I didn't respond. My world had abruptly shrunk, encompassing only the cell phone clutched in my hand.

"What's happened?" I asked, my voice sounding alien to my own ears.

"It's Santou. I'm afraid that his plane has gone down."

The lights now whirled out of control in a deranged kaleidoscope that bounced around in my head. In fact, everything surrounding me spun in an orgy of delirium. I began to pass out, when Eight-Ball shoved the packet of root under my nose, jerking me back to consciousness.

"Rachel, are you still there?" Guidry demanded.

"Yes. Is Jake dead?" I asked, barely able to say the words.

"We don't know yet. He was on a military flight that had mechanical difficulty and was forced to land in the Florida swamp. There hasn't been radio contact with the craft. We can't say anything for certain until a search-and-rescue team reaches the crash site." Guidry hesitated, as if instantly regretting his choice of words. "I mean, if there was a crash. We're using high-tech ground-penetrating radar to try to pinpoint the plane. I'm afraid our only access will be by helicopter or small boat."

What was Guidry saying? That he suspected Santou's plane had sunk into the swamp?

"But Jake took off last night. Why are you just assembling a search team now?" I demanded, wanting to believe that he was somehow wrong.

"Santou's flight was delayed due to bad weather. His plane didn't take off until today."

My mind now raced, as I began to play the morbid game of *what if*. What if the plane hadn't been delayed? What if Santou hadn't followed me to Georgia? What if he was alive, but stuck inside the craft and couldn't escape? Everglades water is dark and murky, filled with gators, slime, and thick muck. Other planes had gone down in that swamp. Sometimes there were survivors, but mostly there were not. I grew cold at the thought of Santou as one more restless ghost in a watery grave.

"I want to go along as part of the search team," I insisted, knowing that I couldn't just sit around.

"Sorry Rachel, but that's a no-can-do."

"What the hell are you talking about?" I nearly shouted, my eyes filling with tears.

"You're too emotionally involved. I don't have time to worry about you, along with everything else going on."

"That's a pile of bullshit!" I angrily retorted.

"No, it's not," he snapped. "Listen to me, Rachel. Santou's tough. Remember, he's Cajun and the swamp was his playground as a kid growing up. If anyone can walk away from a crash and survive, it'll be Jake. But this is going to be done by the book. And that means you can't come along."

Guidry was clearly controlling what he chose to tell me. Still, I had no option but to believe there was hope.

"I'll call you with any updates. But right now, I've gotta go."

With that, he hung up.

I sat staring into the night, seeing nothing but Jake's face before me. Part of my soul had been stolen, and in its place had been left a cavernous void.

"Someone you care about been hurt?" Eight-Ball questioned.

I nodded, refusing to give the news further credence by saying the word *yes* aloud—not that I could have spoken over the lump in my throat. The world had suddenly become a movie, and I just one more bit player, stuck in a role I didn't want. My life was crumbling around me and all pretense of control was now lost.

"But he could still be alive, right? Then that's what you gotta believe in your heart."

It's what I tried to keep telling myself, though my demons whispered it wasn't so.

"We don't have to do this right now, if you don't want," Eight-Ball offered. "I can always get you into DRG another time."

I could easily have gone home and curled up into a ball. But I was afraid that if I did, I might very well lose my mind. Not only that, but I now wondered, more than ever, why Jake hadn't bothered to call when his flight was delayed. Had he not wanted me to worry? Had he simply been too busy with work? Or was something else going on?

"No, let's go ahead as planned."

I threw the vehicle into gear, and pulled back on the road.

DRG soon appeared up ahead where the plant's smokestacks rose like ominous ghouls in the sky.

Eight-Ball jumped out and unlocked the gate. Then he waved me in, and I took my foot off the brake, so that the Ford slowly rolled down the drive. Though I tried to park in the shadows, the moon spilled its light across the asphalt, exposing a throng of anguished souls that walked the night.

Wraiths, specters, hobgoblins, bogeymen—call them what you will. They were each acquaintances of mine, having stalked me all my life. They came along now, as I got out of my vehicle and followed Eight-Ball inside.

The long hallway furiously whispered as we walked by, the linoleum floor chattering beneath our feet. I'd have given anything to know what was being said. But only one word filled my head, *Santou*.

"Where do you want to go first?" Eight-Ball questioned.

He must have felt the spirits around us, as well. Even *his* voice was subdued.

"Drapkin's office."

We walked inside, and I immediately headed for the filing cabinet next to his desk. It proved to be locked, just as I'd expected.

Eight-Ball looked at me and shrugged. "Sorry, Miss Rachel but I'm afraid I can't help. Mr. Drapkin don't give me the keys for that sorta thing."

No problem there; I always come prepared. I pulled out my Leatherman multi-tool, and promptly began to jimmy the lock.

So focused was I that it took a moment to realize numerous eyes were bearing down on me. I quickly looked up. There was Howard Drapkin in all his posed glory, scrutinizing my every move from the photos on his desk. I leaned to the right and then to the left. Each set of eyes followed along, as if accusing me of being somewhere I didn't belong.

Tough luck.

The lock finally popped and I yanked open the drawer. Stashed inside was the file that Drapkin had shown me. I bypassed it to skim through yet more neatly written reports addressed to the Georgia Environmental Protection Division, declaring the amount of mercury discharged by DRG to be well within the legal limit.

It was time to see what the next drawer held. But first, I snuck another peek at the photos. Drapkin's mouth now seemed to have turned from a smile to a frown. However, he wasn't the only one in the room who wasn't happy.

Damn, damn, damn!

I couldn't get the bottom drawer open. It was as though I'd lost my touch. I started to sweat so much that my shirt stuck to my back and my hands shook. The problem was, I couldn't stop thinking about Santou. The next thing I knew, Eight-Ball was kneeling by my side.

"Why don't you let me give that a try, Miss Rachel?" he gently suggested.

I nodded and watched as Eight-Ball adroitly picked the lock.

"There you go," he said and opened the drawer.

I plunged in, anxious to find something in which to drown myself. It appeared I was in luck. A notebook lay inside that was marked STRICTLY PERSONAL. I pulled it out, and thumbed through the contents.

It now began to seem as though DRG were two completely different companies. The first chlor-alkali plant, as depicted in the file Drapkin had shown me, played by all the rules. However, this notebook detailed a company that had totally run amuck. Corporate records revealed a startling fact—the plant regularly purchased ten thousand pounds of mercury every few months. Even *I* didn't have to be a scientist to know that meant something was terribly amiss. DRG shouldn't have been buying *any* mercury at all—not unless vast amounts of it were being lost.

I continued to flip through the pages, increasingly astounded, as I now discovered what I'd been searching for. There was no question but that the reports filed with the Georgia Environmental Protection Division were totally bogus. In reality, the daily average of mercury being discharged was *fourteen times* the permitted amount!

I stared in disbelief, certain that I had to be reading the numbers wrong. But the figures refused to change. Instead what I saw amounted to nothing less than felony conspiracy. DRG had dumped 850,000 pounds of liquid mercury into the neighboring marsh over the last ten years.

I removed the pertinent papers, and let my fingers do some more walking. It wasn't long before I hit upon yet another gold mine—a folder marked CONFIDENTIAL, with each of its letters underlined twice.

Ooh, baby, baby. Your secrets are safe with me, I lied and opened the file. What I found completely blew me away. Enclosed was a summary stating that the plant was a "hazard" and "in total disrepair." In addition, DRG posed a serious threat not only to its employees, but also to the community at large, due to mercury and poisonous chlorine gas leaks. At least ten million dollars was necessary to correct immediate health and safety problems. An attached note, signed by Sterling Engineer Consulting Firm, guaranteed that the information would be kept strictly confidential.

But there was still more. Yet another report revealed that

DRG's treatment tank was too small. In reality, it was half the size the company had originally claimed it to be. Also included were copies of memos sent from Drapkin to the plant manager, urging him to "keep this place running. Money is important. We don't want to lose one single dollar."

I couldn't believe Drapkin hadn't shredded this stuff. Either he was stupid or outrageously arrogant, or had the balls to think that he could actually get away with it.

This time I didn't bother to pick and choose among papers, but took the entire folder. There was still one last item in the drawer that I now opened—a small blue accordion file containing canceled checks. Each was in the amount of fifty thousand dollars. But what caught my interest were three of the recipients—Mrs. Joe Fellows, Mrs. Ralph Moore, and Mrs. Bill Norris.

"Eight-Ball, aren't these the names of those men you mentioned? The ones who died shortly after having been involved in accidents here?"

Eight-Ball held the checks between his wrinkled fingers and squinted at them. "They sure are. Well, ain't that nice of Mr. Drapkin to help their womenfolk out like that."

Uh-huh. Except for the fact that I was suspicious this was hush money.

"Why don't we head over to the nurse's office next?" I suggested, overcome by the sudden urge to take a good hard look at employee health records.

We closed the door to Drapkin's room and proceeded down the hallway.

It's a good time to die. It's a good time to die, the linoleum whispered each time our shoes hit the floor.

Oh, God! Could this have been a warning about Santou all along?

I leaned against the wall and closed my eyes, struck by an unexpected bout of dizziness.

"You okay?" Eight-Ball asked.

Santou's face loomed before me, and I knew I'd never be okay again, unless he were found alive.

"Fine. Just give me a second." I took a deep breath and straightened back up. "Okay, let's go on."

We entered a room that was even more bland and sterile than the hallway.

"This is Verena Harper's office."

It should have been easy enough to guess. The walls were painted a nauseating shade of hospital puke green. I made a beeline for a pair of filing cabinets, picked the locks, and immediately got down to work.

Inside were the health records of every DRG employee. Rather than stored alphabetically, the charts were arranged according to work areas within the plant. So much the better. I swiftly targeted the files of those men in the cell buildings.

Each employee's folder contained a list of health complaints ranging from headaches and shakiness to memory loss and lack of equilibrium. Results of urine samples revealed the amount of mercury that was filtering through their kidneys. The acceptable government level was no more than one hundred fifty micrograms.

I examined the records closely, wanting to make absolutely certain that I knew what was going on. But there was no mistaking the information before me. These men were walking time bombs. Every cell worker averaged over four hundred micrograms of mercury in his system. All except for one poor sucker, who carried the notation *living dead* next to his name. He was walking around with over one thousand micrograms inside him.

I couldn't believe the ramifications of what I'd just found. DRG employees had plenty of ammunition with which to file one hell of a lawsuit. I felt like Norma Rae preparing to lead a workers' revolt. That is until my eyes fell upon a large manila envelope with MEDICAL RELEASES written across its front in bold red letters.

My fingers trembled as I fumbled to remove its contents. Stuffed inside were a wad of release forms; one for every employee. I quickly read their gist. They acquitted DRG of all responsibility for any future medical problems that should arise from having worked at the plant.

"Eight-Ball, did *you* sign one of these things?" I tersely questioned the man beside me.

He looked at me blankly. "Well, I don't rightly remember, but I suppose so."

"You *suppose* so? Do you realize what this means for all of you in this damn place?" I angrily snapped.

Eight-Ball remained quiet for a moment before he finally spoke. "You know, Miss Rachel. Just 'cause we're poor don't make us stupid. Sometimes it don't matter how angry or scared we get. We still got no choice but to turn a blind eye. Too many folks around here need the work. When it comes right down to it, men gotta feed their families."

My face burned in embarrassment. Eight-Ball had deftly put me in my place with just a few choice words. None of these men were lawyers versed in the legal mumbo jumbo of signing away their rights. Most probably didn't remember having put their John Hancock on these papers in the first place. After all, that's what happens when you're constantly exposed to mercury—you tend to forget. What it *did* clarify was that Drapkin was one clever son of a bitch who had shrewdly covered his ass.

I gathered what information I'd found, fully determined to figure out a way to take this bastard down. Then I headed outside, where I stashed the papers in my Ford.

"Where you wanna go next?" Eight-Ball asked, turning on his flashlight.

Between being sick with worry and consumed by growing fury, I was ready to explode. But my obstinacy refused to let me stop. I caught sight of two abandoned railroad cars up ahead. "What's inside those?"

Eight-Ball scuffed his shoes on the ground, as though there were something he hated to admit.

"One's filled with a whole lotta bad liquid. You don't wanna go fooling with that stuff."

"What about the other car?"

Eight-Ball shrugged. "It's basically used for storage. You know, odds and ends like old tools, spare parts, and bags of pesticide."

That last item caught my interest. "Let's take a look in there."

We crossed a field that was quiet as a graveyard, in which no crickets chirped and no cicada sang. It was Silent Spring all four seasons of the year, a place where nothing alive seemed willing to remain.

Eight-Ball and I placed our hands flat against the railroad car and slid the entrance open. The portal emitted a long, low groan eerily reminiscent of a Cheyne-Stokes gasp—the last gasp one makes before leaving this earth and entering death's door. Then he flashed his light inside, where I caught sight of fifty-pound bags heaped in a corner. One of the gunny sacks was slit open, and a mound of tiny brown grains had spilled out.

I would have thought it was birdseed but for the dead rats that lay about. All except for one that still nibbled hungrily at the grain. I pulled out my own small flashlight and shone it on the bags. No wonder so many rodents were dead. They'd eaten Temik, one of the most potent pesticides on the market. I'd come across it out West, where some ranchers had illegally used the poison to kill coyotes, eagles, and wolves. The question was, what did DRG need it for?

"Why does Drapkin have all this Temik around?"

"Maybe it's 'cause he don't like rats and mice?" Eight-Ball answered my question with one of his own.

I was pondering that when the rat eating away at the grain suddenly froze. Then its rear leg uncontrollably twitched. From there the tremor rapidly spread to the critter's torso, gripping its entire body in a seizure. Relief came only when the rodent lay dead.

My body reacted just as quickly, breaking into a cold sweat, as a wave of nausea swept through me. The scene had been all too visceral, a sharp reenactment of Gary's own final moments. There was no controlling what happened next, as I abruptly turned away and threw up.

"Maybe we oughta forget about this for now and go home," Eight-Ball suggested, handing me a tissue. "Something tells me this ain't such a good idea."

I looked over at Eight-Ball to find he'd turned pale as a ghost. I wondered what had scared him most—my reaction, or realizing just how toxic this place really was. Maybe his painkiller was wearing off. I felt bad for the man. But we'd both have to tough things out. No way would I give up now. Not after what I'd just seen.

"Do you have your pain pills with you?"

Eight-Ball nodded.

"Okay, then. You've done more than enough by bringing me here. Why don't you take another pill and wait for me in the car? That way you can give your leg a rest."

"It ain't my leg that's bothering me," Eight-Ball obstinately retorted. "I got a bad feeling, is all."

I had a bad feeling, too. I was now convinced that Drapkin was responsible for Gary's death. Harry had said as much, himself.

Eliminate the biologist and nobody can say that DRG is causing the marsh any harm.

"Anyway, it's not me that I got a bad feeling about, Miss Rachel. It's you."

An icy hand clenched my stomach, twisting hard as a wave of nausea tore through me again. Even worse, I could swear that a tremor now sped through my limbs. I held my breath, wondering if I might be next, and how it was that I'd come to be a victim. But the sensation quickly passed, leaving me more determined than ever to nail Drapkin. Besides, anything was better than the news I feared could be waiting for me at home.

"Don't worry, Eight-Ball. I'm like a cat with nine lives."

"Oh yeah? What number you up to now?" he smartly retorted.

"I don't believe it's quite nine yet," I tersely joked.

"That's close enough. Might as well tell me where you plan to go next, cause you ain't going alone."

Cell Building Two loomed dead ahead. I pointed to it.

"Let's head there."

It was as though I were pulled by an invisible cord past the outfall pond and weir to the man-made lake. I paused for a moment, remembering this was where Gary had taken his last sample. Then steeling myself, I headed toward the entrance of Cell Building Two, when five bony fingers latched onto my arm.

"Hold it, Miss Rachel. You can't go in that way."

"Why not?"

"You'll see soon enough. Follow me."

However, rather than proceed, I illuminated the area with my flashlight, curious as to what the problem might be. A trickle of liquid seductively caught its rays. Reflected in the light was fluid seeping from under the cell door. I aimed the beam along the ground and followed where it led.

A fresh batch of silver mercury bubbles lay percolating in the mud. They gurgled and squirmed like newly evolving life forms, leaving mc with an uneasy feeling of dread. Soon the mercury would become gaseous and easily inhaled—a disturbing sign as to what awaited us in the building.

"Miss Rachel?" Fight-Ball called out again.

I hurried to catch up with him. Rounding a corner, I found Eight-Ball climbing a set of stairs. Our footsteps echoed hollow in the night, swallowed by the marsh, as we made our ascent skyward along the side of the building.

Each tread reverberated within me like a death knell as my mind strayed to Santou. I wondered if he was alive, trapped inside a metal coffin somewhere deep in the swamp. Drops of rain now fell, nipping at my skin like diminutive bits of steel as if the night were crying, its tears fragments of Santou's plane plummeting from out of the sky.

I began to climb faster now, desperate to escape the vision. But my demons had hold and refused to let go, reveling in my anguish. I prayed this would all prove to be nothing more than a bad dream. I'd almost begun to believe it was so—until Eight-Ball's voice shattered the spell, jerking me back to reality.

"You gotta put these on. Otherwise you can get burned real bad inside," he said, handing me rubber boots as we reached the top of the stairs.

I donned them, while he slipped a pair onto his own feet.

"If that happens, make sure to take a shower right away over there."

My eyes followed where his finger led—to a small structure standing off by itself.

"What about face masks?" I asked. "You must have to wear those."

Eight-Ball stared at me as though he'd never heard the words before. Then he reached into a box near the cell door.

"You mean these things?" he asked, pulling out a couple of flimsy paper masks.

I took one and put it on. The mask loosely covered my nose and mouth, offering no more protection than a placebo.

He unlocked the metal door and flicked on the lights, as we stepped inside a space the size of a football field. The first thing to hit me was that it was hot as hell in this place. A thermometer on the wall confirmed I was right. The temperature hovered at one hundred and ten degrees of sweltering heat.

It's funny how information from the past chooses when to come wafting back. I now remembered something an old science teacher had taught me. Haze, smoke, and gas rise under such conditions. That lesson reaffirmed Harry's recent words of warning.

Breathing in all those mercury vapors can cause irreversible brain damage.

I could already feel my IQ begin to drop. The trick was to snoop around, see what I could find, and get out.

One look established that there were at least fifty electrolytic cells on the top floor, each the size of a large dining room table. I could only imagine how hard it was to keep them clean and running. Eight-Ball must have read my thoughts, as he now began to walk toward them.

"See here, Miss Rachel? This is part of the problem."

I bent down, took a good look, and nearly plotzed. *Problem* didn't begin to describe the situation. *Disaster* was more like it. A number of cells were steadily leaking mercury that puddled on the floor.

"What happens is the mercury rolls toward those support columns and then escapes down through the cracks," Eight-Ball explained, pointing to the large concrete pillars around the room.

I listened closely and imagined I could hear the drops *plink, plink, plinking* onto the ground below. Stepping back, I held my breath, wondering how many brain cells I'd already blown.

"But where we got bad trouble is on the bottom floor. You sure you really wanna go down there?" he asked. His shaky fingers wiped a trickle of sweat off his brow.

I hadn't come this far just to wimp out now.

"Absolutely," I said, hoping I sounded braver than I felt. My legs had begun to tremble from the heat, which made me feel weak.

Buck up, I told myself. *You've still got plenty of brain cells left. So what's a few more?*

I followed Eight-Ball down a flight of metal steps, and instantly realized why the lower door had to remain closed. The bottom floor was flooded with a good eighteen inches of corrosive water. Even more frightening was that this was where the control valves, electrical panels, and circuit boxes were housed.

I stared in disbelief at all the exposed wires dangling loosely from electrical pumps. Then I flashed my light onto the liquid below. Glistening strands of mercury lay strung across the floor, where they hypnotically swayed like long silver snakes.

"There's lotsa bad stuff in that water," Eight-Ball spoke above the sound of running motors. "So just try not to get it on you."

That was the general idea. "Workers don't have to wade around in it, do they?"

"Sure," Eight-Ball confirmed. "How else we gonna fix things? Mr. Drapkin had catwalks put in a while back. But a lotta pumps sit on the floor and there's no other way to get to them."

No wonder those DRG employees had died after receiving bad shocks. What had their wives thought when they'd seen the singe marks? Had they realized their husbands had been electrocuted? I now understood why Drapkin had paid to shut them up.

"Besides, there's not always water down here. We vacuum up mercury that's lying around when the floor ain't so wet. Mr. Drapkin likes us to try to put it back in the cells and re-use it."

Drapkin really was the ultimate miser. The best I could wish was that he'd wind up in prison and his wife would sue his ass off—at least, for a start.

"Where can we walk?" I asked, wanting to get off the steps and take a better look.

Eight-Ball pointed to the catwalk below. Constructed of large railroad ties, it stood three feet above the cement floor jutting into wharves that wove their way between the equipment.

"Are there hard hats we can wear?" I asked, dodging a tumbling drop of mercury.

"There used to be a couple, but Lord knows where they are. Mr. Drapkin said we don't really need them."

I added another black mark onto Drapkin's growing list of misdeeds.

"Here. You can stick this on your head." Eight-Ball handed me what looked like a rainbonnet of heavy plastic.

I felt like a Jewish grandmother as I tied its two ends under my chin. Then evading the falling raindrops, I stepped onto the makeshift platform. If I'd thought my legs were shaky before, they were definitely wobbly now.

I looked down at the water below. The caustic liquid lapped at the railroad ties, patient as a gator awaiting its next meal. I began to take a step, only to hesitate. The entire surface of the catwalk was dotted with shiny, silver beads.

Stop being such a wuss and get on with it, commanded the maniac living inside me.

Taking a deep breath, I placed one foot in front of the other, careful not to lose my balance.

Eight-Ball pointed to a group of corroded motors all sitting together. "There's some stuff that needs to be fixed."

I imagined down-and-dirty workers slogging through this water, trying their best to keep it from splashing. Black or white, it made no difference. All of the workers were disposable.

"How much water do you suppose is down here?"

Eight-Ball tilted his head and squinted hard, as if that might help him to think. "I seem to recall someone saying this area holds two hundred thousand gallons. That's when it's usually released. Looks like there's just about that much now.

Release caustic water? Where the hell did it go? Then I remembered the lake just outside. The only thing standing between all that water and this flood was the steel door.

I aimed my flashlight at the barrier and took a closer look. Whadda ya know? The door had been built so that it didn't touch the floor. Instead, the bottom was an enormous mound of dirt that rose about two feet high and a foot wide. The building had been transformed into a man-made lake.

"Is that how the lake out there was formed?"

Eight-Ball nodded his head and chuckled. "Yep. We call that Lake Mercury. Ain't nothing to do but open the door, break that dirt berm, and let the water run out when the room gets like this."

I gazed around, barely able to believe what I'd just heard. *And all of this is going into the groundwater*, I silently realized.

"None of us like it. But what else can you do when there's no money to fix the place?" Eight-Ball questioned.

There would have been plenty if Drapkin weren't so greedy. But what I still couldn't figure out was how this witches' brew was reaching the marsh so quickly.

"Eight-Ball, is there any other way in which DRG gets rid of excess liquid?"

"Well, we got sewers that drain into six underground pipes. Sometimes we dump a bunch of the waste down there."

"And where do those pipes lead?" I carefully questioned.

"They run into the marsh and Purvis Creek."

Bingo! Drapkin was getting rid of corrosive water every which way that he could.

Eight-Ball cocked his head and glanced toward the second level. "Sounds like one of the cells upstairs might need to be checked. Let me see what's going on, and I'll be right back."

I paid little heed, my attention fully focused on the nightmare around me.

"Sure, no problem."

I found it mind-boggling that Drapkin had gotten away with this for so long. Plenty of palms must have been greased, and knowing eyes discreetly turned. Equally troubling was that my Regional Director, Bob Montgomery, seemed to be part of it all.

"Do you think the Reverend will testify as to what he knows?" I asked, upon hearing Eight-Ball's footsteps return down the stairs.

I received a fierce whack across my back in response, followed by a sharp jolt of pain. My first thought was that I'd been electrocuted. My second was to wonder what had happened to Eight-Ball as I started to lose my balance. I couldn't stop my body from leaning forward too far. I just prayed that I didn't fall in face first as I continued to slip, all the while struggling to keep the world from turning topsy-turvy. Guardian angels must truly exist, for they now came to my aid. Though I fell into the water, I managed to land on my feet.

Nineteen

A mixture of laughter and tears exploded within me, duking it out in a hodgepodge of emotions. Though I was relieved to be alive, I was angrier than ever at the world for possibly taking Santou from me. I opened my mouth to scream, only to have all thoughts swept away as my legs began to tingle. Pinpricks of heat pierced my skin with the intensity of miniature smart bombs, and I swiftly glanced down to find that my jeans were soaking wet. A shot of cold fear gripped me by the scruff of the neck, and my survival instincts kicked into gear. I had to get out of here and head for the shower immediately.

Turning around, I placed my hands on the catwalk, only to find a pair of boots planted on the railroad ties before me. Why was Eight-Ball just standing there and not bothering to help? I received my answer as I looked up to find Howard Drapkin sneering down at me. Gripped in his hands was a wooden board, which he swung back and forth like a baseball bat.

"I thought for certain you'd be smarter, Agent Porter. You should have realized that your friend's death was a warning."

I stared at the man with his perfectly coiffed hair, and every ounce of my rage found its target.

My hand slowly reached around to grab the 9mm tucked in the back of my pants. Suspecting Drapkin of having killed Gary was one thing. Hearing the admission was quite another. I'd never fatally shot anyone before. However, if there had to be a first time, Drapkin was the perfect candidate.

No longer was I aware of the sting in my legs, only of the itch in my trigger finger. Drapkin represented everything that I'd come to hate—power, greed, and corruption. Who knows? Maybe by killing him, I'd stifle the blind ambition that had begun to eat away inside me. But more than anything else, I'd be exacting revenge for Gary.

I knew I'd never be able to kill the bastard, even as my fingers wrapped around the gun. Still, I didn't see the harm in maiming him a bit. And there were such an interesting array of places for which to aim. What the hell. I'd be helping Venus out and settling a score for his wife, while I was at it.

"You're no genius yourself, Drapkin," I responded, feeling pretty damn empowered as I swung my weapon around.

But Drapkin's reaction surprised me. Instead of being cowed by the sight of my gun, he appeared to be absolutely delighted.

"Now!" he shouted at the top of his lungs.

I wondered if Drapkin was a lunatic with a death wish. However, that was as far as I got when the exterior steel door flew open, and I realized he had an accomplice. After that, everything happened with lightning-fast speed.

A metal shovel glinted where it was raised high, suspended against the moonlight. Then a pair of arms flung the tool down, deftly ripping through the thick berm of earth. There was no time to think, much less act, as a solid wall of water came hurtling behind me. The liquid locomotive knocked me off my feet and onto the ground, tearing the gun from my grip. Falling onto my hands and knees, I lifted my head while closing my eyes and mouth in an attempt to protect myself. But the flood cynically laughed as it roared past with a fluid shriek.

The caustic water tore through my clothes and into my flesh, setting my arms and legs afire. Hot quivers morphed into a mob of angry throbs, and I knew that my skin would soon begin to blister. If that weren't enough, the force of the water now propelled me forward. My body was carried along like so much flotsam in the direction of Mercury Lake, and out of Drapkin's sight.

I could see him laughing in my mind at what he felt was my just fate. Screw him! I refused to knuckle under without one last fight. No way would I give Drapkin, Williams, and Montgomery the satisfaction of believing they'd so easily won. Instead, I focused on trying to find a way out of this mess.

The doorway stood directly ahead. I no longer battled the water, but allowed myself to be hurled toward the entrance. There would be only one slim chance to get this right.

I waited until the very last second and then flung my arms out wide, my fingers scraping against cement and steel. Even my fingernails ached as I clawed to grab hold of the doorway. Sheer willpower won out as I managed to get a firm grip on each side.

I clung on for dear life until the water subsided. Then pulling myself to my feet, I stumbled outside knowing I had to hit the shower immediately. All the while I kept an eye out for Drapkin, though he must have thought I was dead.

I ran into the corrugated tin shack, my hands trembling as I turned on the shower. Then I stepped under the bone-chilling water, grateful for every drop that ran down my hair, limbs, and back. The stream steadily quelled the fire, reaching through skin and muscle to calm my nerves.

Though I was tempted to strip off every stitch of clothing, it would only make me more vulnerable with Drapkin and his cohort still on the loose. Instead I washed off the taint of DRG as best I could, hoping to stop my burns from growing any worse.

I stepped back outside to find that the rain had stopped, and the night was clear. Clear enough to allow me a glimpse of the vehicle racing hell-bent out the front gate. A new moon revealed it to be a Lexus SUV—one that looked strikingly similar to the model that Clark Williams drove.

"Rachel!"

My thoughts were torn away from earthly matters by a voice so intimate that I believed my prayers had been answered.

I spun around, certain Santou was calling to me. Instead, I spied a vehicle parked at the edge of the marsh where none had been before. Drapkin was still on the grounds. The man had to be caught, only my body ached as much as my heart, and I knew I couldn't do it alone. For once, I needed help.

I pulled my cell phone from my belt, planning to call the local police and request backup. Only it had been damaged by water and no longer worked.

It was then I spotted Drapkin in the flesh. Except that he wasn't alone. He was dragging a body toward the marsh, and I knew that it had to be Eight-Ball. I suddenly remembered the car phone and ran toward my vehicle, knowing there wasn't a moment to lose.

Yanking open the door, I shoved a hand deep into my

pocket to search for the car keys. My burnt flesh scraped
against the denim fabric, and I nearly passed out in pain.
However, the keys were nowhere to be found. Not only
couldn't the phone be turned on, but now there was no
chance of leaving to get aid. Action had to be taken immediately and I couldn't afford to lose any more time. A sob rose
in my throat. I wanted to cry, but there was no time for that
either, right now. Eight-Ball's life hung in the balance, and
he was depending on me.

"*Rachel!*"

There it was again—a voice calling me to the marsh. Be it
Santou, Eight-Ball, or my demons, I had no choice but to
follow.

I rummaged furiously inside the Ford, searching for anything to use as a weapon. A large five-cell flashlight lay on
the floor. It would help me to see and could also serve as a
club. Picking it up, I headed to where I'd last caught sight of
Drapkin.

I passed the cell building, the newly flooded lake, and the
railroad car with its dead rats and Temik. A silver Mercedes
sat directly ahead. Flashing my light inside, I saw where a
Manatee Mania sailor's cap had been thrown on the floor. I
found it hard to believe Drapkin would wear anything that
flattened his hair, much less something so pedestrian.

I aimed the flashlight on the ground and now spotted
where the marsh grass had been trampled and flattened. It
left an easy track to follow where the cordgrass grew high. I
walked with noiseless precision, aware that the silence was
yet one more creature, and the solitude hypnotic. So much
so that I involuntarily jumped as a night heron loudly
squawked and flew away, startled by my presence.

I stopped and held my breath, not wanting to tip Drapkin

off to the fact that I was on his trail. At the same time, I listened for any sound that he might make. But all I heard were the munching and grunts of critters, fish, and birds crawling everywhere around me. I saw one now that was being steadily pulled down into the mud. I couldn't pry my eyes away, but watched in morbid fascination. That is until the bile rose in my throat and I started to gag, having realized the prey wasn't animal, but human. My heart raced, fearing it was Eight-Ball.

I raised my flashlight, bathing the inanimate form in its beam, to discover an oar was being used to roll the body deep into black mud. Only it wasn't Eight-Ball that was being consumed, but Wendell Holmes.

I stared in alarm as the black gunk rose up and wrapped Holmes in a smothering embrace, as though the two were lovers. Only this was no Casanova, but Hannibal Lecter at work. The mud slowly swallowed Wendell up to his shoulders. I blinked, and the ooze seemed to take shape, as though it were a creature come to life. Goosebumps broke out on my skin so that I shivered in the heat of the night. I almost forgot about Drapkin, until his voice nailed me like a spotlight in the dark.

"For chrissakes, Porter. Aren't you dead yet?"

I didn't respond, but watched in stunned horror as Wendell continued to sink beneath the mud.

"Don't worry. He died a few hours ago and doesn't feel a thing. Besides this really is all your fault," Drapkin calmly informed me.

If I hadn't thought so before, I now knew the man was crazy.

"How do you figure that?"

"Well, you're the one who got him all worked up over this

manatee business, claiming the park would fold." Drapkin leaned the oar against one leg and wiped his hands on his pants. "I didn't have much choice after that. Who'd have guessed he'd begin to care about those stupid things? For chrissakes, he was even calling them by name. Holmes was bound to cause trouble sooner or later. Now I'm going to have to find someone else to run the water park. You interested in the job?" Drapkin asked, with a malicious gleam in his eye. "I hear you don't have much of a future with Fish and Wildlife."

"Who told you that? Your friend, Bob Montgomery?" I responded, using anger to regain my composure.

Drapkin raised an eyebrow in surprise, but didn't rise to the bait. "I understand you've also been filling Candi's head full of nonsense. You really ought to lighten up, Porter. Manatees are just ugly, stupid animals. So what if a few die? There are always more."

"Is that how you view your workers, as well?" I countered. "Disposable help that can be replaced?"

"More or less," Drapkin conceded. "Chalk it up to the cost of doing business."

"And what about the fact that you're destroying the marsh and everything in it?"

"Nature is a renewable resource. Or haven't you heard? It'll heal itself. Besides, it's not what people care about these days."

"Really? Then maybe they'll be interested to learn of the health problems that DRG has created."

"First it has to be proven," Drapkin challenged. "You would do well to remember what this administration preaches. Compromise isn't the answer some of the time. It's the answer all of the time."

The circle was now complete. I'd heard that same quote from Clark Williams, my superiors at Fish and Wildlife, and now Drapkin.

The mud let out a gurgle as Wendell disappeared from sight.

Drapkin turned to me with a satisfied smile. "It was much easier disposing of your friend, Dr. Fletcher. But then, what better way to eliminate a contaminants expert than by using a contaminant? The best part was, I didn't have to haul his damn corpse around the marsh."

The rat from the railroad car twitched in my mind, and I knew exactly what had happened. "You used Temik."

Drapkin nodded. "But the artistry came in how it was done. All it took was a teaspoon of Temik dissolved in alcohol, and spread on the handle of his horse's curry brush with a knife. I even added some DMSO from Fletcher's stable to speed the reaction along. The mixture absorbed into his skin as soon as he touched the brush." Drapkin wrinkled his nose in distaste. "The only downside was the smell of garlic that got on my own hands from the liniment bottle."

So that's what I'd smelled on Gary's breath.

"Of course, none of this would have been necessary if you'd just kept your nose out of my business."

My hand tightened around the flashlight. It would have to do in place of a gun. "You son of a bitch. I'm really going to enjoy taking you down."

"I believe it will be the other way around," he smirked, and started to lunge.

I readied myself for a fight, but Drapkin stopped short. His left foot was stuck in the mud.

"Goddammit to hell!" he raged, struggling to break loose, as I weighed my options.

Though I wouldn't kill him, I also wouldn't come to his aid, and I began to chuckle.

"What the hell's so damn funny?" he snarled.

"Having you for a midnight snack might just be Nature's way of healing itself."

Drapkin tried to grab me, and I sharply whacked his hands with the flashlight.

"Where's Eight-Ball?" I demanded.

"Screw you, Porter!"

That did it. Drapkin could stay put to mull over his fate, while I went and found my friend. I spun around and began to walk away.

"Where are you going?" he panicked. "You can't just leave me here like this!"

"Sure I can. You'll be good company for Wendell," I responded, not bothering to look back.

I trained my flashlight on the ground and retraced my steps, careful to skirt each patch of mud. Now that the adrenaline rush had subsided, I realized I could have walked into Drapkin's office and used his phone all along. I planned to do that now, fully confident that the police would arrive in time to pull him out of harm's way. I wanted Drapkin to rot in jail for years to come, in return for what he'd done to his employees, Gary, the people in this area, and the marsh.

A flood of excruciating pain tore through me as my clothes rubbed like sandpaper against my skin with each step. Its agonizing throb shot straight to my brain, while uncertainty over Santou's fate played havoc with my emotions.

I tried to focus on the evidence I'd found, keeping my eyes glued to the small patch of illuminated ground, when a pair of legs suddenly appeared before me. My heart jumped into my throat, and I instantly took note that only one foot was clad in a boot. The other was bare and muddy.

Every particle of air disappeared into a black hole of fear, as my demons now sprang to life and danced about me. Had Drapkin possibly broken loose to circle around in an ambush? Lifting the flashlight, I confirmed that my nightmare had become a reality.

Drapkin blocked my path, his face contorted in fury, brandishing a muddy oar above his head. I swiftly raised my arms to fend off the attack, but nothing could stop the momentum of the oar, as it sliced through the night and found me.

A searing pain shot through my skull, and the sky whirled madly about, bringing Van Gogh's *Starry Night* to life, as the ground rose up to grab hold of my body. I felt certain I'd been set ablaze as I was pulled through the marsh by my legs, the anguish so intense that it was a relief when I finally passed out.

Twenty

Cool beads of moisture coated my skin from the crown of my head to my toes. I was once again a child at my grandmother's house, rolling around in the morning dew.

Take off your clothes before the sun comes up, while the grass is wet and new. Then tumble about until your freckles are gone and left behind in the dew.

Even now, I could feel the paper-thin skin of my grandmother's hands as she rolled me about. Or maybe I was wrong, and they belonged to someone else. They became Santou's hands as he floated into my thoughts. I wondered where he was, and if I'd ever see him again.

Perhaps he's dead and is waiting for me here right now, knowing that I'll be dead too.

I found something oddly comforting in that. Except, what if he was alive, and it weren't true?

I now realized it wasn't hands that I felt, but a wooden oar biting into my side. Then I heard a grunt. Howard Drapkin was using the paddle to flip me over, as I was rolled through the marsh like a log.

The ground was soft and squishy beneath me, the earth oozing like an open wound. My head cleared, and I gingerly lifted a hand, relieved to find I was alive and not yet stuck in black mud. However, another good roll, and it could be too late. If I was going to take action, it had to be now.

What would Santou do? I asked myself.

And then I knew.

I continued to lie limp, not wanting Drapkin to know I was awake, until I was again flat on my back. Then as he began his final push, I grabbed hold of the oar and gave a hard tug. Drapkin stumbled toward me and started to fall, having been caught off-guard. Spinning a half turn, I firmly planted my foot in his stomach and flipped him over my head, so that he landed behind me smack into a pool of black mud.

Drapkin immediately realized it, and began to flail wildly about. I guess he'd never learned that the harder you fight, the quicker the mud pulls you down. He was already enveloped up to his waist, and I knew there was nothing I could do to help him now.

Instead, I scrambled onto my hands and knees in an attempt to get away. But Drapkin wouldn't let me escape.

"If I'm going to die, you're coming with me!" he seethed, his arms wrapped tightly around one of my legs.

I was afraid that he was right. I couldn't free myself and was beginning to sink along with him. At the same time, the water was starting to rise. It wouldn't be long before the tide rushed in, drowning us both, if the mud didn't smother us first.

Panic grew in my chest, clawing like a trapped creature, as the stink of the marsh invaded my nose.

There's no point in fighting. Your death will only be more painful. Instead, you have to let yourself go.

For once, I realized that my demons were correct.

A soft coolness enveloped my legs as the mud caressed my limbs, taking away the sting of my burns. Maybe death wouldn't be such a bad thing after all. Why was I even resisting? I tried to conjure those I'd loved and lost, wanting to believe they'd help ease my way.

Hold your breath until the very last second before exhaling. Then a final inhalation and you'll become one more siren of the deep, forever entombed in the marsh, a voice seductively whispered in my ear.

I wanted to believe it was Santou as I closed my eyes and pictured him for the last time, sure that his arms were around me. The imagination is a powerful thing. I now began to hear him calling.

"Rachel! For chrissakes, Porter! Wake the hell up!"

The raspy voice pierced my daze and my eyes flew open, having realized it wasn't Santou. There on firm ground stood Spud Bowden, looking every bit the weasel with a greasy ponytail, jeans hanging off his butt, and a tee-shirt falsely advertising THE BIG ONE across his scrawny chest. I'd never been so happy to see such a crude dude in all my life.

"Hold onto the end of the oar and push it toward me!" he instructed.

I did so, as Spud sprawled on the ground and stretched to reach the paddle.

"You gotta push a little farther!"

I felt sure every blister on my body would erupt as I tried, but Drapkin doggedly held me back. I attempted to kick him with my free leg, only to feel his arms entwine around me even tighter.

"Come on, Porter! I've got hold of the oar," Spud shouted. "Get yourself free. You're running out of time!"

I took a deep breath, and salt water rushed into my mouth. The tide was on the rise. It was now or never. If I was going to live, Drapkin had to die. I knew what I had to do as I took one hand off the oar, and quickly unzipped my pants.

"Pull now!" I yelled, shoving my heel hard into Drapkin's face.

"You bitch!" he screamed, and momentarily loosened his grip.

Then I was being dragged out of the mud, leaving my jeans and boots behind for Drapkin to remember me by. I heard an anguished cry as Spud pulled me to safety, and I turned to see Drapkin for the very last time.

The mud voraciously swallowed first his mouth, then his nose, and finally the terror in his eyes. Soon all that was left were his hands. Then even those fell limp and disappeared, buried beneath the incoming tide.

Epilogue

"Here, dear. Drink this. It will help you feel better," Marie insisted, handing me a cup of tea as we sat on her deck.

I held it between bandaged hands. My arms and legs were also lightly wrapped in gauze after the events of last night.

Spud had immediately called the police upon pulling me from the mud. Then we'd searched the cell building, where Eight-Ball lay unconscious on the floor. After that, Spud carted us both off to the hospital as the police swarmed the scene, with the EPA and Georgia Environmental Protection Division hot on their heels.

The doctors had treated Eight-Ball for a concussion, while I was wrapped up to resemble the bride of the Mummy. According to them, I was lucky. DRG's shower had done its job. Oddly enough, so had the mud. Otherwise, my burns would have been far worse.

Less than twenty-four hours later, a full-scale investigation of DRG was under way. Word had it that it was already being dubbed the South's Love Canal, and would no doubt end up a Superfund site. Cleanup was expected to take decades, with the cost running hundreds of millions of dollars.

The downside was that there'd probably be no evidence implicating Clark Williams in the scandal. However, his run for office would most likely be put on hold. In the meantime, I planned to do everything possible to end Golden Dreams' land grab along Mamalou Lane and Harrington Road.

Candi had called earlier to inform me that my friend from Sea World had arrived in plenty of time. Most of the remaining manatees had received low enough doses of mercury to allow for appropriate care, and would soon be moved to a rehab facility. She planned to go with them, hoping to attend a nearby school and earn a degree in marine biology. Spud had agreed to accompany her upon learning that police informants are paid more money in Florida.

I'd even received a call at home from my boss, Jim Lowell, with news that the Regional Director had just announced his early retirement. Though Montgomery claimed to be sad about his decision, I imagined he'd be consoled by a suitably large pension. Everything seemed to be falling into place. That is, except for my heart.

"Did you hear anything more from that nice man at the FBI yet?" Marie asked.

I shook my head no. Guidry had called a couple of hours ago. The only news was that they'd finally located the plane, and a search-and-rescue team was now on its way.

"Don't tell Alfred, but I had a little tête-à-tête with Thomas before," Marie confided. "He tells me that he hasn't seen any sign of Santou in the afterworld, and that you shouldn't give up hope."

Considering that Thomas was her dead husband, I suppose he would know. Besides, I was eager to take solace where I could find it.

Marie brushed a lock of hair from my eyes, and my tears started to flow. Why did life have to be so tough? Why do any of us have to die or grow old? I'd lost my mother only two years ago. If Jake were taken from me now, it would be more than I could bear.

Marie linked her arm through mine and gently kissed my hair. "We'll just sit here with the Waving Girl until you get word," she said, referring to her sculpture of the girl looking out to sea.

But my gaze was focused on a flock of pelicans that flew overhead, as I remembered Santou's words.

Always take refuge in nature. It's the one constant in life that will never change.

I soared along with them, my soul nestled on their wings, until the very last bird disappeared.